# Thylacine

Peter Hassebroek

Upbound Solutions

# Also by Peter Hassebroek

*Upbound*

*Melange and Other I. T. Stories*

*The Dancer's Spell*

*Greenplays*

# Thylacine

# Thylacine

Published by
Upbound Solutions
Whitby, Ontario, Canada

This book is a work of fiction.
Names, characters, places, and incidents either are products of
the author's imagination or used fictitiously.

ISBN: 978-0-9866640-6-9 (Paper)
ISBN: 978-0-9866640-7-6 (e-Book)

www.peterhassebroek.com

# Thylacine

*The impossible creature sniffs for food amid the char, embers, ash, and decay that litter a clearing normally littered with the upright beasts perishing inside their blackened den. Despite the roar from the orange flames, innate caution demands deliberate, quiet steps. A yawn. As its jaws close, a whiff of life emerges, coming from a beast separated from the others. Unmoving but possibly alive, hence dangerous. A flashing under its head draws the creature closer to this beast than it's ever been to one before. A drop of saliva falls on the beast, which grunts, stirs, then tries to rise upright. The creature retreats. The beast fails but then slithers, slowly, like a dying snake. The beast reaches for something that disintegrates in its grasp, causing the beast to let out a cry before collapsing. Still again, except for tiny flames that dance on a shiny object on its neck. The creature, not afraid now, but wary, settles near the beast to await its imminent expiration and claim the prize. The beast shifts now and then, in spastic bursts, as the sun falls away. The creature holds its ground, the deterring brightness of the great fire keeping it at bay. Only the fire doesn't look to diminish before a new sun will appear on the other horizon. Impatience prods the creature to snatch the shiny object. It succeeds just before a bizarre wail urges it to scurry back to its rainforest haven with its prize, lest any beast discovers the impossible creature is possible.*

# 1

The school bell, its persistent ting weirdly warped by a passing police siren, startles Christopher, as it triggers a rush of motion. Kids, all in blue shirts, stop bragging about their Christmases, breaking up cliques as they scramble to recall their new term homerooms. Lunch boxes drop, papers fly, locker doors slam shut. Two boys bump into each other by accident, then shove each other on purpose before arranging a hasty date for a fight that no doubt will be forgotten by day's end. Thuds, squeals, clangs. So much commotion. No wonder Christopher, despite his size, is ignored as if he's invisible. Just as he prefers. It's why he's crouching in the first place, taking care to keep the new khaki pants his mom had to buy to meet the dress code off the floor.

Of course he can't stay there, he has to respond to the bell too. Problem is, he can't remember which classroom is his. This is a big school.

The hallway is emptying, unblocked bands of sunlight from the exit doors merging. How easy it would be to follow that light and escape to the wide open outside. His muscles twitch as if urging him to do so; his mind tells him no. His mind will win this time because it will convince him the snow and cold will make sure he doesn't get far and that someone's sure to find him coatless and send him back. And that would upset his mom and he's trying hard to stop upsetting her.

She was so relieved, almost thrilled, when she found out this school would take him, and in such a good mood this morning when she had to drop him off early because of that job interview. He hates schools but he really should make an effort for her, this time. Not troubling her about Willie forgetting to pack his lunch doesn't count.

He knows there are two fifth grade classes, but which is his? No one's around to ask. Wait, that cute girl with pitch black hair? Is that Jennifer? Yes! He shifts from his spot and treads lightly like an animal after the girl, his lanky frame arched on all fours, as his knees hover over the puddle-splotched linoleum floor. Jennifer checks her watch, speeds up, and so Christopher quickens his pace, eyes fixed on her swirling skirt. He's a prowling creature, a tiger, as he closes in on her. Then she turns into a doorway. He follows her in, then halts.

Mrs. Jackson is watching the students as they take their seats, as if waiting for the right moment to tell them to settle down. Jennifer says hi to a couple of girls before taking the last empty seat in the first row. This forces

Christopher to cross in front of the teacher and the entire class to the only open seat, far from the door, though near a window. He knows he should stop scooting and stand, but he likes moving this way. It feels natural. He senses but ignores the teacher's bug-eyed glower to make sure his hands skip slushy spots and bits of dirt—ugh, did someone step in dog turd?—and avoid the legs of chairs, desks, and humans.

"Young man. What on earth are you doing?"

The classroom becomes utterly quiet. But only a moment before smirks escalate into a roar of all the boys laughing. Big deal. They don't exist, as far as Christopher cares. He's used to mocking, gets it at every school. Usually it's for the shade of his skin: too light for the darker kids, too dark for the paler ones. Or it's for his hair, either too thick and not curly enough, or too thin and too curly. At least now it's for something different.

"Back to the zoo with you, weirdo."

What is the same, though, and what's funny is how the girls always remain quiet. They either just stare at him or watch what the boys are going to do, which is usually nothing because they're just talkers. Some girls look nervous but others, like Jennifer, who he can see from the corner of his eye, have expressions he can't figure out. Kind of like the ones his mom and Willie get when they hear about things that happen at school. Maybe the day will come when he understands what others think. All he can be sure of is that to them he is strange and doesn't fit in, and he has no idea why that's so. He just does what feels right. What's strange to him is why it matters so much what he does. He'd never think what others do as wrong. As long as they don't hurt anyone.

"The big pussy."

"Here kitty, kitty."

The teacher slaps her hand on the desk. "Boys, stop that."

"Come on guys, come pet the pussy."

Christopher feels a rough stroke on his head, then his back. This is too much. Christopher lets out a tiger roar before twirling and swiping at one boy's face, catching skin. Christopher's about to charge at the boy, bite him if possible, when Mrs. Jackson's voice reaches a new shrill pitch.

"Christopher Palmer, you stop that this instant." Now the class is quiet again. "Stand up and come over here."

He does stop but doesn't get up. Not to disobey but to figure out what to do. His mind's mixed up. Sorry, mom, he says to himself as he stays a tiger and moves past Mrs. Jackson to the classroom door. He's a big boy, much taller than the other boys in the fifth grade, but not tall enough to reach the handle from this position. He rises to open the door but Mrs. Jackson intercepts him and blocks the exit with her big body. He lowers himself again, making the teacher nervous, until he's lying on the floor, inciting a new wave of snickering.

"What am I to do with you?" Mrs. Jackson says.

"That kid cut me, send him to Mr. Chambers."

"Kenny, if you're injured, go see the nurse."

Kenny glares at Christopher who scowls back.

It's a puny scratch, if anything at all, Christopher knows. He ignores Kenny, looks up at the teacher.

"I'm thirsty, can I get some water?" Christopher says, feeling he should say something.

"Fine, you can get a drink on your way to see Mr. Chambers."

"Who's Mr. Chambers?"

"Who's Mr. — why the Principal, of course. You know, the man you saw every other day last week."

One of the girls, Jennifer in fact, raises her hand.

"Mrs. Jackson, he's new, he may have forgotten."

Jennifer's caring voice affects Christopher in a funny way. He wants to look at the girl but finds himself too bashful to do it. Instead, he watches as Mrs. Jackson takes a piece of paper from her desk. She leans it against the door, scribbles and folds a note, and holds it out towards the classroom.

"All right, Jennifer, how about you escort this young man to Mr. Chambers' office with this note? Stop at the fountain, if he's really thirsty."

Curiosity overcomes shyness and Christopher now has to look at Jennifer who, no surprise, looks as if she wishes she'd kept quiet. But she doesn't scare easily. He likes that.

"Can Sally come with me too?"

"Me and Greg'll take him," Kenny says. "We'll make sure he gets the punishment he deserves."

"I think Jennifer and Sally can manage it."

A pale red-haired girl Christopher has never noticed before — cute though boyish in her overalls, and definitely not pretty like Jennifer—stands up. The two girls approach the door. The teacher opens it. They enter the hallway and wait for Christopher. Escape at last. To make sure he's let out for sure, Christopher stands up and instantly feels awkward seeing how high he stands over the girls. He follows them out, trying to ignore Mrs. Jackson who he can sense watching the trio make their way down the empty hallway.

They pause at a fountain where Christopher motions for the girls to go first. They hesitate but do so. After Christopher takes a long drink, he walks no more than ten feet before dropping on the floor again, resuming his tiger prowl. The girls look back to the classroom in alarm. A moment later, Mrs. Jackson joins them.

"Never mind, girls, I'll take him. Go see if the custodian can watch the class a few minutes."

The girls gladly obey, leaving Christopher alone with this teacher who he's sure likes him less than all his other teachers before combined. He's messed it all up again but her dislike makes him not feel as bad about it as he probably should, certainly not as bad as he felt the first times.

Because when he thinks about it, what he's done this time can't be nearly as bad as what he used to do. Like in Grade One whenever he took his clothes off and the teacher went berserk; or in second grade when he ripped or broke or smashed things and the teacher would get mad, and even madder when he learned to swear and did so to get reactions; or in Grade Three whenever he pushed or bit other kids and the teacher got scared; or last year, constantly running around for no reason and confusing poor Mrs. Davidson, the teacher he liked least. Until now. But he never did those things to make teachers mad. No, he did them because something inside him told him to do them. Compared to all that, this can't be such a big deal. Mrs. Jackson is overreacting. It's not likely she sees it that way so when she sighs, he decides he might as well stand up.

"Why do you do that crawling? You're not in kindergarten anymore, for crying out loud."

Christopher shrugs and Mrs. Jackson shakes her head, as if expecting him to shrug. They walk down long corridors to an office Christopher would never have found on his own. A receptionist smiles at him, a phony smile. Mrs. Jackson looks relieved when the receptionist has Christopher sit on a plain chair and tells the teacher she can return to the class for the time being. The receptionist opens the Principal's door, says something that gets the Principal to come out. He ushers Christopher in and has him sit in a big leather chair, by himself, and closes the door.

It's a tidy office with a large window looking out onto the poorly cleared parking lot with a dozen or so fancy cars covered with a layer of snow at least a centimetre thick. Beyond is an empty football field, its pure whiteness ruined by boot prints, though a thick patch of fast moving grey clouds promises to fill them in. He'd rather be out there instead of at this clean desk made of a thick, reddish wood that looks very expensive. Affluent, his mom might say.

Christopher's been here before, of course, and he remembers what happened last week now. And he's been in similar offices at other schools. For a long time he thought something was wrong with him, something to make him do the things that get him in trouble. But he's not a bad kid, he's kind to people, he's no cry-baby. It's not like he scratches desks and floors with penknives and paper clips like Kenny and Greg; not like he giggles and points while the teacher's back is turned like some girls; not like he picks on other kids—oh, he can list so many things teachers don't notice.

The only explanation he can come up with is an unhelpful one: he doesn't behave like adults want him to. And that doesn't help because they can never explain how they want him to behave. At least not in a way that makes sense. He just does what comes natural to him. It does make things harder for his mom, who will have to deal with this again, and for Willie too. For them he feels bad because they're always sweet to him and never punish him.

Why don't they?

He can faintly hear the voices of the receptionist and Principal. What's taking so long? Why isn't the Principal back yet to stall until his mom shows up?

Now a panic creeps in. What if they're going to put him on those drugs he's heard about, the ones that keep kids still? Mom and Willie wouldn't stand for it but maybe there's a way for them to go around Mom and Willie.

Has he gone too far this time?

What if they think he's insane and try to lock him away in some institution? Christopher curls up. He yawns a big yawn to try and get rid of a sudden chill running inside him. It'd be much colder outside yet the window, revealing the white and wide open possibilities beyond, beckons him.

# 2

Willie Galloway joins a huddle of a dozen or so employees of Bralen and Son Furniture in an open space separating a set of metal stairs from the prefab offices fronting a large, rather shoddily organized warehouse. A garbage bin overflows with litter from the night shift but nobody pays it any heed beyond kicking aside Styrofoam cups and candy wrappers to clear their path.

Conversations stop as seedy, plump, mediocre warehouse manager Todd Bralen descends the stairs with a clipboard. Todd is Willie's best friend at the company, though that's not saying much, their friendship founded more on their mutual alienation from everyone else rather than natural affinity. The employees, most hired by Todd's father before Todd was even out of elementary school, can't stand the son. A political minefield Willie didn't uncover until a month after getting hired last year, after he'd formed a bond with Todd. The father, Mac Bralen, is aware of the morale-risking state of affairs but, as with the sanitary neglect, ignorance reigns supreme. Indeed, at times it appears to Willie that Mac Bralen provokes conflict for some perverse anti-nepotistic purpose. Some family business. Todd does share his father's arrogance, though it's absent today, judging by his hesitant stride.

The reason is evident when the father appears at the top of the stairs, and stays there to look down on them, wearing his unique combination of smirk and scowl. Their tieless, inexpensive and, in Todd's case, ill-fitting suits clash with the assembly of coveralls and work boots. Clearly not a birthday gathering.

"Seems the Christmas bonus wasn't enough for some," Mac says, then looks at his son who's clearly nervous. As is Willie who stiffens as Todd flashes a guilty look his way. Mac, clearly put off by Todd's lack of temerity, no doubt expecting his son to take up his tone, then adds, "Seems we're the victims of theft, right, my boy?"

Todd needs to consult his clipboard before he can address everyone. His voice cracks at first but then smoothes out.

"Year-end uncovered an alarming number of big ticket items unaccounted for. Mostly appliances, but some sofas and dining sets too. I'm conducting an internal investigation before we call in the police. This is an opportunity for anyone who knows anything to come forward now."

"The only opportunity," his father adds.

It takes a moment for the message to sink in and when it does, Willie begins sweating. The jig is up. Just don't panic, perhaps Todd has it covered.

Then Willie's cell phone buzzes. It's an unknown number. Most likely Christopher's new school, but why would they call him? He hesitates. The buzzing stops and a moment later, a light flashes indicating a new voice message.

"I'll meet with each of you, individually," Todd says. "Right now. No one leaves this area until we have that talk. And turn your cell phones off."

"All of you catch that?" Mac says, as if his son's words demand his emphasis. To the elder Bralen, they probably do.

Willie conceals his phone, sets off towards the darker rows of the warehouse. He doesn't get far before a co-worker intercepts him.

"Didn't you hear Mac? No one can go."

"Just a bio break. Can't wait. I'll be back shortly."

"I'd hold it if I were you."

Willie ignores him, escapes into the warehouse jungle. An aisle blocked by several skids loaded with end tables and coffee tables still to be scanned and stocked provides a haven. When he calls the number, Willie gets efficiently connected to a Doctor Chambers, the Principal who, after assuring him no one was hurt, tells Willie there was an incident involving Christopher. Willie struggles to follow what the man is saying as he becomes distracted by approaching voices and heavy footsteps.

"Look, Dr. Chambers, did you call his mother? I'm in the middle of something."

"We tried, Mr. Palmer. Several times."

"My name's Galloway, actually."

"Fine, Mr. Galloway, I insist you or the boy's mother come immediately. Your son attacked another student."

"You said no one was hurt."

"That's hardly the point as this isn't an isolated incident. I took the liberty of speaking with someone from Christopher's previous school and —"

"Okay, I'll be right over."

Willie hangs up as Mac and old Sully and two more of his most senior employees, surround him.

"I believe Todd was clear no one was to leave."

"Mr. Bralen, sorry, I've got an emergency to take care of at my kid's school."

"What sort of emergency?"

"He was in a fight."

Mac laughs mockingly.

"A dose of reality will be good for him. Now shut your phone off and get back. Ask Todd, kindly, maybe he'll talk to you ahead of the others."

"You don't understand. This is important."

"And employees stealing from me isn't?"

The two colleagues and Sully share a grin. Willie shrugs, without disrespect, although Mac doesn't take it that way. He grabs Willie's bicep to drag him back. Only Willie wrests himself free and in doing so shoves Mac hard into a shelf, knocking the owner's head back against the metal.

"This is an assault," Mac says, checking his head for blood, but finding none. "You all saw it."

Bralen looks at his employees / bodyguards who nod obsequiously. Willie ignores them, pushes his way through towards the exit with Bralen's next words echoing in his head all the way to his car:

"Don't even think about a last pay check, pal, think about a lawyer."

Upon reaching his rundown but sturdy two-tone Le Sabre, something troubles Willie about those words. He's fired, he gets that, but would tough-guy Bralen really charge him with assault? Not likely. Combined with the way Bralen was looking at his own son—more with contempt and disgust than his normal disdain—those words carry a sinister aspect. Willie shakes his head. He has to rely on Todd to handle his father while he finds out what's going on with Christopher.

At the school, he's escorted into the Principal's office, instantly struck by its fastidious contrast to the warehouse. An uncluttered large desk with only a telephone and a small binder with a matching pen. All other pens, pencils, and stationary neatly sorted away in desk drawers, ready to use, no doubt. Three walls crowded by an intimidating array of framed diplomas. The Principal himself, Dr. Chambers, is a decent-looking, trim fellow who must be a good decade younger than Willie. A keener, the type Willie would have bullied for ten years as a kid but who, in a twisted karma, could exact his revenge for many decades after.

"I'm Willie Galloway."

"Thank you for coming, please join us."

Three chairs are squeezed in across the desk from Chambers. Christopher, staring in that dreamy way of his, occupies the one on the left. A mousy, attractive but overweight woman sits on the right. She seems young, under thirty, and appears nervous and defiant at the same time, probably wondering how a blue collar Joe like him, in coveralls to boot, can have a kid at this school.

The seating arrangement compels Willie to take the chair directly facing Chambers. He flashes a smile at Christopher who returns it humbly. The boy seems bored, content to let the adults sort it out. Not unlike how Deborah described past situations. She should be here now. Not instead of him, but with him. No one seems sure how to start. Willie directs a glance at the woman.

"I'm sorry," Chambers says, "this is Mrs Jackson, Christopher's homeroom teacher. Mrs. Jackson, can you please relate what happened?"

She readjusts her chair and clears her throat in a way that makes Willie take an instant dislike to this woman. She reminds him of his own self-righteous grade school teachers whom he holds responsible for his abbreviated education.

"The bell had just rung and I was watching the students file in as usual," Mrs. Jackson says, her tone subtly authoritative, her voice calm. "Christopher was the last, again, and came in crawling on all fours all the way to his seat, like an animal. A boy teased him and

Christopher took a swing. There was contact. When I told Christopher to stand and come to me, he disobeyed. He even tried to leave my class and just walk out the door."

"May I add," Chambers says, "there were several incidents last week requiring my attention."

"I am aware," Willie says, though only able to recall Deborah telling him about one.

"Last week he was so disruptive to my class I stressed out all weekend about what might happen this week. Rightfully so, as it turns out."

"Primed yourself for a gotcha, is that it?"

Willie's remark draws a grunt of amusement from Christopher and a frown from the Principal.

"How about we have your—have Christopher wait outside."

Willie nods, annoyed with himself, and keeps quiet as Chambers escorts Christopher out and takes an opportunity to give instructions to his assistant. During the interlude, Willie tries to regain his cool, though he cannot look at the teacher. He looks out the window where he now notices his car—lodged between a BMW and a Lexus adorned with a thin layer of snow—stands out like a sore thumb, its rust spots a conspicuous stain amid the whiteness. He should have parked the thing farther away. But once Chambers returns and sits down, his head blocks Willie's car from view as it did before.

"Mr. Galloway," Chambers says, "as I mentioned on our call, I contacted his previous schools. Based on what they told me, I think I can help."

"Look, Christopher is different from other kids, true enough, but has he caused any real harm?"

"Such a need for attention ought to be addressed as early as possible," Mrs. Jackson says.

"Need for attention? That's ridiculous."

Chambers glances at the teacher, an appeal for her to keep quiet and let him take charge.

"We ought to refrain from conclusions before we fully understand what's going on. Perhaps someone not so closely involved can help get us there."

Willie doesn't care much for the teacher but this Chambers guy seems reasonable, though he's not sure Deborah would agree. Honouring her wishes is paramount and those wishes are crystal clear when it comes to Christopher: don't ever let an institution try to manage her son.

"How about I just take Christopher home."

Chambers puts up a hand, which stops Willie as he's getting up.

"The sooner we understand what's going on, the sooner we can come to a plan to deal with it."

"Not without his mother."

"I wouldn't dream of that. But as you're the only one here, kindly oblige me a few minutes. Then we can reconvene tomorrow with his mother. At which time, I'll bring along someone more experienced in such matters."

Willie hesitates but decides to sit back down. Can't hurt to hear the guy out. Not like there's any work to get back to.

# 3

Fixes are long overdue: sagging floors, scratched walls, and a chipped stucco ceiling discoloured in spots. The landlord's willing to make fixes but only as part of a full-scale renovation, which would mean moving out for months and, if returning, having to pay higher rent. Deborah can afford this place now but not without rent control. And really the house is no worse than when they moved in three years before. She's taken decent care of it and can continue doing so as long as the owner remains flexible.

Perhaps what's most disconcerting is how the severity of the faults contrasts the elegant Natuzzi leather sofa and chairs procured by Willie with that implausible employee discount. The same generous discount that allowed them to replace the landlord's aging almond appliances with a matching set from LG, stainless steel and loaded with features that, like parts of her native Tasmania, remain unexplored. Mostly because she's a so-so cook, but also because she's unable to shake her scepticism about that too-good-to-be-true discount, despite Willie's assurances it's an accounting strategy used by Bralen and Son to generate turnover, and that the items are either second-hand or factory imperfections.

At least she can suspend her misgivings from time to time. For they are wonderful. Especially the austere but comfy sofa on which she can stretch out and sink in, as she's doing now, to watch a large high-definition television free of sports and nature shows. Only there's not much more on than real estate and renovation shows. Normally she enjoys those but today they nag at her with reminders of what needs fixing in the house. Off. In silence she can better relish the soft leather moulding to her back, an echo of the comfort with which she grew up. Ironic how a luxury she once took for granted and unceremoniously renounced can affect her so once she gives herself in to it. Which isn't often.

She can still take or leave such luxuries, would prefer to leave them, truth be told. It's more a case of appreciating the sentiment of the man behind the gifts. The actual gifts contribute little to how she feels about Willie; their value lies in how Willie feels about himself.

She loves the man not for what he can or can't provide but for his way with Christopher. It seems each year her son gets older he gets better, more normal, something for which Willie deserves much credit. That makes it easy to abide his modest financial contributions.

It doesn't pay much yet but he's had that warehouse job over a year now and the future looks more promising than it has for at least three years.

Which makes it four years since Willie became a fixture in their lives. Four years since she came to accept her existence would never be as affluent as it was in childhood, nor as comfortably middle-class as it was before she lost Dwight.

Beyond the sofa, delicately standing on two legs, her only valued possession: an exquisite handmade Huon pine half-table sturdily attached to the wall. Aside from some photos in an album, the only link to her mother who died when Deborah was a teen. The one piece, despite the incongruity of its old-fashioned light varnish with the new furniture, she'll never allow Willie to replace. Staining it a different colour might help it fit in but would also ruin its rustic purity, its symbolic value. And on that table sits a framed studio portrait of a handsome African-Canadian man in military uniform. Heroic and stoic Dwight Palmer, the opposite of Willie. How those two became best friends when they served together baffles Deborah. Dwight, so rigid and impatient, would have struggled with Christopher but would have tried. Sadly, there was never a chance for them to bond as father and son after Dwight fell victim to an IED and died overseas. Her mother would have taken to Dwight, Willie not so much. But even if her mother hadn't died when Deborah was young, she never could have met either man, for everything in her life would have been completely different.

How she hates when those reflections threaten to turn into regrets. She needs to do something else, think of something else before the tears. Indolence always plummets her into the past, which then leads to sadness, frustration or, worst of all, the second-guessing that ruins her mood. And that would be a shame after coming home in such a good mood, having done so well at the interview they hired her on the spot with a shift in a few hours. That's what she ought to be thinking about. Positive thoughts.

Like her optimism about Christopher's school and how that morning he got out the car and went inside with no fuss, just as that Principal Chambers predicted, as if those incidents from last week never happened. It was strange not to linger as normal. She would have, if not for the interview, so it turned out to be a good test. This school, though public, is somewhat exclusive and reminds her of the private schools she went to as a child, and not just because of the dress code. She's anxious to find out how it's going for Christopher, and frustrated knowing she won't until tonight because of the new job.

She rifles through a stack of magazines under the coffee table, grabs the weekend paper. Willie's left it in disarray, again, and it takes a while to sort the various sections. She stops at an article reporting on a plague of bushfires in central Tasmania, which apparently started months ago and are only now coming under control. More than two dozen people have died, plenty injured. The story doesn't go into details or provide pictures other than a vague map. Only the faintest curiosity tempts her to go online to find out more, to find out if anyone she knew . . . no, if that were the case, someone would make the effort to find her, to tell her. No news is good news.

Now where is that crossword? She finds it but it's completed—Willie's not the brightest guy but he is good with words—so she casts the paper aside. She scans several bills on the coffee table. At least their situation isn't so dire that any are past due.

Her attention is drawn back to the article. She reaches for it but then drops the paper when the front door opens and Willie enters, followed by Christopher. Her immediate joy at having company is trumped by the sense something must be wrong.

"Why are you both home so early?"

It comes out more confrontational than intended but the way they're staring is almost as challenging. Christopher points at her outfit.

"What's that you're wearing?"

Deborah looks down, somewhat with disdain, at her waitress uniform, its gaudily violet top barely covering the cleavage exaggerated by her best bra, and the black skirt highlighting her thighs of which she's still proud.

"It's for my new job. They liked me so much at the interview, I already got a shift this afternoon, so I decided to try it on."

Willie frowns, causing her to put her hands on her hips, knowing what's coming.

"You'll have no trouble getting tips," he says.

"I'll take that as a compliment."

"You do that."

"I know how to handle myself."

"Fine. Never mind. Christopher had an incident at school. I had to get away from work because you weren't answering your phone."

Deborah finds her purse, pulls her phone out, sees the dark screen.

"Right, I turned it off for the interview. Guess I forgot to . . . what kind of trouble?"

Willie shares what he heard from the Principal and teacher. Christopher interjects to correct one or two minor points, and his conclusion:

"I don't like this school, mom."

"Honey, you don't like any school."

"I never learn anything. Can't I just learn at home?"

"We've tried, remember? It didn't go so well."

"It went well enough for me."

"Besides, both Willie and I have fulltime jobs."

At this Willie coughs, then says, "Perhaps I can give it a shot for a semester."

"That'd be awesome," Christopher says.

"Willie, what are you talking about?"

"I guess Christopher and I had similar days."

"I'm supposed to understand what that means?"

"Like I said, I had to get away from work to get Christopher. Bralen didn't like that so much and, well, I kind of shoved him and here I am."

"Oh Willie. Just go back and apologize."

"Won't work."

"Why not?"

Willie hesitates and seems uncomfortable.

"Some nasty stuff going on at the warehouse. Besides, I agreed we'd meet with the Principal in the morning. We need to talk about that."

Deborah can't believe what she's just heard and is about to utter something in haste, but holds back, to measure her tone.

"We've talked about this. Call back, cancel, no, I'll do it."

She turns on her phone and sees several missed calls, two from the school, the others from Willie. She's about to call the school back when Willie grabs her arm gently.

"We should hear Dr. Chambers out. He seems like a good guy, pretty smart."

"A doctor? He's a doctor?"

"Yeah, the academic kind, lots of diplomas."

"Oh, I know the kind. The kind who—"

"Can I go watch TV?" Christopher says.

"Yes, honey, why don't you do that."

She flinches when Christopher gets down on all fours and scurries into the living room, probably as he did in the classroom, as he did in the previous school too. He gets himself comfortable on the floor and turns on the television. She glances at Willie who's watching her son as well. They keep silent as Christopher searches the guide until he finds a show about African wildlife. He turns up the volume, perhaps intentionally to give them privacy.

"Honey, that's way too loud."

"Sorry."

Christopher lowers the volume, puts down the remote, then pushes the coffee table against the sofa to make room for himself to emulate the movements of the animals on the screen. First a lion, then a giraffe. He's clearly having fun and she can't see any harm in it.

Willie had a hard time with her son's behaviours at first but came around once she convinced him Christopher was just being a kid, that he'd grow out of it. So it's taking a bit longer. Perhaps this doctor Principal said something to sway Willie back. If so, she must impress on him that all these academics want is a guinea pig so they can write some paper.

On the other hand, she knows she ought to allow Willie more say in decisions about her son; he's earned it. And she will. Next time. As long as Willie understands her word will always be the final word when it comes to Christopher. He's respected that to this point, yet another of his traits she adores, and there's no reason to fear that won't continue.

# 4

Christopher still has no clue as to the surprise until Willie flicks a finger that starts the tick-tick-tick signalling a right turn into an exit that looks vaguely familiar. His heart jumps. Can it be? Willie parks his light blue car in a parking lot that's largely vacant. Not like his mom in a spot far away from other cars, but between a couple of cars about as old as Willie's, though not as rusted. They get out and Christopher can't believe it. All the times he's bugged his mom and Willie to go to the zoo, never expecting them to give in, knowing they're afraid he'll act up, he's here at last. He has to wonder if his mom knows they're here. Considering her mood just before she left for work, probably not.

She used to take him all the time whenever she was sad, which used to be often. That was long ago. Long before Willie was around. Christopher doesn't remember much of those visits, except it was usually sunny and never this cold. Though he can recall the last time because of his acting up and his mom getting mad and embarrassed. Funny, he never felt bad about it then but does now, maybe because of what happened at the school this morning and the fact that instead of a punishment he gets a reward.

But wait, is it a reward? Maybe it's a test. If only he'd listened while she and Willie were talking. But he's not like that. Adult conversations confuse him and bore him because they take so long and use so many words to say simple things.

Christopher follows Willie to the entrance where a big sign says there are pandas. And a newly born polar bear cub. How he's longed to see animals that aren't dogs or cats or squirrels.

"So what would you like to see first?" Willie says, after shaking his head at the cost.

"Doesn't matter, I want to see everything."

Willie laughs. "Not sure we'll have time, but I'm game to try."

They set off towards the right, following a sign indicating the pandas are close. So is some animal pooping up a storm. Thankfully, the smell vanishes once they go through an exhibit with lots of boards talking about pandas. With just a look, they agree to ignore them and go straight to the action.

Outside again, Christopher sees how few people are around this time of year. Plenty of space for him to wander and run around. The only obstacles to avoid are women leisurely pushing strollers filled with quiet and behaved children. Seeing this now that he's older makes him understand why his mom was embarrassed by his behaviour, and only adds to his determination not to be like that today.

The fur on the giant pandas isn't as white as Christopher expects but the big animals are just as adorable. They'd be more adorable if they didn't sit there like round logs. Christopher's starting to get bored but, because the pandas are such a big deal, he stays a few minutes longer.

More interesting are the red pandas, constantly running around, climbing trees, their little shoulders bouncing back and forth, their black and thick tails sweeping the dirt ground behind them.

"Kind of like squirrels," Christopher says, "but cuter, though not as quick."

"You want to stay and watch them or should we move on?"

"Move on."

The farther they go, the emptier and quieter the zoo seems. The unoccupied cages seem abandoned, creepy. So few animals, so few humans. Those that are there, of both kinds, move slowly, if at all. It's as quiet as a library that's cold and smelly. But it is peaceful, with the iced-over river to the right tempting Christopher to slide. He doesn't and is pleased with himself at passing a test.

"Where are all the animals?"

"Many can't handle the Canadian winter."

"But the ones who can should be moving about to keep warm, right?"

Willie shrugs. Christopher can tell his mind is on something else. He wonders if it's about what he and his mom talked about. He wants to ask but figures that whatever it is, he may not care to know, at least not yet.

The two-humped camels are doing nothing, maybe waiting for food. Same with two animals he's never heard of: tur and chamois. A snow leopard is moving and Christopher resists an urge to copy it. He succeeds. Not from self-control but because it's doing nothing more than pacing back and forth. Boring. The sheep on a steep, rocky hill are more lively. It's neat watching them, wondering how they keep their footing. He discovers these are the culprits making the pooping smell before, which is stronger now and drives them away.

At the Australasia Pavilion, they go inside for a break from the cold and the stench. They're greeted by colourful birds freely strutting about, although they're not really free as they have no way of getting out of the building, so it's not much different than being in a cage. There's a wallaby and a wombat but, guess what, they're sitting around. Kind of scrawny too. Suddenly Christopher finds it too warm, too humid, too closed in. The fans are loud and muffle an odd ringing sound that turns out to be Willie's cell phone.

"What's up, Todd? As if I didn't know."

Willie's voice, usually smooth and confident, sounds angry, even scared, as his free arm shakes slightly. Who could he be talking to, Christopher wonders, who is this Todd? Willie then notices Christopher, points to the phone, and steps away.

Christopher's tempted to retreat back outside but instead follows Willie to an aquarium tank filled with tons of small brightly coloured fish doing laps. Christopher likes all animals but, now that he thinks about it, he's never cared much for fish and sea life. Nor even for birds and especially not snakes and insects. The sooner they get out of this building, which is full of these things, the better. Then he hears Willie's raised voice:

"You sold me out, didn't you?"

Willie's voice lowers and now Christopher's not sure where he is in the dark interior, let alone where Willie's at. Let's go, Christopher thinks, wishing he'd done so on his own. Why didn't he? Oh right, he's behaving, and doing a pretty good job of it. At last, Willie wraps up the call and finds him.

"You all right there, sport?" Willie says.

"It's too humid. If Australia's like this I'd never want to go there. Can we get out of here?"

"We should at least see the Komodo dragon."

Lizards, ugh. Fortunately, Willie gives in when Christopher pulls his hand to take them to the exit.

Willie's mood has changed since the phone call. He's unusually quiet and only says anything when he's answering Christopher's questions. He's pretty much letting Christopher guide them. No doubt he's still watching me, but I'm doing good, Christopher thinks. It's actually not that hard. All the uninspiring animals doing nothing helps.

"Enjoying yourself?" Willie says.

"Yeah," Christopher says, though not really sure.

He wants to ask about the phone call, but that's not what's bugging him. Then it comes to him. "Willie?"

"What's up?"

"What do these animals think?"

"They're animals. They don't think."

"I know. Don't you ever wonder if they know they're in cages? Like, maybe they think they're free and that we are the ones who are in cages and just roaming by."

"I doubt that. Most would have been captured, and would understand being captured."

"Even those born here? Like the polar bear cub? The ones who've never been anywhere else? Can't believe he's not out."

"Probably feeding. We need to eat as well. Hope something's open."

That's right, Christopher thinks, all the eating places they've passed, which usually would be filled with people, are empty. Lots of picnic tables tied up with chains and ropes. Willie stops to ask a woman with a stroller who points in the direction they're heading. Minutes later, Christopher and Willie are sitting in a warm building, each with a hot dog and a small Pepsi.

"Who was that on the phone?" Christopher says. "Was it about my school?"

"Uh, no. But now that you mention it, when I was talking to your Principal, he said something you've said before. That he doesn't believe you do the things that give teachers trouble because you want to give them trouble. Or for attention. Or even to be defiant—I mean to intentionally not fit in."

Willie pauses. It's as if he's spent all this time at the zoo figuring how to say this and now wonders whether he should have. Or maybe Willie has been waiting for Christopher to act up and since he hasn't done so, decided to say it anyway. If the Principal did say that and does feel that way, it would be the first time someone other than Willie and his mom shows understanding. Maybe that's a good thing. Maybe it isn't.

"This Principal, Dr. Chambers, he says he knows someone we can talk to."

"Mom won't like that, she won't allow it."

"She might if you tell her you want to fit in."

"You want me to go back to that school?"

"Not necessarily. I just want to—I don't know—I just want to figure out what'll work best for all of us, you know?"

"You said you would home school me."

"I did say that, but we both know it wouldn't work. I'm not smart enough to teach and I do need to find another job. Which is why it might help to look at other options."

Poor Willie, Christopher thinks, he's going to get it when Mom finds out about this conversation. Christopher will never forget an argument between his mom and a neighbour who used to be a friend about sending Christopher to a specialist with some fancy title. In fact, it happened not long after that last zoo visit. His mom got as mad at the woman as he's ever seen her. Christopher will keep his mouth shut, or say what he must to help Willie who is trustworthy and might be on to something. It would be nice to get along with kids his age, especially girls like Jennifer.

Willie seems in a better mood after lunch and the talk, which puts Christopher in a better mood. It helps most of the clouds are gone and the bright winter sun is making it warm enough to unzip the tops of their coats. They enter the African zone and pause to watch the hyenas, which are bigger than Christopher expects and, because they're roaming swiftly and not pacing, more interesting. Then they come to a pair of lions sitting side by side. Male and female, king and queen, though Christopher senses weariness more than majesty.

The earlier feeling returns and develops into an overall sadness for the animals. They need space to move around. What they have here isn't even close to enough. Not like what they'd be used to based on what he's seen on nature shows. No one needs a helicopter to find the animals here. He used to think they were happy having all the food they wanted and all that room seemed like a lot then.

It starts to aggravate him. He feels an old energy building up inside, an urge to be among them, be one of them. The signs warning people to stay off the rocks—many more than he remembers—make him think twice. But not a third time. Christopher puts one hand on a rock, pulls himself up to grasp another with the other so that now he's covering up one of the signs. But as he pulls a leg up . . .

"What are you doing?" Willie says, calmly but firmly, making Christopher freeze. "Pay attention to the signs."

With that, the urge vanishes completely, and it seems it was never there. Christopher steps down, acting as if he never intended to actually do it.

"I bet those signs are for me," Christopher says, making sure it doesn't sound like bragging.

"For you?"

"I used to climb the rocks. Almost got in a cage once. With a cheetah. That's why mom hasn't taken me since."

"Since? When was the last time you were here?"

"I don't know, when I was four or five?"

"Is that so?"

It's obvious by Willie's face this is news to him. Surprising because Christopher thought his mom and Willie told each other everything.

They move on and find a cheetah—the same one?—behind large panes of Plexiglas, pacing like the rest of the animals, but with great impatience. It's mad about something.

At this point, any desire within Christopher to climb the rocks and join the animals disappears. He doesn't want to be with them, or be them. No matter how much space they have, they are in cages. Maybe it's better in summer with more people and more animals about. Now it's so stark. He wouldn't want to be caged and unhappy like this. He wants to be like the ones on nature shows, the ones that find their own food without the help of humans. And this is the problem, this is what's bugging him: what he feels for the caged animals is exactly what he feels at each and every school he's ever attended.

They continue through the Africa section, which is large but empty because animals like the zebras are gone for the winter. Where would they go? Two giraffes and a rhino are indoors in an even smaller cage, although cosy and warm, and the building's high ceiling makes it look roomy.

Their last stop is the best as it's tense watching a graceful Bengal tiger from overhead. The way its orange body with black stripes sways proves to be Christopher's biggest test: he's itching to copy it, to imagine stripes on his back twisting with the same rhythm as this cat. He's not sure if it's self-control or because he feels down but he overcomes it.

Though he's pleased he did well, it wasn't as hard as he thought it would be.

On the way to the car, Christopher looks back at the zoo entrance, a wall of ticket booths and gates and fences keeping those who live there inside and those who don't belong outside. That those gates, like gates everywhere in the world of people, built by people, and not natural gates, are, to him, in a way, somewhat sad.

Because if he thinks about it, isn't his house, or the house of anyone for that matter, just another zoo? A place where one can visit humans and cats and dogs and hamsters and other domesticated pets? The difference is people in houses can leave them, of course, but they can never really be free of them, can they, because they have to come back? Or just find another one.

What about schools? How are they different? They're just temporary zoos where he feels trapped.

Willie holds the door while Christopher gets in the front seat.

"Thanks for opening my cage."

"What?"

"Nothing."

"Are you all right?"

"Yeah. Thanks Willie, for taking me to the zoo."

"You bet. We'll go again on a nicer day, okay?"

Willie says it, as if he's the reason Christopher feels down, which isn't true. But all Christopher can do is nod.

# 5

Deborah wants to lash out at Willie. The same Willie who poured her a glass of Chilean Cabernet after her shift and asked how it went, listening intently as she summarized—tiring but promising with middle- class clients less shy about tipping than those at that dingy Irish pub in the dingier downtown location—making a decent though imperfect effort to contain his theories on the motivation behind that tipping, then insisted she relax on the sofa while he reheated the plate of pasta he had prepared for her in case she hadn't eaten—she hadn't—then rejoined her with a refill and a Moosehead for himself, but not before putting on her favourite Moby CD. Which is when he ever so casually let her know about the zoo visit.

"I see," is all she can say.

Nothing more comes to mind in the long silence that follows during which she finishes most of her food, the impulse to unleash a stormier reaction kept in check. Not so much by the risk of waking up her son, but by a sense of guilt stemming from having led Willie to believe she took Christopher to the zoo from time to time, a deception he likely uncovered.

Truth is, she hasn't taken Christopher to the zoo since he was four or five. Or was it six? She used to revel in her son's joy at each new creature they encountered. Their visits provided a happy escape from whatever emotions were plaguing her at the time. Until she began to fear his actions could lead to disaster. All his impetuous behaviours—taking off his clothes, emulating animal movements, but especially running amok over the rocks and almost getting in once—intensified at the zoo. The time he nearly got himself mauled by a cheetah marked the end of their zoo excursions. Willie's report that Christopher was subdued, that he stayed on his feet the entire time—a claim she doesn't fully buy—pleases her as a sign of progress but also deepens the guilt for making Christopher miss out on the experience all this time. So in the end she can't be angry at Willie for taking him to the zoo; if anything, he's done her a favour on that account; if anything, she's the one deserving of that lashing.

Perhaps for more than just this. Though she can rationalize the many difficult decisions she's made on behalf of her son to herself, she's not so confident she could defend them to others. It's difficult to surmise the links between those decisions and his behaviours. He's always been different, even before she was called on to make certain choices. The idea she's a poor mother, rather than simply an imperfect mother who's completely self-reliant and estranged from the familial resources other parents take for granted, is one her pride might not withstand. She puts a hand to her mouth, almost choking on the last tangled forkful of spaghetti— what does her pride have to do with the welfare of her son?

Willie's keeping quiet, letting her eat in peace, giving her time to process this, perhaps awaiting a lashing. As he should. Despite her own guilt, she is and legitimately can be frustrated with Willie for having done this in her absence without her consent. Was this an effort on his part to fortify Christopher's affection, as if he needed it? It would be with the best intentions, of course, not traitorous, and most definitely not an indictment of her parenting abilities. Still, he can't do such things unilaterally and, if only to ensure they remain on the same page, she's got to nip this in the bud.

"I wish you'd told me beforehand."

She swallows the last bite, accidentally dropping the fork on the plate, making a loud ting.

"I didn't think of it until you were at work."

"I see," she says, his quietly confident matter-of-factness confusing her. "But next time . . ."

"Deborah, listen, you may not like this . . ."

He pauses to wait for her to set down the plate and take a sip of wine before revealing bringing up seeing a professional directly with Christopher. He intercepts her reaction with the claim her son is open to it, eager to improve his social interactions with other kids. Hard to believe, yet Willie's saying it in such an assured way she finds it hard to refute as well. When he says he intends to see the Principal in the morning, alone if necessary, it's not as a provocation—if it were she'd know how to react—but rather a reasonable, even sensible, plan against which her pride is powerless.

"But you said Christopher was fine at the zoo. So today's incident could have been the last one."

A weak argument, she knows. Willie shakes his head slowly, in a way that makes his features rather handsome.

"I think the extent of the change from how he was at the school to this afternoon at the zoo makes it more important to understand, with help, what's going on, as soon as possible. Before he gets much older."

She fears he's right. She's always feared this and has always hid behind her own feelings. This is why she appreciates Willie's presence in her life. She needs a man who possesses the patience he does to get past her denials, her fears, her pride. To shake her out of her comfortable delusions. Contrary to her thinking until now, she needs Willie to be fully and directly involved with Christopher. Time to face the reality she can't do it alone.

"All right," she says, softly. "I wasn't happy you took my son to the zoo but now I'm glad you did."

By his smile it's clear he's surprised at his success.

They sit quietly while finishing their drinks. The wine's going down smoother than usual and she's feeling better with each sip, proud of herself for letting go. Then, expecting to see a similar humour in Willie, she looks up to see him sullen, his eyes staring down at her uniform. He's had a few beers and it's likely he's not aware he's doing it.

"Don't tell me you're still upset about what I'm wearing."

"You could have had the decency to have changed by now."

Can't quit while ahead, can you? she thinks, as she tries to keep her cool while he tips his beer glass to take the last swig.

It frustrates her he can't accept he is and will continue to be her only man. That his caring nature, simple needs, and humble character are enough for her, all she wants, all she needs. Any desire for storybook passion or romance, let alone prosperity, died for her a long time ago. She's not bitter about that, that's just how it is. She wants him to accept he is good enough, in her eyes. Tonight's discussion should have cemented that. For him to transition so readily to this petty jealousy is, well, tedious.

He puts his glass down and now he's smiling, acting as if he was kidding. Funny guy, she thinks, let's test this.

She stands up, tugs at her skirt hem, and walks over to him. She bends low to takes his empty glass to the kitchen where she pours another. She returns and stands next to him, her thigh almost touching his cheek as she slowly sets the glass down. She stays there until he grabs at her leg. Her reflexes  surprise him as she swipes his hand away and steps back.

"I am sorry, sir, but I have a man at home."

"Is that so?"

"To whom I'm faithful, even if he's not confident I can make sure of that myself."

Willie laughs.

"I can assure you he was a fool, but no more, and that he's confident now."

"And how would you know that?"

"Because that man is me."

"I see. I suppose that changes things."

She sits on his lap, grabs the beer and puts it in his right hand, then takes his left hand and puts it on her leg.

# 6

It's early as Willie probes his way downstairs, keeping the lights off so as not to wake Deborah or Christopher. Outside, it's oppressively dark. No way Todd's up yet so Willie kills time tidying up, first collecting the remnants of Deborah's uniform. Good thing Christopher's still asleep. He picks up the skirt, sighs.

He nearly blew it last night by letting out his true feelings about this ridiculous outfit. Somehow, he had the wits to make light of it. He can't help himself. He's no catch and it's easy to imagine it not taking much more than good looks and impressive tipping to cast him aside. He knows thinking this insults Deborah, as she repeatedly and often sharply reminds him. But it's a realistic assessment of his situation, has been since their friendship developed into a romance.

It was much easier when he first met Deborah, when she and Dwight, his best friend, hit it off at that bar in

Australia. When he could admire her beauty knowing the romantic possibilities were nil. Even after Dwight's death, their friendship stayed platonic for some time and that only changed when Willie started to develop a close relationship with Christopher who was unusual from the get go. He could envision Dwight's disappointment in his son had he survived the mission. Dwight would have fixated on the oddities in the boy's behaviour and be blind to the fact there was much more to the boy. Christopher has an inexplicably positive impact on people or at least on those open to it. That Deborah kept her son sheltered meant Willie was a benefactor of that charm, from which a parallel bond formed with Deborah. It was organic too and might have happened had he met her some other way. Because of that, neither he nor Deborah viewed their coming together as a betrayal. End result, he found himself with a wonderful woman who would ordinarily be out of his league.

His insecurity is fuelled by another factor, his inability to contribute more financially. Deborah seems comfortable with their modest lifestyle, lack of friends and social life. Indeed, sometimes it's as if she delights in it, as if rebelling against the comforts she grew up with before coming to Canada. But can anyone sustain that forever? Maybe Deborah can. He ought to trust her faith in his relationship with Christopher to whom he's almost a father.

This was never more evident than last night. Even without the passionate ending, their talk went far better than Willie could have hoped. He expected Deborah to aggressively resist his attempts to have them see the Principal. That she relented says a lot, including her dramatized insistence he has nothing to worry about in terms of her job. She's right, he knows, but it may take time for it to register to the point where he can contain his jealousy enough to stop saying the stupid things he says. To handle it instead as he did last night, with humour. Given those results, that time will come sooner rather than later. Now, if only he can be as confident about not doing stupid things like getting involved with Todd and his schemes.

Willie hears movement from upstairs, a toilet flushing. Christopher, no doubt, a much earlier riser than his mother. No chance to try Todd now. Willie goes to the kitchen to prepare breakfast, getting out Christopher's bowl and spoon, his Lucky Charms cereal. Then the orange juice and milk.

How will he react to hearing they're going to the school this morning? They don't have people to call on short notice in such situations, so they'll have to bring him along.

"Morning," Christopher says, groggily.

Once Christopher settles in at the table and starts eating, Willie makes himself a coffee, excuses himself, and heads to the living room where he can't be heard. He pauses to make sure Christopher doesn't follow before making the call.

"Todd, give me an update."

"Not a good time to talk, Willie," Todd says, the fear in his voice palpable.

"Why not? What's going on?"

"We'll talk later."

Then, just like that, Todd hangs up. It leaves Willie in more of a mental mess than after the call at the zoo yesterday when Todd revealed his father's warning to get a lawyer was not because of getting shoved, but because he had become aware of the furniture scam. Apparently the old man intended to reclaim all he'd lost one way or another, every last penny's worth. When Willie reminded Todd they were partners, Todd said his father wouldn't see it that way. Obviously, Todd had put it all on Willie and when Willie threatened to reveal the son's part, Todd laughed, then warned Willie to keep scarce and not answer the door. Something in Todd's voice now makes that warning even more ominous.

It also makes the appointment at the school a welcome distraction. Only it's barely past eight and the appointment isn't until eleven. Nearly three hours for him to speculate various scenarios. Fertile ground for paranoia. Enough time to pay a visit to Todd but he can't go to the warehouse. If Bralen saw Willie there, no doubt the cops would be called.

He checks on Christopher who's eating slowly and seems caught up in his own concerns.

"What's up, Christopher?"

"Am I going to school today?"

"Let me get your mom. We'll have a little talk."

This seems to satisfy Christopher who clearly has no desire to go to school. To him, the more they linger, the greater the chance he'll avoid it.

"Can I have another bowl?"

"Sure."

Willie pours it for him then goes upstairs. He pauses when a siren sounds. It gets louder, closer, then drifts off. Willie takes the stairs two at a time to look out the master bedroom window, which faces the front. Nothing.

"Morning," Deborah says, smiling contentedly at him. "What time is the appointment?"

"Eleven, but Christopher's awake. The sooner we tell him he has to come, the better."

"Right, I'll be down shortly."

Shortly doesn't mean the same to Deborah as it does to Willie as she takes a good forty minutes to shower and dress. His impatience to get away from the house, even though they still have nearly an hour to make the ten-minute drive, starts to bear down. Cleaning up after Christopher and preparing some toast for Deborah only kills a few minutes.

At last, she comes down and joins her son who's watching cartoons. Willie brings coffee for both of them as they sit down on either side of Christopher.

"What's going on?"

Willie nods for Deborah to take the lead but she shakes her head, motions for him to do it. This is a big moment for him but a pressure in his head, and a tightness in his stomach dilutes it.

The doorbell rings.

Deborah seems to be waiting for him to answer the bell but he can't. In fact, he's petrified, almost about to vomit. When he doesn't move, she goes to answer, gasping as she opens the door and steps back to let in a woman Willie's never seen before. A woman closer to his age, dressed conservatively but with a certain elegance. Not at all like a cop, more like a child welfare agent.

"So you found me," Deborah says.

# 𝒦

A salty wetness contacts the raw, scraped away flesh on his cheek, inciting a painful burning that restores consciousness, as well as unfiltered awareness of the soreness in every limb of his immobile body. It's so intense a return to unconsciousness almost would be welcome. But the fact even one of his senses is operating has to be considered a miracle.

A rustling of movement becomes distinct from the crackling flames. That means he can hear too. He tries to call out to whatever it is but this causes the wetness on his face to run down his neck into his mouth. A sharp foul taste worsened by an even fouler odour. He tries to spit it out but isn't strong enough. He swallows. Fortunately it stays down and he can take comfort in confirming two more senses operating, albeit disgustingly so.

His eyes, however, won't open on their own, his eyelids weighed down by ash. Or by a reluctance to observe the horror around him. But he must know, must overcome it, must face the truth. He manages to raise his eyelids enough to see a low sun slipping away in a sky filled with light clouds darkened by smoke. He twists his neck towards the rainforest from where he thinks the rustling sound is coming. There it is, a shape he doesn't recognize. It yawns.

Impossible. It can't be. He's seen jaws open as wide as this only in photos. Either he's dreaming an outback mirage or his mind is going. He shuts his eyes. When he opens them again, the shape is gone. Gone like everything he is, was, and could ever be.

They're all dead, he knows it. For even one to have survived, let alone to have that one be his son is as impossible as that mirage is real. Drew's death is as certain as his own demise is imminent. He may not perish from the flames, of which he seems clear, but will certainly do so from this excruciating pain a human can only bear so long. When the last breath of Andrew Kiltepper the sixth comes and goes, it will be the last male Kiltepper breath. An inglorious ending to an improbable but glorious dynasty. Sadly echoing the unhappy fate of the Aborigines and the impossible creature he just imagined whose image is on the Tasmanian coat of arms.

Coat of arms.

Andy lifts his head ever so gently, aims his gaze towards the estate where flames relentlessly work at the back rooms. The destruction is like a television show, the screen a gaping doorframe that ought to be filled with the massive front door that for two centuries symbolized the Kiltepper heritage. Crafted by the original Kiltepper from a Huon pine tree he likely cut down himself, adorned with an ornate panel for each generation since the first, where is it? There it is, in pieces all around. Must have blown out. But how? And why is he here and not inside with everyone else?

It comes back. Getting ready for dinner in the bedroom upstairs, putting on and admiring the medallion, then seeing the wide, curvy bands of red and yellow out the window, tearing through brush and ancient eucalypts, rapidly advancing. An angry bushfire intent on destroying an estate that, with its primitive wood, could offer no resistance. It took mere seconds before he heard the terrible screaming, the yells of his brothers, their wives, his nephews, his wife and, of course, Drew. None had a chance. Why didn't he try to help them? Was he standing still all that time?

No, he was trying. The hallway was consumed with flames and impassable. He had to jump out the window and the landing probably broke his legs. He was still able to drag himself to the front door but only got up one step before an explosion blasted the entry away to where it is and shot Andy to where he is to suffer the awful screaming that diminished just before he lost consciousness.

Yet now the unaccompanied roar of the flames seems worse. Why was he spared? Why not Drew? Or one of his nephews? Why only him? An impotent man approaching his mid-fifties. Him and a stupid door, a door he loves, a magnificent tribute to the Kiltepper legacy, yet still just a door.

Its top is nearest the estate, nearest the flames. Andy can faintly make out the wooden disc bearing the mighty "K". The original corporate logo inspiring the one now ubiquitous across Tasmania. Somehow, it's remained attached to the door. From this angle, the way it's charred and marred by the fire, it also reminds him of the Tasmanian coat of arms, at least one side of it. He has to get it, save it. Somehow. If only as a noble last action that can, with luck, also distract the pain.

An inspired effort gets Andy several inches closer. Mixed success. For the pain is terrible, worse than he's ever experienced before. His old trick of keeping still and absorbing the pain until you sort of got used to it doesn't work this time. He holds his position a few minutes before trying again, using anger to help fuel the next attempt to cover the last ten metres to the crest. He makes it. Now he must gather enough strength for one tug, perhaps two. He gives it a pull. To his surprise, it comes off easily and success fuels the strength to drag it and himself as close to the rainforest as possible. Only he can move no more. His legs won't obey. Broken for sure. He clutches the coat of arms tightly, as if to crush whatever remains that's keeping him alive, as if to hasten his end, his family's end, get it over with. Even with his weak grip, as if to symbolize fragility, it breaks apart, crumbles in his fingers. He releases an involuntary cry but stops short of tears. Crying isn't in the Kiltepper blood. Neither is despair. Or sorrow. Not as long as the idea of the legacy remains in his mind.

The rustling returns. In his madness, Andy once again senses the creature nearby. Impossible. Yet Andy hears it, smells it. It knows he can't move but must know he's still alive. It seems to be settling in to act as an audience, confidante even, or an agent of the land waiting to pronounce dead a dynasty. An ignoble finale though impressive if viewed against the origins of Morris Fitzpatrick who arrived at Port Jackson in 1800 from England, convicted of the theft of an item or items that have never been and likely never will be identified by Andy.

The value was enough to warrant a seven-year sentence, but not so criminal as to preclude a chance to sail with Matthew Flinders on a mission to settle Port Dalrymple. A northern complement to Hobart, this new colony would aid England in establishing control over Tasmania and Australia before France. Through hard work, or perhaps charisma, Morris managed to get his sentenced reduced, meaning only a year after he came to Tasmania, he gained his freedom. Instead of returning to England, he chose to stay, acquiring the land that includes the burning estate he built in 1811. The estate where he raised his first and only son, Andrew.

Prior to the birth, Morris changed his surname to Kiltepper, seeing his convict past as an obstacle to his and his family's prospects. How he came upon the name Kiltepper is unknown. It sounds Irish and he could have been from Ireland and just gotten arrested in England. Or it was the maiden name of his son's mother, another person of whom nothing is known. The scarcity of records makes it feasible to suppose Morris never married.

Indeed, Andy would not have known of Morris Fitzpatrick if not for the genealogical efforts he and his father undertook twenty years ago. For Morris was intent on erasing that convict past and, with the help of his son, did a decent job of it. The only information they could find about Morris Fitzpatrick came from public records, some of which took years to locate and access. The estate never offered clues to dispute the claim of the first Andrew Kiltepper that he was an orphan. Succeeding generations took this at face value—if one trait links early generations of Kilteppers, it's their aversion to nostalgia—until Andy and his father, noting the fictive histories of many other Tasmanians, decided to look into it. By this time, convict pasts were coming into vogue. That this particular convict was one of the first to settle and grow the Launceston area only enhanced the mystique. Not only was the Kiltepper family a social and financial powerhouse, they could also claim a colourful history.

As much as the first Andrew Kiltepper did to eliminate what was to him and his fellow citizens a shameful past, with even greater zeal did he aspire to create an admirable, if not prestigious future. He vowed to make this false name a name of pride to be augmented by future generations. He kept these ambitions private, only noting them in a preface to his journal, until he earned a degree of success. One can only speculate the role his convict father played in this as no Kiltepper journal makes mention of a Morris of any name. Public records do document a Morris Fitzpatrick dying in 1825, when Andrew was nineteen, coincidentally the day before the inaugural journal entry. They also record a lease for the land around the estate to a shepherd a month later. This transaction enabled the move to

Hobart where it is assumed Andrew buried Morris. From here on, the Kiltepper history becomes clearer since the first Andrew—claiming ignorance of his past—ensured his descendants would be aware of their heritage via his thorough journal keeping.

The farmland provided collateral to back loans for inventory as he established shops in Hobart that sold alcohol, weapons, and other settlers' essentials. The rental income helped cover operating costs. An influx of new immigrants ensured profitability from the start. Combined with an upstanding manner and regular church going, he found a formula to impress upon his heirs. Once he found a wife.

Alas, finding that wife proved difficult. Andrew, despite his success, was not a popular fellow. His pride rankled some but it was his undefined past that proved the biggest hurdle in dealing with the haughtier, more discerning families. His business acumen was held in regard, as was his reputation as a gentleman, but these attributes on their own weren't sufficient to transcend basic prejudices and elevate him socially. He wasn't an outcast like the Aborigines or convicts, but his status wasn't much higher either. It was in this part of his life he likely developed the forbearance for which the Kilteppers became renowned as he resisted the temptation to find a wife through more accessible but less savoury avenues. He trusted his industry to persevere until the focus shifted from his past to his present. He never faulted others for this treatment: it was how it was then. He saw his dilemma as a rite of passage to achieve his ambitions. He had to trust his situation eventually would change.

It did. Though not in a way Andrew could have predicted. This was the period of the Black Wars and Aborigines were a prime source of trouble and complaint for many. Not for Andrew who spent most of his time working in the city and thus rarely encountered them. He was lucky in that they never set fire to or assaulted the estate though that didn't mean the fear wasn't there. That fear kept Andrew in Hobart and he made only occasional, brief visits to the country. He reasoned the estate's best security was vacancy and was convinced that, had the estate been occupied more often, those attacks inevitably would have touched him too.

Thus he could maintain a neutral stance during the Black Wars, though inside turmoil was growing. As a seller of guns, he couldn't escape the fear that, each time he sold a rifle or bullets, their purpose was to exact revenge for some attack on settlers rather than for hunting food or defending property. Which is why he joined the Black Line and its effort to find and corral the most aggressive Aboriginal tribes to the Tasman Peninsula. It seemed the best solution for all as there the Aborigines could enjoy their way of life without interference from the settlers, and set an example to motivate other tribes to do the same. Uprooting the native inhabitants did not sit easily with Andrew in principle, but the situation would only worsen as long as the Aborigines continued to resist adapting to the colonists. To Andrew, the Black Line was the least violent option; whereas he knew others, particularly near towns where attacks were more prevalent, who would gladly hunt and kill every last one.

What a debacle The Black Line turned out to be. With settlers and soldiers numbering more than two thousand, they managed to capture two natives, one a youth, and kill a few others. Andrew returned to Hobart demoralized at the failure and ineptness, and appalled by the brutal views of some of his fellow citizens. He wasn't alone feeling demoralized. The show of force had an impact on the Aborigines who realized the settlers could continue to conduct such initiatives, perfecting their methods until they reached overwhelming effect. They surrendered and agreed to migrate to Flinders Island. It should have been out of sight, out of mind for Andrew. Only his curiosity led him to discover that, contrary to what he thought, those Aborigines were not allowed to retain their way of life. Instead, they were pressured to adopt British ways, observe British law, learn English, and take religious teaching. To Andrew, as he noted in one of the most poignant entries in his journals, their race was doomed. If not through extermination then through assimilation.

This sad possibility inspired him to redouble his efforts to establish a strong and distinct Kiltepper legacy. The stabilized Aboriginal problem helped as the newfound peace brought more settlers from England. Among the newcomers, Andrew found a wife, Angela, a preacher's daughter from Hull, and the couple married within a year. However, it took five years and three daughters before he finally had a son and heir, Andrew Kiltepper II.

The senior Andrew inculcated the importance of legacy to this son who embraced it. The two were so close it's undeniable to Andy the newest Andrew had to know of Morris Fitzpatrick, for he must have questioned his father about their past. To have none in a world of convicts would have been an unlikely coincidence. Most certainly the elder Andrew disclosed their true past and the two then conspired to keep it hidden. Their strategy involved shifting business focus away from Hobart to Launceston. They began acquiring land to sell to new settlers who sought their consultation. Though immigrants could acquire land for free, many were unfamiliar with the varied geography. Exploiting their local knowledge, they turned into savvy speculators by obtaining strategic lots for which more ambitious farmers would pay a premium so they could make their properties contiguous or frustrate competition. Success increased profoundly once the younger Andrew refurbished the estate and established it as their headquarters. The greater the effort buyers had to put forth to conduct negotiations, the more they would value the product was the thinking. The remote site also provided a firsthand demonstration of the newfound peace in the countryside, assuaging the more fearful clients. Furthermore, the lovely setting and pampered guest treatment ensured civil negotiations. While one couldn't say the Kilteppers were esteemed just yet, they weren't despised either.

The Kiltepper legacy was developing as well as Morris Fitzpatrick's son could have hoped in all but one aspect: an heir. The remote location reduced the opportunities for his son to find a wife. So the two agreed to split the purchasing and selling duties and have Andrew Jr. return to Launceston where he could keep tabs on competition and more effectively lobby officials in charge of granting deeds to do so in favour of the Kilteppers. And seek a wife.

The third Kiltepper generation established itself within a year of Andrew Jr. marrying Susan Baxter, whose family owned the bank holding many of their property mortgages. They had a boy. Then a second arrived, and a third. At his father's behest, though to his wife's chagrin, Andrew Jr. named them all after himself. Thus began the family tradition in which the firstborn male would go by Andrew and be given no middle name while all subsequent males would answer to their middle name.

As the three boys grew up, it was clear only the oldest son could uphold the standards established by their grandfather. The other two boys—Martin and Alan—drank, womanized, got into fights and brushes with the law. Their independent spirits drove them on several occasions to mine for gold in Victoria, always failing and returning to Tasmania to behave pretty much as convicts behaved. How that had to have galled their grandfather who would have seen this as a threat to his legacy. That may be why little is known about them after they left Tasmania for Victoria the last time in 1880.

Andrew did behave as a true Kiltepper ought to, and worked hard to further family fortunes, but he was as independent and headstrong as his younger brothers and in no rush to wed. The Kiltepper name had some cachet in the community by this time so it wasn't for lack of opportunity. It's just he preferred hunting at the estate to socializing. The land around the estate was still leased to sheep farmers and, as he was a good hunter, his presence was welcomed as he ably helped rid the lands of the Tasmanian tigers threatening the flocks.

The 1888 Tasmanian tiger bounty inspired him to organize a competition at the estate. Winner take all. That is, the one who had the most bounty claims won the money for all the claims together. It became a semi-annual event lasting two to four weeks at a time, rendering Andy's great-grandfather virtually inaccessible in Launceston. Those who hoped to do business with the Kilteppers during these events, including the marrying off of a daughter, had better learn to shoot.

Hence, aging Andrew Kiltepper I, declining in health, with little to do other than worry about his legacy, would remain anxious about it through his death in 1895. At least he lived long enough to hear of a marriage a few months before his passing. But he was too feeble to make the trip from the estate to Launceston for the wedding and so he never met the bride. Perhaps this was merciful as the couple had difficulty conceiving. It would take fourteen years before the birth of Andrew Kiltepper IV, in 1909, the last year of the bounty. Also, no one could be sure what his reaction would be to a Kiltepper marrying a woman rumoured to have been born out of mixed parents. Racism was not a Kiltepper flaw, per se, but the historical lack of interaction with natives meant their prejudices had not been tested to this degree. It was never proven if she was part Aborigine, though a distinct darkening in the complexions of Kiltepper males of subsequent generations indicates she was.

Once the Tasmanian tiger bounty was called off, interest in hunting evaporated for Andrew Kiltepper III, replaced by guilt for the certain extinction of this poor species at the hands of his kind. His empathy paralleled that of his grandfather for the Aborigines after the Black Line. He was determined to pass on this sensitivity to his son, Andy's grandfather, and demonstrated it a year later when he came upon a Thylacine that had been shot. He took the animal in and expended great effort nursing it to health. During the healing, the tiger formed an attachment to his rescuer and, at the request of his own son and Andy's grandfather, they kept it as a pet. Sadly, the creature didn't survive long, and its loss was almost as deep as that of a family member. Andy used to love hearing stories about the animal, which carried a nostalgic melancholy each time he was allowed to touch the skin his grandfather kept.

From this point the diligent journal keeping fell off as decades of growth and achievements would be recorded in newspapers and other media instead of private notes. Each generation built upon what it inherited or transformed focus altogether as was done in the earlier generations with the shifts from farming to retailing to real estate. Unlike many family-run businesses that get stuck in tradition, this was encouraged. So long as the Kiltepper name remained untarnished, and the male line continued.

They did have a few more black sheep, as was to be expected in any dynastic family, and there were struggles through depressions and other uncertain times, including the two world wars. But the efforts of Andy's grandfather, father, and of Andy and his quick actions during the global financial crisis a few years back, ensured the Kiltepper lineage would not be threatened by extinction again.

Until now. When all that's left is reminiscences that will dissipate with his own expiration. Even this creature keeping him company, whether real or imaginary, will outlast him. Impossible animal, if you are real, bark or say something to declare if you are actually there. The smell alone is not convincing.

Then again, if the creature could speak, what would it say? Next to its story, the Kiltepper legacy is just hubris, an indulgent tale. Too polished, too sentimental, a sham. Seven generations. What's that compared to the thousands of generations of this creature and the Aboriginal races that survived until his meagre clan came along?

Oddly, this thought is inspiring. For as long as he breathes, as long as he feels, hears, smells, tastes, sees, he can and must forge another future for his daughter, pretty and fair little Carla, who's about to discover she's lost the mother she idolizes. As well as for his rough and tumble niece, Wilma, to whom someone will have to break the news the parents who adopted her are dead. That someone is him. It has to be. He cannot abandon the girls. He may be biologically impotent, the male bloodline may be at end, but he still possesses the Kiltepper drive, which he can instil in others. With luck, the new estate he's building on the other side of this rainforest has managed to survive the bushfires. That slim hope makes it paramount he stay alive as long as possible, and not dwell on the Kiltepper fate.

The sky is darkening, the sun nearly gone. This enhances the brightness of the flames that continue to viciously work away at the remnants of the estate.

Andy hears the rustling again and the smell of the creature becoming stronger. He doesn't want to look at it, doesn't want to believe it exists. He feels a tingle on his skin and then the smell recedes, though leaving behind a wetness on his neck, which he now notices, with great alarm, feels bare.

His consciousness once again slips away, but as it does, he hears a faint wail in the distance though, like his erstwhile companion, it's bound to be a fantasy.

# 7

"Not so as you made it easy for us, Debs."

The woman's voice has the same cadence as Deborah's but the accent is sharper, refined, leaving no doubt about its Australian origin; whereas with Deborah it's not always clear. A facial resemblance is there, particularly in the small curvy noses, but the older sister obviously colours her hair, the artificial auburn a stark contrast to Deborah's natural though thinning blonde. She's plumper than Deborah too, cute but not as attractive, and a bit frumpy.

Willie can relax, certain who it is. Though now it seems his petrified state has transferred to Deborah who's just staring.

"Thought you'd escape us forever?"

The male voice startles Willie. He hadn't noticed a man and leans to look closer. All he can see is a shadow that's tall and thin, not a beer drinker like himself. He sounds like a moderator accustomed to easing tensions. Or like a tiresome salesman from whom one always has to glean two meanings. His accent is far more cultivated than the woman's, bordering on pompous, though with a friendly note.

"Actually, yes, I thought I had, Ruthie."

Deborah's Australian accent comes out now—a sign to Willie she's perturbed—though the response does not rattle the visitors; if anything, they find it amusing. Deborah rarely talks about her estranged sister—has never mentioned a brother-in-law—yet this exchange is pretty much what Willie imagined it might be. Perhaps for them too. Then again, his girlfriend is never one to shy away from sharing her feelings at any given time.

Deborah steps back to allow them in. As they remove their coats, Willie glances at Christopher, only to find the boy staring back at Willie, looking as if he's been doing so awhile. Christopher breaks his gaze to study his aunt. What's going through his young mind? No doubt struck by the likeness, it depends how much his mother told him about them.

Then, without warning, Deborah's guard drops, and she begins trembling. She hugs Ruth, causing the woman to drop her purse and just like that the sisters are sobbing. Willie notices the man's shadow coming closer. He follows suit and the two men reach the women at the same time.

"Oh, hello," the man says, upon seeing Willie, putting out a hand awkwardly around the hugging sisters. "Fred Johnson, pleased to meet you."

Deborah and her sister separate to give the men room. Willie shakes the proffered hand, distracted by the hipster glasses that seem out of place. As does the expensive, impractically thin tan leather coat.

"Willie Galloway."

"Pleased to meet you, Willie," Fred says, then looks at Christopher, plainly happier to greet his nephew than his sister-in-law's common law spouse. "And who might this be?"

"That's my son, Christopher," Deborah says.

"Indeed," Fred says, suddenly animated. "Could he be . . .?"

"No."

The abruptness of the response startles Willie. Deborah breaks away to pull Christopher towards her, then faces the guests while keeping her hand on her son's shoulders.

"Honey, this is your Aunt Ruth and your Uncle Fred Johnson from Tasmania in Australia. Aunt Ruth is my sister."

"Actually, Debs, we live in Adelaide now."

"I must ask then," Fred says, "if this isn't . . . then what happened to—?"

"Fred, not now."

"Of course. Of course. Lots of catching up to do. But young man, tell me, how old are you?"

"He's ten," Deborah says, with an emphasis that seems excessive to Willie.

"You don't say. At that height I'd have pegged him at least a year older, maybe two."

A nudge from Ruth quiets Fred and prompts him to produce a stuffed kangaroo. He holds it out for Christopher who looks at his mom and waits for a brief nod before accepting the gift. Odd that this man, who a moment ago seemed surprised at seeing Christopher, would have a child's gift at the ready.

"Thanks," Christopher says.

"Honey," Deborah says, "why don't you go and get dressed?"

"They're not on school holidays here," Ruth says, to Fred. Then to Deborah, "Is his school nearby?"

"He's not going to school today," Deborah says, the defensiveness in her tone restored. She checks herself before saying more.

"Oh," Ruth says, "is he sick?"

"He's just not going to school today."

The terseness in Deborah's voice is enough to ward off further questioning. For the moment. The two sisters scrutinize each other in a manner Willie suspects was customary when they were younger.

"You two must be jet-lagged, coming all the way from Down Under," Willie says. "How long was the flight?"

"Actually, we've been in Canada for a week."

"Is that so?" Deborah says.

But instead of pursuing this, she takes their coats, hangs them up, then guides the couple to the living room. Christopher, instead of going upstairs to change, parks himself on the floor next to Deborah who appears uneasy in the easy chair. Fred and Ruth are on the sofa.

Willie remains standing.

"It's no palace, though cozy I'm sure," Ruth says, "but these furnishings are high end."

"Willie got us a discount. Otherwise they'd be as drab as the house."

"Forgive me, I didn't mean to knock anything."

"I'm happy with what we have."

"Of course."

Willie breaks the ensuing interminable silence to announce he'll make coffee. In the kitchen, he works silently to get the fancy cups and saucers and wipe off the dust, but can barely hear them. When the water starts boiling it's pointless to try. Christopher joins him and sits at the table.

"What would you like, sport?" Willie says.

"Just some milk."

Willie pours Christopher a glass of milk, then searches the cupboards for a tray to hold the cups. Christopher points to a narrow drawer next to the fridge from which he pulls a plastic tray. It'll do. He loads it with the empty cups, some sugar and milk, and pours the coffee. He heads to the living room while Christopher remains behind.

"I hoped you'd be more pleased we've come all this way," Ruth says. "Guess little has changed."

"Now honey," Fred says, but adds nothing more.

"I'm only asking why you came now, after all these years."

Ruth and Fred exchange looks, clearly making a charade of not having anticipated this question. Willie sets down the tray and sits down. This seems to relax everyone. They help themselves to various combinations of milk and sugar. Their movements seem ritualistic from repetition to Willie who finds the symmetry of it fascinating.

"Daddy's in a hospital," Ruth announces, after a couple of sips.

"A simple letter would have sufficed," Deborah says, with no hesitation.

Willie almost spills his coffee; he's never heard her sound this rude and uncaring before. The rare times she speaks of her family it's never in a positive light, but never this spiteful either.

"We only found your address a week ago."

"When I left, I said it was permanent and I meant it."

"Oh Debs, stop. That's a dozen years ago. You're not saying you don't care about Daddy, are you?" Then, when Deborah crosses her arms: "You're so stubborn, just like him, but I know deep in his heart he wants to mend things."

"What's the matter with your father?"

"He was in a dreadful fire in Tasmania, Willie," Fred says, at which Deborah shifts her body but remains quiet. "One of only two survivors."

"So he's fine," Deborah says.

"No, he's not fine," Ruth says.

"He's really in bad shape, Deborah," Fred says. "He barely survived the airlift to Melbourne."

"There was something in the papers about some big fires," Willie says. "Pretty bad, I imagine."

"Not as devastating as the ones in 1967 but far more traumatic for us," Fred says.

"That's terrible," Willie says, and then glances at Deborah. She's not budging but he can tell she's affected. "Will your father survive?"

"Walter's in and out of consciousness but there's no threat of him dying. At least that's what they told us, which is why we felt now was a good time to come here. Because he . . ."

"Because Daddy wants to make things right."

Ruth's eyes appeal to Deborah for a reaction but, again, none is forthcoming.

Willie's not sure what to do about it, if anything. This cold determination can be an unappealing trait in his girl. Sometimes it's fitting, dealing with certain teachers or customers, for instance. Now it seems cruel and unnecessarily harsh.

"Like I said, a letter would have done."

Ruth recoils. "Of course, we wanted to see you too. And meet your son."

"My son? How did you even know I had a son?"

"We didn't know," Fred says. "We just assumed that, we hoped that you didn't mean what you said when you left Tasmania."

Ruth directs a glance towards Willie.

"Willie knows all about the circumstances that made me leave. Including my abortion."

Deborah did tell Willie about being pregnant before she met Dwight and that she had an abortion. A mere detail in their past. Forgotten. Faded away. Part of the strength of their relationship is a mutual desire to look forward and not probe the past. However now, with the arrival of her sister and brother-in-law, that pact seems at risk, not the least because of his own curiosity.

"Oh Debs, I never seriously thought you'd go through with it."

All this gets from Deborah is a shrug. Fred pats Ruth's hand, as if this is confirmation of a fact his wife has denied to this point. Ruth's face saddens even more. She turns away and Willie can see this isn't easy for Deborah whose voice softens. This time the silence is broken by the sound of Christopher rinsing and putting his breakfast dishes in the sink.

"I was young but old enough to know a child wasn't for me. At that time."

Ruth and Fred together gaze at the kitchen just as Christopher emerges. He pauses, unsure what to do, before heading upstairs. The exchange is odd, to Willie, which adds to his alarm when the telephone rings and precipitates the fear of who the caller might be. Deborah gives him a look that tells him to deal with it. Two rings pass before Willie can reach the kitchen and answer. To his relief, it's Deborah's work. However, she's not pleased when she hears this but takes the phone.

Willie returns to the living room. Fred and Ruth decline his offer for more coffee, which makes it awkward for him.

"So is Christopher your son, then?"

Ruth asks politely and Willie can tell she has a great deal of tact as he's not the least bit offended or insulted.

But anyone can tell by their skin colours Willie couldn't be the biological father. He shakes his head, points a finger at the picture on Deborah's special table and gives them an abbreviated history of his old friend, Dwight Palmer, and how he and Deborah came to be together after Dwight's death. He doesn't mention Fremantle and implies their first meeting was when she and Dwight were a couple awaiting their baby just before the two men shipped off to Afghanistan, on the mission from which Willie returned alone.

Ruth walks to the photo but doesn't pick it up, instead rubbing the two-legged little table it's on.

"Fred, come here, look," she says.

But Fred remains where he is.

"Yes, I noticed."

"I have the same table," Ruth says to Willie, with emotion. "Or rather its sister table. It was handmade by an old family friend. It's Huon pine, a special tree in Tasmania. I'm happy to see Deborah still has it."

"Oh," Willie says, and wishes they'd talk about anything other than furniture. "She values it a great deal. You can see it doesn't match the other pieces, but she insists it stay there."

"She's never talked about where it came from?"

"To be honest, I've never asked."

Ruth hesitates, as if deciding to enlighten Willie. He doesn't encourage it and she returns to her seat.

"So what brought you two together, as a couple, I mean you described the circumstances but what drew you together?"

"Just keeping in touch, honestly. I became kind of a big brother to Christopher and from there, things just progressed."

Ruth looks at him, as if probing for more details. Giving no sign of it but probably wondering how a doll like her sister could end up with a mutt like him. Thankfully, Deborah ends her call, which ends Ruth's silent interrogation.

However, instead of joining them, Deborah goes upstairs without a word, carefully watched by Fred and Ruth. Fred pats his wife's knee reassuringly. A minute later, Deborah comes down wearing a heavy sweater and leggings.

"Why don't I take you for a walk by the lake? It's no Wineglass Bay, and it's rather cold, but pleasant enough."

"Sounds wonderful," Fred says, and Ruth nods.

"What about the school?" Willie says.

"We'll have to postpone it. Can you call them?"

She leaves before he can protest. He's not sure if he's angry or hurt. He closes the door after them, leaving him with Christopher, and a notion they've taken a step backward, a twelve-year step.

# 8

Deborah feels bad for having put Willie in such a position but instinct demanded she usher Fred and Ruth away from the house as quick as possible. Part of it is the fear of information sharing that might put her in a bad light, but mostly it's to ward off this sense of everything closing in on her. She's terrible at multi-tasking when it comes to personal matters.

They reach the end of her street and cross a road before she notices Ruth is shivering while Fred is preoccupied watching the shapes his breaths form. The wind is gustier than yesterday, as if in a hurry to bring in the forecasted cold front and snowstorm.

"We can go back for some sweaters."

"We're fine."

They proceed down her street to reach a multi-use path that's only partly cleared of ice, some of which is concealed by snow.

"Watch your steps," Deborah says.

"Where are we going?" Ruth says.

"Like I said, nowhere spectacular, but it's nice and very quiet in winter."

They cross another street to continue on another path that passes under leafless trees before twisting and curving until it parallels a busier road on which an occasional truck rumbles by. They cross a bridge over a marshy waterway. Dozens of winter birds mingle among ice patches, a few squawking for attention. Beyond the bridge, the floating boards of an eerily empty marina creak as the masts of boats stored for winter chime. The sun, mostly obscured by patches of grey clouds, still casts an occasional bright blue opening large and warm enough to help temper Ruth's shivering.

"Where are you two staying? Our place is small but we could make room."

"Nice of you to offer, Debs," Ruth says, "but we have a hotel and all our stuff's there already."

"In Toronto?"

"No, it's about ten minutes away," Fred says.

So this visit was well planned, Deborah thinks, though she'd expect nothing less from her brother-in-law.

She abandons this thought to focus instead on how their familiar voices hearten her. So much she could take off her coat and still feel warm. She smiles unrestrainedly at her visitors for the first time since their arrival. A natural smile, not forced, her best defence to hold back tears she had given up on ever shedding long ago. Ruth responds in kind and the two share an embrace that lasts a long, cold minute. When they break, Deborah gives a shorter one to Fred who is the one shivering now.

"Never thought I'd admit it," Deborah says, "but I'm so happy to see you two."

"Debs, that means so much to us. I was afraid."

They quicken their pace and stroll along a quay that leads to a pier with a small lighthouse, ignoring warning signs about the patches of ice on the cement surface. Larger, jagged ice chunks float in the water on both sides. Several people are out, a few walking dogs, a senior couple enjoying a stroll, and a pair of joggers. No one is at the end of the pier so Deborah guides the Johnsons there. They stop at a partially protected side of the lighthouse to look out at the lake and its small but choppy waves. Fred points south.

"What's across the lake?"

Deborah points from right to left. "Toronto, Hamilton, Niagara Falls."

"Honey, we must see Niagara Falls before we go back home."

"In winter, Fred? Besides, we only have a week left."

"A mere daytrip. I imagine it's fascinating this time of year. And less crowded."

Fred looks at Deborah who nods agreement, but then has to look away, the rejoice of a moment ago displaced by old feelings. She feels a hand on her shoulder. It's Ruth's.

"Debs, what's the matter?"

She wants to say something but words aren't coming to her, not yet. They're waiting, giving her the time she needs. Which is only fair. They've had however long they took to prepare for this; whereas for Deborah this emotional storm, like the increasing gusts of wind and clouds, came without warning. They're both shivering and a small part of Deborah relishes their punishment. And though it's not what she wants to say, it's uppermost in her mind.

"Okay, out with it. How did you find me? Why did you come? Why now?"

"It wasn't difficult to find you," Fred says, but with no trace of condescension, nor even boasting.

"And we told you why," Ruth says. "We thought you might have read about the bushfires so we had to come in person to tell you about Daddy."

"No, you didn't," Deborah says, despite herself, knowing her rigidity isn't constructive for herself or for her visitors.

"He's our father for crying out loud," Ruth says, her raised voice possibly causing a young couple on a bench to get up and go.

"He's your father, you can have him. Until he betrays you too."

"Oh my God," Ruth says, but her sobbing only makes Deborah cross her arms.

She feels bad for what she's saying it but is able to overcome her guilt by realizing it has to be said, it has to get out and though it may be painful for Ruth, it can't be helped.

"I was quite clear when I left that I never wanted to hear about Tasmania again. Nothing has changed. I'm thrilled you're here, I want to spend time with you, but as far as that place goes, it doesn't exist any longer for me."

Fred flashes a warm smile that compels Deborah to uncross her arms, and then he consoles his wife.

"Ruth, honey, let's be honest. Coming here we knew this might be your sister's reaction. Deborah, forgive us if we've upset you, but we had to see if anything's changed firsthand."

"Now you know."

"You don't want to know about the fire?"

Whenever she hears of events back there, she's always tempted to look but she always resists her curiosity. This time, with Ruth and Fred in front of her, with answers at hand, it's not so easy. On the other hand, if she gives in to sentiment . . .

"Not a bit."

"All right,," Fred says, smiling, as if expecting such a reaction, "let's set that aside, Ruth, and admit we've been looking for an excuse to get over our fear of what might happen and see Deborah for years."

"Fred's right. We just never had—the timing was always—we were always worried about how we'd be received."

"You've been keeping track of me all these years? You've known where I've been?"

"No, not at all. What I meant to imply earlier is that maybe you weren't as careful as you could have been in hiding your tracks. I think it was reasonable for Ruth and I to conclude someday you'd want us to find you. Wishful thinking, I suppose."

"Debs, the point is, the decision to take a chance and come here was extremely difficult."

Deborah looks at them both and it's the first time she can recall ever holding any kind of power over them. She was always the little girl, the one tagging along, but this time they're the ones who seem to need her.

"Okay, I believe you. I appreciate you respecting my wishes for as long as you have. But now what? I'm not prepared to see our father."

Fred suggests they put the matter off and return to the house. The three retrace their path, but once her house is in sight, Deborah changes her mind. Willie won't like it but Deborah chooses to take her visitors to the Tim Hortons nearby. Over coffee, and a bowl of hot soup for Ruth, they delve into happier memories. Such as Deborah's early years when she depended on Ruth after their mother died and their father concentrated on his career. They relive Ruth's on and off again relationship with Fred and how, whenever Ruth was mad at Fred, Deborah would threaten to marry him herself.

But the accumulation of anecdotes connected with Fred and Ruth's often turbulent relationship and early marriage starts to wear on Deborah. She loses interest in talking about the past as nostalgia gives way to melancholy the closer they get to the events that eventually sent her away.

Ruth, bless her soul, seems sensitive to this and doesn't push, knowing this will come up again.

What surprises Deborah is how she doesn't balk at that possibility. In fact, not only does she want them to stay as long as possible, part of her shares this desire to venture into painful memories. Just not yet.

# 9

Ever since his mom left with those people more than half an hour ago, Willie's been moping, restless. Except when checking his cell phone, which he does constantly, he's got a dazed look, probably like the one Christopher thinks he gives off sometimes. Kind of how Willie looked the other day at the zoo, after that odd phone call. This isn't like him. Normally, at least around Christopher, Willie is upbeat, cheerful. Now he's slumped back as they watch the sports highlights on television. Even the rare surprise of a third Leafs win in a row on the weekend makes no difference.

"Willie, what's going on?"

"Not sure. Your mom didn't say anything about your aunt and uncle coming here, did she?"

"No," Christopher says, then shakes his head, because that's not what he meant.

"What do you think of them?" Willie says.

"They seem all right, but I wasn't asking about them."

"Oh?"

"What's going on with school?"

"Right. To be honest, I'm not sure. Depends on when your mother comes back."

"Huh?"

Willie hesitates before telling Christopher about the appointment at the school with the Principal. He reminds Christopher they discussed this at the zoo yesterday. Then Christopher's heart sinks when he hears the appointment is in less than an hour and he has to come along. Willie adds that, because of the visitors, they may have to postpone it.

"Fine with me," Christopher says, which makes Willie laugh.

But it's a nervous laugh and only lasts a moment before Willie becomes serious again. He looks at his phone, at the door, as if he's trying to make a brave decision. It's strange. Even though it might not be a decision Christopher likes, part of him is pulling for Willie to make it.

"Well, it's not fine with me," Willie says, rising with a new energy. "Go get changed. We're making that appointment, even if it's only you and me."

"But mom won't like that," Christopher says to Willie and, to himself: Me neither.

Willie shrugs and it's pointless to argue. Now he misses the moping Willie. Why, oh why, did he have to ask about school? He sulks to himself on the way upstairs, wishing he'd insisted on coming along for the walk. His mom wouldn't have let him but he could have made a fuss that would have made those people, who seemed happy to see him, get her to change her mind.

Christopher takes his time washing his face, brushing his teeth, and picking out clothes to wear. The longer he takes, the greater the chance his mom returns, or the more time Willie has to back out. He buttons up his least favourite but warmest red and green plaid shirt and a pair of jeans. No way he's going to follow the dress code. That would only make it easy for them to leave him there. Now for a fresh pair of socks and he's ready. Except maybe for another pass of his white comb through his black hair. Unfortunately, there's still no sign of his mom returning or of Willie changing his mind. He lets out a sad sigh.

Then the doorbell rings. It's followed by several hard raps on the door. Did Mom forget her keys? Christopher gets to the top of the stairs, then stops, as Willie's at the door, looking out the little window a long time, as if unsure whether to answer.

Christopher retreats to the master bedroom to spy from above. There's a police car on the street, and two officers at the front door, blasts of breath seeping out of their mouths as they calmly talk to each other. They're not acting as if it's about anything serious. They do look impatient, probably wondering why no one's answering. Don't answer, Christopher wants to yell out, but then sees both his mom and Willie's cars in the driveway, and what must be the Johnsons' on the street. One officer points at them as if to say somebody has to be home.

Finally, Willie opens the door and Christopher slides open the window to listen.

"William Galloway?" one officer says. "May we come in? We'd like to ask you some questions."

"About?"

"Sir, it's cold, it might be better if we talk in your hallway."

"The place is in disarray right now."

Christopher keeps still, perplexed why Willie isn't letting them in.

"It's a serious matter," says the other officer who seems bored. "We'd be happy to talk with you at the police station."

"How serious?"

"You know a Mackenzie Bralen? He's the owner of Bralen and Son—"

"Yes, I know him, I work for him, worked for him, until yesterday."

"His body was found last night. We believe he's been—"

Christopher gasps.

"You know what," Willie says, surprisingly calm and cool, "my spouse and her son are out for a walk and are liable to come home anytime. I'll take you up on that offer to talk at the station."

"It wasn't an offer but very well."

Christopher's mouth remains open, which he only realizes when a drop of drool falls down his chin onto his arm. He wipes it away. What's going on here? Should he say something? Should he go down to help? Willie doesn't seem upset and now he's smiling, saying something to make one of the policemen smile. Maybe Willie is trying to make it look that way, knowing Christopher's watching.

The officers keep a close eye on Willie as he opens the foyer closet, at an angle that blocks their view to upstairs, and grabs his coat. Willie puts it on and flashes a wink upstairs before exiting and locking the door behind him.

It's quiet now. The police car is gone but Willie's Buick is still there. This is disturbing. But exciting too. They never leave Christopher by himself. And now he's like that kid in the Christmas movie. Willie must really trust him, which is funny because a moment ago it seemed the opposite.

Christopher spots an object on the floor that looks out of place. Aunt Ruth's purse. Wonder when they'll be back. They've been gone quite a while and it's cold so it could be soon. Christopher checks the door. It's locked so he'll have warning when they do come back. He shouldn't do this, he knows, but can't help himself. He squats onto the floor, opens the purse.

There's a wallet full of colourful money, a mix of Canadian bills and Australian bills, which are just as colourful. Aunt Ruth's driver's licence photo looks just like his mom's driver's licence photo. Where they live, Adelaide, is in South Australia. Is that like a province?

Next he uncovers another wallet filled with photos. All are of people he doesn't know, some kids, some adults. There is one of a dark-skinned girl with thick black hair who looks about his age. She's unusual looking, wild but pretty. Kind of how Jennifer might look if she were more athletic, less girly. There's another photo of the same girl with another girl who is younger and as pale as his mom. Neither looks like Aunt Ruth or Uncle Fred or each other. Probably close friends.

He finds a picture that's not as shiny as the others. A wide shot of three people—he recognizes his mom right away even though she's really young there, as well as the Johnsons—standing in front of a humongous rock with nothing else around. The sky is perfectly blue except for a stray cloud shaped like a dog. It's the first picture he's seen of his mom from before he was born. He flips it over and someone's written: 1999. That was before she even knew his father. Who would have taken it?

The photos spill from his hands and he struggles to put them back together in the same order. At any moment the door will open and he could be caught. His haste only makes it take longer putting them back but he finally does so. It's too risky to explore the purse any further, but then a folded newspaper clipping falls out. Who brings articles on a trip? He skims it between glances at the door. It's about those fires in Tasmania. A lot of people died in them, important people it sounds like, though Christopher doesn't recognize any names.

He's pushing his luck if he explores further. He refolds and replaces the article and reassembles the contents of the purse back as best he can remember.

Christopher gives up after repositioning it three times. He checks the window, the coast is clear, and then turns on the television and gets comfortable on the couch. There's a nature show on. Would be neat if it was on Australia, and even neater if it showed that rock. But it's not. It's about somewhere in North America. Lots of moose and reindeer, which are all right but he sees shows about them all the time. Worse, the narrator sounds like a male Mrs. Jackson. He dozes off and doesn't wake until he hears the door unlocking.

"Where's Willie?"

It's the first thing his mom says, as if knowing something's wrong. Christopher keeps still, faking sleeping. He doesn't want to get Willie in trouble, if in fact he is in trouble. But now his mom stands over him, and repeats the question.

"He's not here."

"I can see that."

Her voice is calm but she's angry, Christopher can tell. Probably trying to disguise it because of the guests who are behind her, taking off their shoes.

"Well? Where did he go?"

"He went with the police."

"The police?"

"Yeah."

His mom pulls out her cell phone and presses a button. Willie's ring tone sounds from the kitchen. She rushes to it and makes the ringing stop. She says a little curse, takes a deep breath, then goes to Aunt Ruth and Uncle Fred, who are still at the door, and escorts them into the living room. Doesn't look like they're going to leave for a while. Christopher vacates the sofa for them and climbs into Willie's easy chair. Only his uncle sits down.

"Thank you, young man. So what is it you're watching? Wait, I know this show. Don't believe I've seen this episode, though."

"Everything all right, Debs?" his aunt says from behind him.

"Christopher, give Uncle Fred the remote."

"Deborah, it's fine. I'm interested in this."

As his mom and aunt talk quietly, Christopher and his uncle, who clearly didn't say it just to please Christopher, watch together.

"Do you know where this is?" Uncle Fred says.

"Alberta? Jasper?"

"Ah, I have seen it. Know how it ends?" When Christopher shakes his head: "The antler did it."

"Oh Fred," Aunt Ruth says.

Christopher doesn't get the joke but his aunt's reaction makes him laugh. She sounds like his mom but with a stronger accent and softer voice. He likes the combination and decides Aunt Ruth is nice. Uncle Fred, he's not so sure about yet though.

"Just kidding," Uncle Fred says, and moves to Christopher as if to rub his hair. Christopher swipes at the large hand, but misses, which makes Uncle Fred chuckle but his mom angry.

"Christopher Palmer, apologize right now."

"I'm sorry."

Christopher hopes his mom doesn't send him to his room. Normally, he'd be happy to escape there with visitors around but this time he wants to stay in case she needs him or Willie calls.

"That's all right," Uncle Fred says. "You just met us. Let's shake hands."

Uncle Fred puts out his hand and Christopher shakes it and this makes his mom happy. She then says she'll make sandwiches and goes to the kitchen. Uncle Fred offers to take them to Macca's and when Christopher realizes he means McDonalds, he jumps out of his seat, only to fall back when his mom says she wants to wait for Willie to return.

Now that he thinks about it, Christopher does too. The program ends and Christopher goes to his mom, not comfortable enough with these strangers yet to be alone with them. He helps getting plates and napkins out and puts the bread properly away.

"He'll be okay, Mom. It wasn't like they took him in handcuffs."

She pauses, and it seems he said the right thing, but then his mom shakes her head and he feels like he said the wrong thing. You never know with her.

"That's not what's on my mind. Well it is, but, I don't know."

"You thinking about the school appointment?"

"What?"

"Willie told me about seeing the Principal at that school, only that's when the police came."

His mom sighs, shakes her head again, but says nothing. She gets Christopher to put the finished plates on a tray while she makes lemonade. They come out together and put the drinks and tray on the coffee table, which Aunt Ruth has cleared. How did she know to do that? And how did his mom know what kind of sandwiches to make for them without asking? Apparently his uncle figured out the remote control as now the news is on.

"Looks delicious," Aunt Ruth says.

Christopher is enjoying his sandwich when his mom gasps. She stares at the TV while shushing his aunt and uncle. She grabs the remote and turns up the volume to a level she would scold Christopher for. The story is about a man who was found dead near the zoo yesterday. The zoo? Yesterday? That's why the police are talking to Willie. But they didn't see anything or even hear any sirens.

Then his mom's cell phone rings and she rushes to the kitchen to answer, though she forgets to keep her voice down.

"What? Oh for crying—okay—I'll be right there." She hangs up and rushes back, upset.

"What's going on, Debs?"

"That was Willie. I need to go get him."

"Where is he?"

Christopher puts down his sandwich, rushes to put on his coat.

"Oh no, you're staying put."

Christopher reluctantly puts away his coat and returns to his seat, dejected.

"As long as your aunt and uncle don't mind watching you."

"No worries, I'll watch him but Ruth, maybe you should accompany your sister."

"Absolutely."

His mom hesitates as if not sure about this but then, as if she has no time to argue, she agrees to let Aunt Ruth join her.

"He'll just watch television or go to his room."

Just like that the women are out the door, which leaves Christopher alone with his Uncle Fred who he just met. He can't remember the last time his mom left him alone with anyone other than Willie, if ever. She must trust Uncle Fred a lot. What's weird is that Christopher feels he can trust these people too. He feels an unusual connection to them, similar to how he felt when he first met Willie.

Christopher looks over at his uncle who seems to have been watching him. Uncle Fred smiles and hands over the remote.

# 10

Deborah backs her trusty green Civic, still holding up after a dozen years of her aggressive driving, out onto the street. Quicker than usual, before it fully registers she's leaving Christopher on his own with an adult he barely knows. She never gave it a second thought in the moment—it's Fred, after all, whom she's known nearly her entire life—forgetting that, to her son, her brother-in-law is a stranger. It might make her son uneasy and behave unpredictably.

Way to go Willie.

What has he gotten himself involved in? He was never a choirboy, has spent a night or two in prison, but for petty issues like fights and a little larceny, events that occurred before he became a constant presence in her life. Nothing close to murder. Such an idea is preposterous. Yet she has a bad sense he's in a situation beyond him.

She races to the main road but the pedestrian light flashes, indicating the traffic light is about to turn yellow. She rushes it, catching a patch of snow that causes her wheels to spin, almost trapping her in the intersection. She recovers though not without inciting a honk from a left-turning vehicle. Out of habit, she readies her middle finger but, as she's trained herself, she uses it to crank up the hard rock station playing Led Zeppelin. The song barely lasts one verse and chorus before Ruth turns it down.

"Debs, I can't believe you still listen to that kind of music. And for goodness sake, please slow down. We don't want the police to stop us."

"Where do you think we're going?"

"I don't understand."

"Neither do I, but I intend to."

Ruth lets out a brief sigh as she shakes her head. Deborah now sees how annoying her habit of vague snap responses must have been to her sister growing up. Thankfully, this time her sister doesn't get upset, maybe realizing herself how it upset Deborah when Ruth got upset, or simply to ensure Deborah keeps her eyes on the road.

A rash of slow drivers, slush-marred streets, and a parlay of red lights conspire to slow their progress, which increases Deborah's agitation and aggravates her frustration at not leaving Ruth behind. What was she thinking? The last thing she wants is for her sister to see her in trouble. Bad enough for the Johnsons to witness her humble living conditions and assume, incorrectly because if Deborah can do one thing it's make the most of what she has, she and Willie are deep in debt.

Deborah groans as she encounters yet another red light, giving her an opportunity to consider another troubling thought: what might inquisitive Fred be extracting from her son?

"It'll be all right, Debs."

"You two picked a bad time to come."

"On the contrary, seems we picked a great time to—"

"To rescue me?"

"Everything always has to be so dramatic with you, doesn't it? The circumstances back home are what brought us here, not any knowledge of your situation, of which we had none. But if not for Fred, you might still be waiting for a sitter or having to take Christopher along. I'm guessing you wouldn't have wanted to take him to a police station."

"Sorry for putting you out about that."

"Nonsense. Nothing would please us more than to help out, even if . . ."

Ruth's voice trails off, as it tends to do when she's about to say too much. Deborah's tempted to press her on it but decides against it.

"Why didn't you and Fred at least tell me you were coming?"

But as Deborah asks the question, she knows the answer: She knows, depending on her mood at the time, she would have considered prior notification as a warning, would have found some way to avoid seeing them. A side trip to a park, perhaps, timed for their arrival. No, the only way for her sister or anyone from Tasmania to guarantee seeing Deborah again would be by surprise. No one would know that better than Ruth.

"We'll only stay as long as we're welcome."

Just then a truck cuts them off from making a right turn, and Deborah swears.

"Sorry, that was for the truck."

"I know."

The truck finishes turning and Deborah follows, resisting a temptation to ride up alongside and then cut it off too.

"How come Christopher's not at school today?" Ruth says. "Forgive me if I'm prying. I was a teacher, remember, so I can't not ask."

"Of course," Deborah says, partly wanting to tell her to mind her own business, but also happy to have a female ally. "He's had trouble with schools. Teachers. Certain teachers."

"Is that why you're so on edge? I mean, I sensed it before, on our walk."

Another red light delays them at an intersection where Deborah points out a square structure at one end of a plaza surrounded by cars.

"That's where I work," Deborah says.

Ruth smiles in a patient older sibling way that sees through such diversions but chooses to let them go.

"At the restaurant? What do you do there?"

"I'm a waitress." Deborah pauses for a comment, verbal or otherwise, but Ruth only nods. "Hardly the career I had in mind when I was at uni, right? Should be owning or running one, instead, right? But this is a decent place, quite popular as you can see, and the clientele—well, I've worked in worse."

Ruth pats Deborah's arm. "Honey, I'm not here to judge."

Which only makes Deborah feel foolish for her self-conscious rambling. She keeps quiet and during that silence something strikes her in what Ruth said. No, not what she said, but how she said it, as if the sentence was a fragment, missing a clause along the lines of, "you think you have it bad?" Must be her imagination, perhaps a reflection of her own latent bitterness at what she herself gave up.

"Then why are you here? I know you talk about Dad and wanting to find me and all that, but I'm sensing there's more."

"So sceptical. Aren't those reasons enough?"

"I suppose. I don't know. I guess things must be pretty good with you and Fred, to just up and away like that?"

Ruth chuckles and hesitates, the way she used to when she and Fred were just friends on the cusp of romance and people asked if she liked him, and she needed that extra moment to prepare an answer.

"We're doing all right. Fred retired last year and I gave up teaching two years ago. We hope to travel, see the world, you know. You could say Canada is our first stop."

"I'd hardly consider a plain suburban town like this travelling."

"The lake was pleasant this morning, with the ice and all."

Deborah laughs. At least that's something that hasn't changed. So like Ruth to try and make things sound better than they are. That positive outlook could have helped her so many other times.

At last she pulls into the police station, finds a parking spot, and unbuckles her seatbelt.

"Let's see what Willie's been up to."

Deborah's cell phone rings with a number she doesn't recognize. Instinct tells her to ignore it but instead she ignores her instinct, answers, and wishes she hadn't. It's the school—the good Dr. Chambers himself—wondering where they are, that's it's been over an hour since their appointment, whether they intend to show. Behind the understanding manner, Deborah senses a threat. She's about to get angry when Ruth grabs the phone.

She introduces herself, gets an understanding of the situation, then provides vague but plausible reasons for the absence. After a minute of back and forth, Ruth apologizes on behalf of Deborah, and hangs up.

"There, problem solved."

"How did you do that?"

"I've learned a thing or two from my husband on getting people on my side. Knowing how schools and schoolmasters operate doesn't hurt either."

"And?"

"He was quite insistent but I told him this was a stressful week for you, because of our unexpected arrival, and told him you need to spend a few days with

Christopher at home before such a meeting."

"He bought that?"

"He wasn't thrilled. He'd brought in some expert from a university. But yeah, he bought it."

"Ha, an expert, just as I figured. Ruth, you're a life saver."

They enter the police station and find Willie in the lobby by himself. He's wearing an everything-is-fine-let's-worry-about-dinner smile that doesn't fool Deborah. When he sees Ruth, his smile drops just enough for Deborah to know he's full of it.

"Where's Christopher?"

"You think I'm going to take my son to a police station? What if you were in handcuffs? He's at home with Fred."

"Handcuffs, that's crazy. I came voluntarily to help them out on something."

Deborah laughs but she's not amused. She wants to call him out and reveal what they know of the murder and his connection to it, circumstantial as it might be. Instead, they exit as a flurry of thick flakes descends on them. Ruth is walking quicker and gets ahead, allowing Deborah to hold Willie up.

"What were you thinking leaving Christopher alone this morning?"

He's ready for the question and explains that since the cops didn't know Christopher was home, Willie felt it was better to leave him be. He figured the cold weather would bring Deborah back soon enough, meaning Christopher would be alone only minutes. He adds he didn't want to call her as that would have alerted the police to Christopher's presence.

"Considering your view on your son's presence here, I think I made the right decision."

She can't argue this point. She also can't release her frustration yet and admit as much. She rushes to catch up with a shivering Ruth and open the car door for her sister, leaving Willie to trail behind.

# 11

Fred observes Christopher operating the remote control, going back and forth between different channels, until settling on the Bugs Bunny cartoons he started with. Once the boy's attention is fully on the show, Fred turns his to the framed photograph.

Deborah with a black man. Unexpected, but that is only indicative of how few non-white people were in their lives in Australia. The son's skin colour almost evenly blends Deborah's paleness and that of the man in the picture, though leaning towards the latter. Beyond that, all similarity between the boy and Dwight Palmer ends, as far as Fred can tell. Christopher's soft, pleasant features are consistent with Deborah's, but he is big and tall, unlike his mother. Perhaps in that he takes after this man. Impossible to be sure from a studio head shot.

The Huon pine table the picture sits on has been kept in wonderful shape, better than its other half at their home in Adelaide even. Sentimentality is such a scarce trait in his sister-in-law, this has to be taken as a good sign. Things have gone better than he and Ruth could have hoped, so far. Deborah seems to have weathered the shock of their arrival well. Behind her stoic posturing, she seems glad, possibly even relieved. What a relief for them too. Perhaps an indication the past twelve years can be classified a separation rather than a severing? He hopes so.

The stress they see in Deborah may not be due to their visit; it could reflect her daily life. Her living conditions are substandard compared to what the girl they knew would have tolerated. But her claims of being content sound sincere. The same could be said of her attachment to this Willie Galloway, her caring reaction to his situation evidence of that. Perhaps her stress has to do with the boy as well who, from what Fred knows about North American schools, ought to be in class. Whatever is going on, Fred's been granted a chance to observe her son firsthand, with no risk of having to reveal his intent.

Fred rejoins Christopher in the living room. The boy seems at ease but he is a kid and, based on Fred's experience with children, it's best to approach cautiously. For a long time he and Ruth tried to have a child but eventually gave up. They're blessed with plenty of nieces and nephews and friends' children whose company is delightful, in small doses. Fred wonders how long this dose might last.

"Did your mom say where they're going?"

"No, she didn't say, but I know they're going to the police station."

"Police station? Is Willie in trouble?"

Christopher shrugs, a response that annoys Fred for a moment. Patience, he tells himself, and forces a smile.

A Tasmanian Devil cartoon spurs Christopher to whirl like the cartoon character while trying to emulate its guttural sounds. Fred stares at the boy, unsure what to make of it. He stops, perhaps self-consciously, and looks at Fred who again smiles.

"You like animals, don't you?"

Christopher nods.

"Better than people?"

"No, some, maybe."

"How about that one?"

"The Tasmanian Devil is one of my favourites."

As if to affirm it, Christopher spins again.

"You know, the real ones don't behave or sound like that."

"How do they behave?"

"They're nasty little things that scamper around and eat just about anything. They climb trees when they're young and then go around them rather than through them. Their voices are raspier too and they kind of sound like sick dogs."

"How do you know all that?"

"Your Aunt Ruth and I used to live in Tasmania. Just like your mom."

"My mom?"

"She never told you about living in Tasmania?"

"No. I don't know. Maybe she did."

"Well, it was before you were born, I think. How old did you say you were again? Was it twelve?"

"I'm ten, like my mom said."

"Right, you're right. Forgive me, you just seem big for ten. Where were you born?"

"In a hospital."

Fred laughs. "No, I mean, what city?"

"Ottawa."

"Ottawa, right. I guess you don't see many wild animals in Ontario."

"Willie and I went to the zoo yesterday."

"Those are hardly wild animals, are they?"

Christopher looks up at Fred, as if searching for a connection. He smiles gently, as if Fred's passed an inspection. The feeling is mutual and, in this shared gaze, Christopher is no longer a stranger to Fred, but his nephew.

"That's so true. It wasn't as nice as when I used to go with my mom. It's winter so there were only a few animals but a lot of them seemed unhappy."

"Why is that?"

"They want to be free. They should be free."

Free. Interesting, Fred thinks, before something strikes him about Christopher's words. That news story Deborah reacted to, a murder at a zoo. Is there a connection? How many zoos can there be around here? There's the big one in Toronto, but are there others? Could it be a coincidence?

"When did you say you were you at the zoo?"

"Yesterday."

That's too much a coincidence. This Willie Galloway seems nice and reminds Fred of guys who might have been bullies as kids but, like scorpions with their stingers removed, are no threat now. He is somewhat a scruffy character though—back home some might call him a bogan—who could associate with questionable types.

And Willie's certainly not the type of fellow they expected to find Deborah with, though the man's bond with Christopher is undeniable. Would that be enough? Such a quality would be important to his sister-in-law whose appreciation for luxury could never trump that for loyalty, even before she experienced the betrayals that drove her here. Willie might prove a complication and Fred needs to find out more about the man and their relationship. Of course, asking Christopher would be pushing his luck. Kids' instincts are sharp and he cannot risk alienating his increasingly compelling nephew.

A car door slamming interrupts Fred's thoughts. Christopher rushes to the front door, opens it. Willie enters first, followed by Deborah, then Ruth. Fred can tell his sister-in-law's furious. Willie's fortunate Ruth was there; otherwise it would have been a hellish ride home. Christopher gives Willie a hug before the man can take off his shoes. Fred follows to help with the coats, though Willie seems put out and chooses to hang up his own.

"Are you in trouble?" Christopher says. "Did they treat you badly?"

"I'm not in trouble, and they treated me fine. Just asked a few questions. Nothing to worry about."

Only Christopher's not convinced and continues to press.

"Was it about that murder and the body at the zoo?"

"What are you talking about?"

"It was on the news when you called mom."

"I see," Willie says, looking at Deborah.

She offers nothing in response, which Fred finds curious. Is there a bigger issue here?

The five remain standing in the foyer with only Christopher unaware of the awkwardness. Fred can sense Willie wouldn't mind them staying to delay Deborah's wrath. Deborah, on the other hand, seems anxious for some privacy.

"Honey, we ought to go," Fred says, getting his own coat and then Ruth's.

"I do have to get ready for work soon."

"We could drop by tomorrow," Ruth says.

"I've a better idea, honey. Tomorrow, let's go see Niagara Falls. We can drop in after that or wait until Thursday. Then we can spend an entire evening with all of us together with fair warning."

"Sounds great," Deborah says, visibly relieved. "I'm scheduled to work Thursday, but I'm certain I can change shifts."

After wiping off the snow and warming up the rental car, Fred manoeuvres the underpowered but otherwise comfortable Hyundai through patches of slush seemingly affixed to the main street. It's busy with rush hour traffic now. He's never driven in snow before and each bump and jostle unnerves him, though the car's tires keep their grip well. Ruth, several times, expresses her frustration at leaving so abruptly. But Fred's pleased at the chance for he and his wife to compare notes.

Though it explains why the boy was at home, he's surprised to hear about Deborah's troubles with Christopher's schooling. To Fred, Christopher is a fascinating lad, quiet but affable. Just thinking about sharing his nephew's company, even for those one or two hours, fills Fred with an agreeable emotion. He shares this with Ruth who is pleased to hear it but points out that, apparently, his school absence today is not unique, and that his sister-in-law has an aversion to consulting professionals, for which Ruth had to intervene and bail her sister out. They agree it's odd Deborah has no close neighbours or friends to call upon to look after her son on short notice. Unfortunately, Ruth's time with her sister wasn't as illuminating about Willie.

"It didn't seem right to grill her about that?"

"I suppose."

"No, Fred, really. She seemed intent on avoiding the subject. It was quite strange, actually."

"What was strange?"

"That she didn't tell Willie what we saw on the news, that she let him go on about how the police wanted him as a possible witness on an insignificant matter he never offered to explain. You saw that by his reaction when we got back."

Fred copies the swerve of a car ahead to avoid a patch of hardened snow; he's getting the hang of it.

"Yes, I did notice that. Try to find a news station. Maybe we'll hear something about that murder."

Ruth turns the dial but gives up after a series of commercials, weather reports predicting a respite from the snow, traffic reports, country music, pop music, and at least two heated call-in shows focused on ice hockey players named Kessel and Phaneuf. Fred frowns when she nudges him while pointing at a nondescript shopping plaza.

"Honey, I need to concentrate on the road."

"No, that's where Debs works. She's a waitress."

Fred slows slightly to look at the dark, square brick building. Restaurant? Pub? Hard to tell. Not the sort of place Deborah would have frequented, let alone worked at, back in Tasmania. Fred's saddened at how her standards have fallen.

"She says it's a nice place," Ruth says.

"Maybe we ought to find out."

"What?"

"Oh, just thinking it's odd how we came here just as all this is going on in Deborah's life. Or do you think this is how it's always been for her here, the usual course of events?"

"I hope not."

"Honey, we need to find out more, and find out soon, before this gets too complicated."

Ruth nods, as if understanding, but when they arrive at the hotel and he clarifies he means visiting Deborah at her restaurant, she backs off.

"Too soon. Too smothering. Too . . . sneaky?"

"Is that so bad? We need to understand all that's going on. This Willie fellow, for instance, who seems all right for the most part, could mess things up with this police situation. If he is in serious trouble, we may want to adapt our approach."

"I'm sorry, I wish I could have gotten more out of her while I had the chance."

He sits her on the bed, puts his arm around her.

"I'm not reproaching you. Deborah is your sister and, despite what's at stake for us, your relationship with her, and now her son, our nephew, is what's most important. We can't leave without trying our best, at least we'll know we've done that. Besides, we have to eat somewhere tonight."

She keeps quiet but offers a wan smile he takes as agreement. He turns on the television to a news station. They just miss a report on the murder but catch enough to find out the police are still looking for suspects.

Ruth prepares for dinner and when she reappears, so does her hesitation. Fred suggests they eat at a finer restaurant close to the hotel—he wasn't relishing a meal at an unknown entity anyway—and Ruth happily agrees. Over a fine lamb chop, Fred brings her back around to stopping at her sister's work for a drink.

"We can make it seem a coincidence," he adds.

"No, I want to be upfront as much as possible."

"You mean ask directly about Christopher?"

"Well, maybe not that just yet, not there."

Driving in the snow in the dark is harder than it was earlier but at least there's far less traffic. They pull into a parking lot shrunken by piles of snow on its perimeter. They spot Deborah's Civic far away on its own. Fred parks the rental close to it but regrets doing so as it means traversing perilous chunks of hardened snow and black ice all the way to the entrance.

"How can she put up with winters like this?"

"Ruth, we need to come across positively, which means banishing even the most innocent thoughts that might question her motives."

"You're right, Fred, you're right. Though I'm still not sure this is the best approach so soon."

"Trust me, it's best we do it now."

"Aren't you the one who's preaching patience all the time?"

"There's patience and there's stalling."

"It could look like we're ambushing her."

"We're consulting her."

"You may be retired but your corporate BS is as strong as ever."

He chuckles at his wife's remark but an odd movement in his stomach makes Fred pause at the door. He hopes it's from the lamb but fears it's due to the lack of a plan.

Fred pulls the door to allow Ruth to enter first. No one is there to greet them. They look around, Fred towards the bar, Ruth towards the restaurant area. The place isn't that bad, kind of intimate, the clientele reasonably dressed. Still, not the sort of establishment he would patronize by choice. But it is clean. And calm. Save for several loud patrons fixed on a bank of television screens, all but two showing an ice hockey game. Just then a team scores, inciting a boisterous cheer. A jovial atmosphere even Fred, never a big sports fan, can appreciate. He feels better about this decision. Even more so when Deborah spots them and comes over. Other than surprise, she gives no indication their dropping in troubles her. If anything, it's the opposite, based on her cheeriness.

"Well, isn't this a coincidence. Or is it?"

Fred and Ruth say nothing, neither expecting Deborah to be this high-spirited and, dare he say it, happy to see them. Then, as if to erase her words, she hugs them both warmly.

"Just kidding. As if you'd voluntarily come to a place like this."

Fred chuckles, taking the remark as benign, but Ruth remains quiet, confused. It takes a moment to realize it's because of her sister's alluring outfit. Fred can't help being impressed at how good-looking his sister-in-law still is in her mid-thirties.

Deborah escorts them to a booth, adding she has an hour to go on her shift, but brings the each a glass of red wine first. Ruth fidgets, only takes tiny sips, prompting Fred to hold her hand to settle her down.

"This is not at all what I expected," she says.

"The wine's not that bad."

"No, I'm talking about this place."

"What did you expect?"

Instead of answering, she points with some alarm towards the bar behind Fred. He turns. Two men in their forties, one fat, the other only slightly overweight, like Willie, are accosting Deborah. The fat man's distracting his sister-in-law while the other tries to grab her behind. Deborah's wise to it and manages to evade contact. The bartender looks as if he's intentionally ignoring the situation. Deborah glances back and he and Ruth turn away quickly, probably not quickly enough. When they look back, Deborah is out of sight.

A few minutes later, his sister-in-law shows up with a glass of water in one hand and her coat slung over the other arm, acting as if nothing's amiss, and takes a seat next to Ruth.

"You two are good at tracking me down."

"You showed me, remember," Ruth says.

To Fred, it's fairly obvious Deborah's continuing the joke and wanting to keep things light, but Ruth is struggling to do the same.

"Ice hockey's big here, isn't it?" he says.

"As much if not more than footy in Victoria, I reckon," Deborah says.

She adds she's grown to enjoy hockey, but isn't nearly as avid a fan as Willie. Fred wants to pursue this and ask about their favourite team, but Deborah spots someone or something at the bar and says she has to attend to a few things and then she can end her shift.

Fred uses the time to try to figure out what's going on with Ruth who's clearly uncomfortable. It doesn't take long. He's so concerned with achieving what they want to achieve, it's easy to forget he also needs to keep aware of the toll this is taking on his wife. How painful it must be for Ruth to watch her sister work, to witness Deborah fending off reprobates or acting subservient to those who ought to be beneath her. It's likely Ruth is unable to accept that her sister has changed, and changed for good.

Deborah rejoins them, this time with a draught beer. A beer. Fred can't remember ever seeing either of the Pollard sisters drinking a beer.

Ruth is a little more at ease now, though still distant. He sticks with the small talk—weather, hockey, things to do around the area—and it's rather enjoyable, like old times. Deborah echoes this.

"So easy between us, isn't it? I never thought that could happen again. I think Tasmania was the problem all along. I wasn't getting away from you as much as I was from that place. Sad, isn't it?"

"Sad?" Fred says. "In what way?"

"Because Tasmania is beautiful, a place I used to love. It's just not for me, not anymore. And because I haven't realized that until now. Better late than never, I suppose."

Ruth grabs her sister's hands.

"Come back with us, Debs, if only for a short while. Don't worry about the expense, we can cover it. Of course, that includes Christopher as well. He'll love it."

Fred's taken aback. This is not the way he would have approached it. Fortunately, Deborah is calm, maybe too calm, almost as if she expected this.

"Christopher can come. What about Willie? You don't much care for him do you?"

Fred shakes his head.

"On the contrary. Other than what that police matter is—I have no intention of prying—he seems a decent fellow. And clearly he's close to Christopher. What I'm trying to say is, we're open to a variety of arrangements."

Deborah nods and her expression tells him she anticipated such a proposal, but also that she hasn't formulated a clear response.

"You said Dad's in Melbourne, right? Not in Tasmania."

"Last we checked, your father's condition is the same. But he won't be in Melbourne forever."

"Tell you what, I'll think about it. I'll need to talk with Willie and Christopher, as well as sort things out work-wise. Come by after your visit to Niagara Falls, like you said."

For the first time in hours, Ruth smiles.

"That went better than expected," Fred says, upon leaving the restaurant.

"I feel we're still deceiving Debs," Ruth says.

"In what way?"

"In not telling her all about the fire, for instance."

"You know her better than me so I'm not going to dispute that, but I suspect she'd rather not know."

"Why would she not want to know?"

"Let's just take her at face value and not reveal anything until she prompts us to."

"How's that not deceiving?"

"Okay, we are deceiving her. I won't deny it. As long as you don't deny the part her deceptions have played."

"Oh Fred, that's so . . ."

"Petty? Yes, I'm being petty. But listen, the worst that can happen is she says no. Then we'll still have reopened communication. If she says yes, and those details distance us, we'll still have more then we did before coming here. And also, if she says yes, we can help many people. Including us, need I remind you."

"You're right. I'm too worried about what might happen later when everything comes out. Especially if we're wrong."

"Keep positive. If we're right, and I'm inclined to think we are, things will turn out well for everyone."

"You think she'll come, Fred?"

"We'll have to see, won't we?"

# 12

Probably not wise to park close to the warehouse where , someone might recognize his Le Sabre. But this vantage point is the furthest from which he can still keep sight of Todd's MGB. Willie turns up the radio to the sports call-in show. They ought to rename it the Leafs call-in show in winter.

It comes as no surprise Todd decided to go to work today. It's bound to be less exhausting than staying at home, faking mourning for a father he despised. Then again, who is Willie to say what their relationship was like? All Willie can go by is the complaining. All families do that about each other. It's possible Todd is grieving and needs to escape his guilt and get away from his house. Just as Willie needed to get away from his this gloomy, cloudy though still snow-less morning.

Deborah dropped a bomb on him at breakfast when she told him about the Johnsons surprising her at the restaurant last night with an invitation to Australia. Her and Christopher. Such a possibility entered Willie's mind the moment she answered the door and only grew once he heard about the father's situation. Deborah's defiance in front of her relatives never fooled him one bit. If there's one thing he's learned about people, the more emotionally and irrationally anyone declares their resistance to something, the easier it is to break that resistance down. Deborah's a tough cookie but not even she is immune to that.

His frustration isn't with the asking but with the underhanded manner it came about. And he made no attempt to conceal his annoyance to Deborah about that, leaving the house in a huff, unwilling to discuss how it might be handled if she were to go. Not even after Deborah suggested there might be a way for Willie to join them. Come on! No way that would ever happen, no way her relatives would go for that, let alone pay for it. All saying that did was expose her desire to go. His natural inclination is to accede to her wishes in things as much as possible, but this time his selfishness is lobbying for the opposite. He doesn't want her to go. He doesn't want Christopher to go. He needs them. They're his support system during what he fears will turn into the worst few days, or even weeks, of his life.

There, someone's exiting, a man in a black coat and pants. He's too far to identify but he is heading towards the reserved spot with Todd's car. The man stops, stares at the car, stoops over it, spits on it. Got to be old Sully, Todd's godfather. He's reaching into his pocket, pulling out a key, pausing in temptation. It passes and Sully moves on. Wow, if Todd's having to deal with this, he won't be at the office long.

Maybe the same kind of resentment is in Willie's future if he blocks the trip to Australia. He might not feel so strongly against it if not still bothered by Christopher's taking to his uncle so readily. His envy isn't much different than what he feels about Deborah at times. In a way it's worse, as Willie can't shake the idea that this Fred character purposely engaged Christopher to sway Deborah. Also, Willie must look like an idiot in the eyes of the school Principal; it's unlikely they'll explore that avenue. Though, as Deborah tersely pointed out, missing the appointment was as much his fault as that of her relatives. Good thing he left when he did, before the discussion deteriorated further.

So much tension between them lately. The New Year started off so promisingly. She was excited by that new school, which turned out to be a dud. And then this Bralen business. He's not happy she didn't reveal knowing about the murder when picking him up at the police station. Letting him go on, saying she didn't want to get into it in front of her sister. Okay, fair enough. But she should realize how foolish this makes him feel. Only when he says that, she claims she feels like a fool too because he's not telling her everything. That's only partly true. His chat with the police was as benign as he described it. Indeed, they were open and pleasant when they told him Mac Bralen was murdered here in Durham and that the body was only dumped near the zoo. Which is why they're running the investigation, and not the Toronto police. He's still not sure why they had to point out that distinction.

Willie glances at his watch, it's close to noon. How long should he wait? Usually Todd would be on his way to lunch by now. What's holding him up? Perhaps he's getting hell from Sully's pals who would intentionally delay Todd to annoy him. It's tempting to walk in there and rescue his partner from that abuse. But he can't.

He can't because of what he didn't and won't tell Deborah. How the police intimated, subtly, that Willie might have helped dispose of the body, at the same time revealing, while remaining careful not to accuse, awareness of the little side business he and Todd have going. At no time did it sound like they suspected Willie of killing Bralen, although being at the zoo yesterday is a troublesome coincidence, one of those that can land an innocent but unlucky guy like him in jail.

From this, Willie can only conclude the police suspect Todd who stands to inherit a decent fortune and a business. And by inheriting that business, Todd can more easily conceal certain activities. Only Willie doubts Todd has it in him to murder anyone, let alone a mob-connected father he feared far more than he hated.

All these questions, all these uncertainties, make it imperative he talk to Todd. So here he waits and will continue to wait until—now two people come out the main door. Todd and someone Willie doesn't know. Looks like a lawyer. They stand by Todd's car a moment before Todd gets in, alone.

Willie starts his car and drives off to avoid being seen, not bothering to watch Todd, knowing where he'll go. His habits will get Todd in big trouble one day, Willie knows, but at the moment he's glad he never gave his partner that advice. Willie takes a right turn on a small street, then a u-turn in time to catch a glimpse of Todd's car. Sure enough, he is headed in the direction of his favourite daytime bar. Willie can hang far back and out of sight.

Willie finds the MGB in the parking lot, empty. He parks on the opposite side of the building and enters to some dreary country music. Todd's usual table is occupied and Willie has to scour the place before finding him alone in a booth, his first pint of Coors Light two-thirds finished. Willie slides in the seat across Todd who is not as surprised to see him as Willie expects. He's unusually subdued, in fact, not at all the frazzled mess one would assume of a murder suspect. A waitress stops by. Willie orders a pint of Guinness as Todd lifts his glass for a refill. When the drinks come, Willie raises his glass.

"My condolences."

"Cut the crap," Todd says, not raising his.

"The police came to see me yesterday."

"Sure, I told them you were at the zoo."

"Why would you do that? Why would you even bring my name up?"

"I didn't bring your name up. Someone at the warehouse told them about your altercation with Dad. Pretty stupid of you."

"Did you do it, Todd?"

Todd shakes his head, though not with much conviction, in Willie's view.

"I have an alibi."

"Then what was the point telling them I was at the zoo?"

"Just cooperating."

The terseness of the response, his calm honesty, his whole demeanour, strikes terror within Willie. If the cops see Todd as cooperating, as civil, this could turn against Willie.

Of course, Christopher can provide an alibi too, but can he rely on the boy to do so when facing an aggressive prosecutor? It's an irrelevant question as he would never put Deborah's son through that.

"You might want to find a decent lawyer," Todd adds. "Just in case."

"You know I can't afford a lawyer."

Todd reaches in his coat and pulls out a wallet out of which he extracts a stack of hundred-dollar bills that he hands over to Willie.

"Don't say I never looked out for you."

Against his better judgement, Willie pockets the cash. A different, more attractive waitress comes by—in a modest skirt and golf shirt, Willie can't help notice—and sets down a plate of fish and chips. She looks at Todd who shakes his head.

Willie takes the hint and leaves. Nothing more he'll get out of Todd, at least not now, and he gets the sense that ignorance may be his best ally.

Outside, the clouds are dispersing, opening up to an expansive blueness. Yet Willie feels his world contracting. Just as he opens his car door, he spots a standing police car with two officers in it. He exits, checking the rear view mirror frequently until, to his relief, it's certain the police car isn't moving.

A little farther along, Willie wonders whether that's a good thing. For that matter, is Todd looking out for him or working against him?

A more immediate concern: where does he go now? Going home is not the best idea in his current state of mind. It would have been nice to stay in the bar, have a few drinks with Todd. Like it was a year ago when the buzz from the alcohol improved the company. But those days are gone, gone forever; he must think of the future. Less his own than of those he cares for. Old times may seem appealing in the present but there was plenty of loneliness in there too, periods in which he had no one.

He sniffs. He sensed a cold coming on last night, which is why he took a couple of Echinacea tablets with him. Only they're deep in his pocket. He pulls over onto the shoulder and parks. He has to exit the car because his pants are getting too tight again. Just as he pulls the tablets out his phone rings and, in reaching for it, he drops the tablets in a pile of slush.

"Hello."

"Willie Galloway?"

The accented voice sounds familiar but Willie can't place it.

"Yeah. Who's calling?"

"It's Fred Johnson. I was wondering if you could oblige me some of your time for a chat?"

Even though he knows what his response will be, Willie preoccupies himself with an unsuccessful search for the dropped tablets, before giving it.

# ℋ

The bones have mended, the scars have healed, the cuts have scabbed, most of the burned skin has recovered, the infections have cured, the headaches have cleared and now, at last, the pneumonia has run its course. One painful wound to nurse. Not a wound that inhibits buttoning his shirt or putting on his trousers, nor one that pains him in any physical way. No, this wound is the discovery Andy is not the only survivor and that he is joined by Walter Pollard. Of course, Andy is pleased for Walter and his family, and he takes no solace in knowing the old man's injuries at his age could hospitalize him indefinitely. He just wishes it was his son, a nephew, or a brother instead. The wound is the miserable sense of feeling cheated, and it's one that will persist long after his release from the hospital today.

Andy finishes dressing and sits back on the bed, until a male orderly knocks, opens the door, and rolls in a wheelchair.

"Your driver is downstairs. Would you like me to take you to him?"

"Thank you, but no, please ask him to come up."

Andy's voice, an essential and effective tool for negotiating, sounds weak still. Will it stay that way? Will everything be weaker than before?

"Just promise you'll use the wheelchair?"

Andy nods and the orderly leaves. Wheelchair. Well, at least he gets to leave the hospital, gets to leave Melbourne. The ability to go to people instead of having to entertain them might temper the bitterness he's cultivated all this time in the hospital towards his fellow survivor. Might.

Another knock. It's his assistant, Crane, the most affable and cheerful Aborigine Andy's ever known, whose infectious smile brings one to Andy.

Crane has worked for the Kiltepper family in various capacities as long as Walter Pollard did, and has contributed as much in personal ways. What bonds Crane with the Kilteppers, particularly with Andy, is a shared sense of bloodline. Crane's pride in his many millennia of Aboriginal history puts to shame the measly two centuries the Kilteppers can claim. Which makes Andy value Crane's empathy as much as he does.

"Ready, sir?"

"Yes—wait, I want to make one stop."

"Room 231."

"Thank you, Crane."

Andy's assistant guides the wheelchair forward and helps Andy climb in. The aching pain reminds him these are essentially the first movements of his atrophied muscles, the result of postponing, not always voluntarily, physiotherapy until he's home. They go down the hall quite some distance before Crane pushes open a door, wheels Andy in partway, and steps away.

There lies Walter Pollard, unconscious, tubes running from his small, aging body to machines making soothing but tense beeps. Seeing his dead father's best friend in this pathetic condition does nothing to diminish Andy's resentment. He figures out how to manoeuvre the wheelchair and brings himself closer to this man who is a part of Kiltepper history, albeit a volatile part.

Andy's always liked Walter, has always thought of him as an uncle since the Pollards immigrated to Tasmania in the sixties when Andy was just seven. Humble Uncle Walter and Aunt Amy with their two distinct North American accents—Walter's from Chicago, Amy's from Toronto—and their baby daughter, Ruth. Possibly the first non-Tasmanians Andy ever met. Aside from that, Andy saw nothing special in these newcomers. It was only once he got older that Andy came to appreciate Walter Pollard's importance to his father and their family.

For the Kilteppers, all the way to and including Andy, have an aversion to Hobart. A quirky bias transcending the natural rivalry between Tasmania's two largest cities.

From their genealogical research, Andy and his father theorized it had to do with Andrew Kiltepper I avoiding Hobart as part of his effort to erase the Fitzpatrick origins. However, that doesn't explain why this was carried forth so staunchly with each generation's treatment of Hobart as a mere satellite. No Kiltepper, prior to Andy's father, would concede Hobart was superior in generating revenue, despite fiscal evidence to the contrary. It's Andy's belief there was a lingering psychological effect from the Black Line, both its execution and failure, in how it brought out the worst in fellow Hobartians in his ancestor's eyes. One that entrenched a pathological and hereditary partiality leading to decades of bad administration in the capital.

That ended with Walter Pollard, a modest yet capable man with no desire for glory, only a knack for setting up and buying new businesses, as well as knowing the right time to sell them. He was also a close, trusted friend of Andy's father and so the perfect man to run operations in Hobart.

Under Walter's aggressive leadership, at any point over the next decades, the Kiltepper family would own or operate department stores, gas stations, automotive shops, real estate companies, art stores and, for a short time, a highly profitable credit union they sold for ten times what it cost. Walter's broadminded instincts were almost magical. The only businesses Walter shunned were those having to do with guns and weapons, for he was a pacifist. A rebuff of the family's origins, certainly, but one tolerated because Walter was, in all respects but name, a Kiltepper.

After thirty-five years, perhaps due to a mid-life crisis or repressed naïveté, Walter, in search of new challenges, took his earnings and old world business acumen and applied them to the stock market. An unfortunate decision for all concerned. Walter failed and his personal fortune suffered. Only his gut warning him to get out saved him from utter ruin.

The Kiltepper businesses suffered from this decision too because Walter's replacement—it still pains Andy to recall his name—could never match his predecessor's ability. It wasn't all the successor's fault. Walter had adopted dozens of proprietary methods and short cuts over the decades based on his instincts. But if his successor had possessed even a smidgeon of that instinct, warning signs would have emerged before major damage was done. The end of the smorgasbord of Kiltepper companies was at hand as this started the serial downsizing Andy may have to carry on as the sole living Kiltepper.

Furious as that made Andy, he was particularly angered when his father refused to cut ties with the Pollards who, due to his resentment, Andy couldn't stand the sight of anymore. But Walter was Andy's father's closest and dearest friend and would always be welcome at the estate.

Which is how Walter Pollard came to be there during the fire. Andy can recall little of their rescue other than those moments when the two survivors were waiting to get put on separate ambulances for the short ride to the helicopter that would take them to Melbourne. Walter was conscious and Andy can recall hearing him utter a few words. He heard them then but lost them. What were they? For along with the words came a strong sense they were important. Revelatory. Promising even.

"Walter," Andy says

He waits several seconds before repeating it, several times. Nothing. He gives up and backs out.

Andy almost gives himself a headache trying to recall those words while Crane drives him to the

Melbourne airport. From there, a short flight gets them to Launceston.

Good to be home, Andy thinks, as he settles into the passenger seat of his Cadillac Escalade. Crane drives away from the airport towards the house.

"How are Carla and Wilma?"

"Anxiously awaiting your arrival."

"They know I'm coming back today?"

"Each time I go to the house they ask if today is the day. It was nice to finally give them the answer they wanted."

"Good."

Andy's eager to see them too, to see how they're coping firsthand instead of the fluffed-up reports he hears on their hospital visits. Only something else is tugging at him.

"Crane?"

"Yes sir."

Andy directs his assistant to take a detour to the old estate. He obeys without a word. They turn off the main road but Crane slows down before the turn for the Kiltepper private road.

"Are you sure you want to do this now?"

"Crane, you know when people share both good news and bad news and are told to give the bad news first?"

"Yes."

"I'm doing it with good vibes and bad vibes."

"I don't understand."

"That's all right."

Crane turns onto the private road. Aside from a few fallen trees and windblown ash, one wouldn't guess such a ferocious fire came through here. The pains that had diminished return once the car hits the windy, bumpy uphill section that leads to the paved driveway of the estate. Not even the SUV's suspension can protect Andy's sensitive bones and muscles.

The driveway is littered with black brush and black ash, grim frontage for the skeleton of the pride of the Kilteppers, which has been reduced to a few stubborn frames in a grassy area covered in debris. Incombustibles such as appliances, parts of toys and bicycles, shattered dishes, warped tools, and broken kitchen items pollute the fine lawn and front porch, transforming the lovely site into a garbage dump. Someone should have cleared this, Andy thinks, then recalls it was his direction that not be done and he's glad they listened.

Andy takes his time to exit the car, stubbornly shaking off Crane's help, and walks around the area, poking with his toes at various items, turning them over or shoving them aside. He's certain Crane is wondering what he's looking for. No way Andy would divulge his recollection of seeing a Thylacine. He's not sure he believes it now. But he can't get out of his head the stripes, the jaws opened much wider than he's ever seen an animal do. He won't share the experience, let alone believe it, without the proof he may find here.

In his recollection it was the tiger that took his beloved Cessation of Transportation medal, a family heirloom handed down every generation since the second Andrew Kiltepper who received it as a boy. It commemorates the termination of the practice of transporting convicts to the colony, and celebrates the fiftieth anniversary of the settling of Tasmania. A fitting token of his family's tie with the island. Andy was wearing it that day to pass on to his son, only to have it snatched away. If he can find that piece, a worthwhile endeavour based on sentimental value alone, then he can prove, if only to himself, his mind was playing tricks.

However, it's hopeless to find anything so small in this mess, in his condition. Andy does spot an old axe that might be the one that belonged to the first Andrew Kiltepper. A shooting pain stops him as he tries to bend to pick it up. He'll get it later. Andy pokes around a few more minutes before giving up, vowing to come back and do something.

"Now for the good vibes," he says, at the car.

This time Crane seems to understand as he smiles.

Only he doesn't understand and starts driving towards Andy's house in Launceston. Again, Andy redirects him, this time to the new estate, on the other side of the same rainforest. Its access road is steeper but better sealed.

What luck it was spared from the fire, given all the exposed wood. Andy's infirmity has set back its completion date but the contractor has promised to get the project on track to have it ready before the holidays. Though it'll be a sombre Christmas, just he and the girls. At least the delays give him an opportunity to make some appropriate redesigns.

They drive close enough to confirm the reports that it's undamaged.

"I don't need to get out," Andy says. "I'm ready to go home. Please don't mention the detours to Carla and Wilma."

"I wouldn't think of it."

Crane pulls the car around and back down the hill. Andy is as content as he could hope to be. Even his anger at Walter for surviving is receding, except there remains that nagging frustration: what had the old man said?

The pain has lessened too. Andy notices Crane driving tentatively, especially when cornering the sharp turns, which may be the reason. He's driving like Drew did when Andy let his twelve-year-old take his first attempt at handing a vehicle, just as his own father did for Andy, though for Drew it would be his last attempt.

Andy slumps back, succumbs to the emotion.

Half an hour—maybe forty minutes given the careful way Crane is driving—will be long enough for him to indulge in sorrow, knowing the promise of seeing Carla and Wilma will prevent a complete meltdown. As will a new determination, driven by his concern for those girls, to change many things.

# 13

Sporadic dark shapes pop up on the horizon, adding variety to a sublime flat fiery landscape of yellow, orange, and red dotted by sparse green vegetation. Oblong formations, silent and unassuming patrols, that seemingly say: move on, nothing for you metal-encased humans to linger for here. You kangaroos and other bouncing, crawling critters, on the other hand, feel free to bound about. And they do.

How nice to be on the ground again, enjoying such a vista at eye-level instead of trying to catch glimpses from above through breaks in the clouds. It's taken nearly two weeks but Ruth's roundabout suggestion—which Deborah thought frivolous at first—to split their journey into three legs—London, Dubai, Perth—turned out to be a stroke of genius as the altitude and claustrophobia made Christopher ill on each leg. Fortunately, he only had to resort to the air sickness bag once, on the last leg.

Seven, maybe eight, hours it seems is the maximum for him. The timely stopovers—three days in London, two in Dubai—were just long enough for him to recover and prepare for the next leg. And they got to shop, see Buckingham Palace, and take a camel ride as a bonus. Had they flown direct, Christopher might have suffered too much. Maybe he could have made it—he never complained or cried when he did get sick—but then it would have been Deborah who would have suffered from worry. But at last they are on terra firma again and, though confined in a train, they have cabins—Platinum Service at that—and so far he's been fine. More than fine.

"Gin," Fred says, spreading out his cards.

"Already? Glad I'm not playing for money."

Deborah collects the cards and starts shuffling, expecting Fred to say his unlucky-at-cards comment like he did in her youth. He doesn't. Even the littlest things seem to be going her way at the moment. As they should for any tourist, which is how she's approached this journey, at least the initial part.

As a tourist, their stops in London and Dubai were terrific but pale in comparison to this, the real thrill, riding across Australia on the Indian Pacific, a train trip she yearned to take as a child. The cabin she shares with her son is more luxurious than the ones in those dreams. Fred and Ruth seem anxious about making everything right for her and their nephew. In a way it seems too easy, too tailored. As if Fred and Ruth were certain she and Christopher would come. Is she being railroaded? She chuckles at a bad joke that might amuse Fred.

"What's so funny?" Fred says.

"Oh nothing," she says, and deals out the cards.

A few days ago she might not have laughed so readily, might have nurtured such a silly thought into paranoia. Maybe she left her suspicious nature behind with Willie.

Leaving him was the hardest part of the decision to come here, the only negative aspect that remains. Now that the whirlwind of travel of the past week has subsided, his absence is more deeply felt. The phone calls she made from London and Dubai did little to fill that void. She can tell, despite his words to the contrary, he's troubled by the police business. Lonely too, though that didn't come through as strongly. Maybe she shouldn't read too much into how he sounds over the phone and accept at face value his assurances the situation is in hand.

Sweet man. His unexpected declaration this trip would be wonderful for Christopher, would give her son a practical education while also keeping him immune from Willie's troubles, means a lot to her. He's sacrificing a great deal and without complaint. Quite a turnaround considering the argument that ensued that morning when she broached the idea of coming to Australia.

It's the reverse of Christopher whose initial excitement at seeing other places, not to mention not having to go back to that school, blinded him to the realization Willie would stay at home. When he did grasp this, Christopher began bounding around the house with more intensity than before, spicing his actions with unusual guttural sounds. Only Willie could calm him down. Perhaps Christopher hoped they would see Willie was needed. It didn't work.

Fred lets out a polite cough and Deborah notices she's been absentmindedly discarding and taking cards, barely looking at them. She picks up a jack, discards it right away, before recalling Fred picked up another jack the move before. Or was that the game before? He says nothing but smiles knowingly as he picks it up and discards a useless six of clubs.

"Thanks again, Fred, for all this."

"Oh stop it. Don't act as if this isn't meaningful for us either."

"This slow re-immersion into Australia was a great idea. I loved London and Dubai, and I'm sure Christopher did too, but this train, it's fabulous."

"Again, don't make a fuss. It's how we intended coming back all along. We've got the time so why not travel at our pace? No hurries, no worries."

She likes the sound of that. And Fred is such a meticulous organizer, a complex trip like this would have been a breeze for him to put together, as well as a joy.

"You and I are taking it easy. What about your wife?"

"What about Ruth? She's in her element."

"It's wonderful of her to give it a go, but I'll bet she'll find it hard."

"Don't underestimate her, my wife's up for the challenge. Grateful too. She misses teaching."

"She didn't have to retire, did she?"

"She misses teaching. Not the schools. Not the bureaucracy."

"What about you, Fred? Never thought you'd retire this young."

"A lot has happened since . . . since we last saw each other."

He looks at her, as if provoking her to ask. Not yet, she thinks, don't let anything spoil this ride.

Fred grins sardonically as Deborah lays down another jack, which he picks up. He rearranges his hand, lays it down for another win. Deborah collects the cards, stacks them in a neat pile, and puts them back in their sleeve.

"That's it for me."

She declines his offer of tea and he leaves her on her own in time to catch movement on the horizon in the form of a troop of kangaroos hopping in their direction. As they get close, she's able to make out a female with the tiny head of a joey peeping out her pouch. The image is so pleasant, so nostalgic, so ephemeral, as the train whisks by.

Soon enough, they will reach their destination, the journey will end, and real life will return. She'll have to face people, face her memories, after vowing never to return to this land. Does her presence now make her a failure? Prodigal?

Or is she a nomad? Is this another move rather than a trip? Maybe her lot in life, and her son's, is akin to that of the Aborigines, uprooting from time to time, place to place, giving up everything to seek peace and restore a way of life somewhere else, all the time facing the fear of ending up in one's own Wybalenna.

Only for Deborah the choices are hers, and such a fate is avoidable for her and Christopher. In a way, though, that makes it more frightening.

She looks out the window and can't resist the sensation that, were this train to glide forever along these smooth rails across this peaceful desert, she probably wouldn't mind.

# 14

"Three thousand, six hundred fifty-three."

"That was quick," Aunt Ruth says. "Are you sure it's correct?"

"Pretty sure," he says, not hiding his pride.

Aunt Ruth takes his paper.

"Let me see—oh, we do have to work on your penmanship."

"I know."

As she tries to make sense of what he's written, Christopher looks out the window in time to spot more kangaroos bouncing into the horizon. So many of them. Nothing else, really, and he wonders how they survive out there, what they eat, where they get water with all those river beds dried out. He's heard it explained on nature shows but he doesn't always listen because the voices put him to sleep. He bets Aunt Ruth could explain as well as those narrators. Better. And she'd make it sound more interesting too. Or maybe Uncle Fred since he knows so much about animals.

When his mom told him about going away he was thrilled until he learned Aunt Ruth was going to home school him. The idea of home schooling was okay—better than a real school—but he became worried when he found out she used to be a teacher. He's never cared much for teachers, especially lady teachers. He doesn't know why. He couldn't say much, though, because his mom would have given him only one other choice, which was to not go on this trip and to go back to that school and face Mrs. Jackson again. So he said okay and suggested Willie could teach him instead, or at least assist Aunt Ruth. Then he found out Willie wasn't coming. Boy did he not like that. Only when Willie explained he had to stay because of things he had to take care of, did he stop making a fuss. However, the way Willie talked, saying he was counting on Christopher to look out for his mother, as if they would be separated a long time, bothered Christopher. He made Willie promise that if they weren't back by spring, he would come to them. He made Willie re-promise it on the phone calls from London and Dubai.

Being without Willie was hard the first few days and Christopher missed him so much, he got sick a few times. Everyone thinks it's because of the planes but those didn't bother him. Or maybe they did. He's not really sure what made him sick except it always happened when he thought about Willie and how, the farther away they were, the greater the possibility of never seeing him again seemed. He did feel better after they landed in Perth and has been fine since they boarded the train. Maybe they were right, maybe it was the planes.

The space outside is so big and unchanging that Christopher's attention always drifts off after about his third kangaroo sighting. That makes it easier to pay attention to Aunt Ruth whose gentle voice with its soft Australian accent draws him in to whatever she teaches. No matter if it's English, Mathematics, History, or even her testing him on the things they saw in London and Dubai. He's actually having fun learning stuff.

She seems to be having fun too—most of his other teachers didn't look like they were having fun—especially coming up with puzzles. Like this one she says Uncle Fred thought of to get him to figure out exactly how many days old he will be on his upcoming birthday. She suggested adding up the days and months, including all the February twenty-nines. But he decided to add up all the years instead to go faster. And for ten years that just means adding a zero to 365 and figuring out there have been two leap years in his life so far and there will be another one this year. Although something tells him he may not want to look too smart.

"This is good, Christopher, very good," Aunt Ruth says, and she sounds surprised.

"Thanks."

"I thought you were having difficulty at school."

"Not with lessons."

"Then what?"

"You'll have to ask my mom."

He turns away, not wanting Aunt Ruth to see he's playing dumb. It makes him wonder: would he have been different at school back home if Aunt Ruth was his teacher? Maybe, but probably only if the other kids were gone. He would want Aunt Ruth all to himself. Because he did like it when his mom tried and there were no other kids. It's just too bad his mom wasn't very good and got frustrated easily when his attention would drift or he would get something simple wrong. Aunt Ruth has a way of knowing what to say and how to say it. Although now she seems puzzled.

"What's wrong, Aunt Ruth?"

"You seem too smart for Grade Five."

"Really?"

"Yes, you're too advanced for the materials I picked up in London. We've got two days left on the train and I'm not sure what to cover next."

She adds that where they are is so remote there aren't any schools or stores with the materials she needs. So instead she works with him to improve his penmanship. He hates this and has always hated this. But now he wants to impress his teacher, his Aunt Ruth, and so he lets her guide his hand to write neater letters and numbers.

She pauses to check his work giving him a chance to look out the window again. This time the beauty surrounding the train hits him in a new way.

The fine redness in the endless sand, the small green bushes, the giant rocks that crop up out of nothing far away. He's never seen anything like this. Not up close. The TV shows can't make it look this good. The more he sees, the more the idea of staying appeals to him. If he impresses his teacher, who happens to be his mom's sister, that will make his mom happy, and if his mom is happy then this trip can continue long enough to force Willie to keep his promise and join them, instead of them having to go back there. That would be awesome. For that he will try as hard as he can.

But hold on. What if Aunt Ruth tells his mom he just needs to move up a grade or two? His mom might think that was the problem all along, meaning they might return sooner, not later, so he doesn't miss a whole semester. That can't happen. Maybe he's been too smart, too eager to please, too happy to get all the answers right and quickly. It might be too late to fix that but there may be another way to get what he wants.

"We haven't done geography."

"I didn't bring any materials on geography."

"You can teach me about Australia. You have to know that."

His aunt smiles.

"I know all about Australia. But I like to prepare my lessons and have an approach before I teach."

"Okay, but can you at least tell me what you know about that famous big rock?"

Aunt Ruth looks out the window.

"No, the really famous one. The one that's in the middle of the country."

"Oh, you mean Ayers Rock. Uluru."

"Airs raw cooler ooh?"

Aunt Ruth takes a piece of paper and spells out the names.

"Uluru, that's what the Aborigines call it and we call it that now too. Ayers Rock is what it was called for a while, named after an important Australian."

"Uluru sounds nicer."

"It does, doesn't it?"

"Do you have a picture of it?"

Aunt Ruth reaches for her purse but then stops, her face blushing as if caught doing something she shouldn't. He knows the picture's in there but she doesn't seem to want to share it. Of course, he can't let on he knows it's there.

"I'm sure there's a picture on board somewhere."

Why won't she show it? Is it because she doesn't want his mom to know about it? That's silly, his mom's in the picture. Though it is an old picture and Christopher knows his mom doesn't like to discuss old things. She doesn't like old memories and that's probably an old memory. Makes sense. But it only increases Christopher's curiosity, especially the most intriguing question: who took the picture?

There's a knock at the door. Uncle Fred pokes his head in to say it's time to get ready to eat as he's made a reservation. Aunt Ruth looks at her watch and gives him a look. He then says that, because it's a full train, the dining car might be less busy now.

They leave Christopher alone to change but he's not sure what to wear. Then his mom comes in to recommend the tan dress pants and blue and white checked shirt—thankfully no tie—they bought at the fancy London department store. The same store they made him go to because the wait to get on the giant Ferris wheel was too long. The same store where she bought the fancy jeans she's put on. Christopher can almost hear Willie's voice saying they're too tight.

At the dining car, Christopher discovers Uncle Fred was wrong. It's full. A cylinder packed with dull humans in grey and white and brown and black in the middle of a lovely yellow, green, and red wide open space under a blue sky. They're squished in so tight it reminds him of the zoo, but in reverse. A waiter guides them to the last empty table at the far end.

Most of the diners are older than Uncle Fred but some tables, including the one across from theirs, is packed with large men who look like they could be friends of Willie's, except not in jeans and flannel shirts, but just as loud and ugly. They're swearing a lot too. At least their plates are empty and they're about to leave. But then a waiter arrives with a tray of filled beer glasses. He sets it down, collects the empty dishes, then distributes the drinks.

The waiter drops off menus for them, including a kids menu Christopher declines. He tells them, above the clinking glasses at the next table, today's special is kangaroo steak, which sounds tasty until Christopher spots one in the distance.

"I thought you said the restaurant car would be empty," Aunt Ruth says, as the waiter leaves.

"My mistake," Uncle Fred says. "I forgot the train will stop at Kalgoorlie soon."

"What's in Kalgoorlie?" Christopher says.

"What's in Kalgoorlie?" one of the beer drinkers suddenly says. "Why the Super Pit, of course."

His rough tone startles Christopher, Uncle Fred, and Aunt Ruth, but not his mom who gently shakes her head and ignores the speaker.

"What's the Super Pit?" Christopher says.

"Why, nothing but the greatest gold mine in the entire world."

A second man points his glass at Christopher's mom, and speaks in a low but sneaky voice.

"I'd be honoured to give you and your sister a private tour."

"I'm her son," Christopher says, just as his mom taps his shoulder to hush.

The man studies Christopher up and down, grins and winks at his mom whose face remains still as she continues to ignore the man.

"No worries, lass, I'll fix you up with one of proper colour."

"That's enough," Uncle Fred says.

This makes the men laugh and encourages the second, ruder one to step across the aisle and stand over them. Christopher tenses up, his instinct telling him this is a threat, telling him to attack. He's about to drop to the floor when something inside him—a new instinct, a superior instinct—stops him, tells him: not now, not here. Christopher becomes aware of others watching as the whole restaurant car gets quiet, making the man's voice louder.

"What do you say to that? Fancy a private tour?"

Christopher's fists clench and again he struggles to hold himself back, surprised and more than a bit proud he's succeeding.

Good thing too as several men approach from down the aisle, including the conductor, the waiter, and a man in a suit that's nicer than Uncle Fred's.

When the brutes see this last man, they shut up instantly. Wow, Christopher wonders, how did he do that? The four men follow this other man out, leaving behind half-finished beers. Good riddance.

"Animals."

His mom's sudden comment, as well as a scary glare in her eyes, catches Christopher off guard. So much so he decides to keep to himself that what she said is an insult to animals.

Once the gawkers around them stop gawking, they order their meals. Then the well-dressed man returns, looking as embarrassed as he should. From behind his back he pulls out two bottles of red wine and sets them down on their table.

"My humblest apologies. Rewarding those men with a luxury train trip was clearly a mistake. Please accept these as a token."

"Just boys being boys, right?"

His mom says this in a weirdly bitter way, as if she's angriest with this man who, to Christopher, is the good guy.

"Right," the man says.

He gives a bow and departs, no doubt happy to get away. His mom is still upset and something is distracting her. This is as good a time as any to do his test. He may end up feeling bad about it but he has to, if only to see what happens. Who knows, it might help make sure they don't go back too soon.

"Mom, Aunt Ruth is a good teacher."

"That's wonderful."

"Yeah, except she needs to find some pictures or anything about Uluru. Have you ever been there?"

# 15

The station at Cook is the most barren place Fred has ever seen. Nothing but dirt and desert and a few defiant wildflowers swaying in the warm breeze with a purple hue that would be gloomy elsewhere but is cheerful here. Christopher is about a hundred metres away, happy to loiter in the emptiness, no doubt hoping to spot a kangaroo or emu or even a camel during their two hour stop. The flat horizon ensures he can keep tabs on the boy for some distance and it's reassuring to see him heeding the advice Fred forgot to provide to avoid bushes and rocks that might conceal snakes and spiders.

It's nice to get a dose of fresh air, even in this midday heat. Still nearly twenty-four hours before they reach Adelaide. To Fred, it would have been much easier and more pleasant for them, for him, to have flown. But this was the best way to acclimate Christopher and re-acclimate Deborah to Australia. How Ruth's been able to withstand the slow pace is beyond him; she must really be enjoying teaching Christopher. The boy's surprised them all with his willingness, even eagerness, to learn. So far his wife has probably spent twice as much time with their nephew than she has with her husband. It wouldn't surprise Fred if Ruth said she'd love to continue all the way to Sydney.

What can Ruth and her sister be doing? There's only an hour before they re-board for the last leg. They ought to be out here, taking the opportunity to stretch in the open air. He wouldn't mind returning to the train, which is not feasible while his nephew is out here. Though he shouldn't complain as this is one of the few moments he's had with the boy since Perth.

A moment ago he was envious about the time his wife was spending with a nephew she's known barely two weeks. That envy is less about the time lost with Ruth than for missed opportunities to get to know a child who is nothing close to what they expected. Their fondness for Christopher is growing with each day, each hour. Had he and Ruth ever considered adoption, they would have balked at a kid like Deborah's son based on first impressions. How ignorant and short-sighted that would have been. How much they would have missed. How lucky to have this chance, notwithstanding, of course, the unfortunate circumstances of the fire that brought it about.

Deborah and Ruth emerge. Christopher rushes back to call his mom over. Ruth is about to follow them when she spots Fred waving his arms to call her over.

"Thank goodness, I doubt I could keep up with that boy."

"What have you two been doing? The train is about to leave soon."

"Just talking. Deborah's still upset about dinner last night."

"Yes, that was unfortunate. Now I see why they hire charter flights for those miners."

"No, no, she's used to that type. I meant when Christopher asked about Uluru."

"You're not serious."

"Just the way he asked, it troubled her."

"Women's intuition type of thing?"

"No need to mock. His was a pointed question. And you know she's only been to Uluru that one time. With us. With . . ."

"Surely a coincidence. Uluru is the most famous place in Australia. Its picture is on every map, every brochure, every pamphlet imaginable. I'm sure that's how it got into his head."

"It's possible you're right."

"Of course."

"Only, just before we ate, while I was teaching him, he also came out of the blue with a question about Uluru, asking whether I had a picture of it."

Ruth produces the photograph of the three of them in front of Uluru.

"I forgot you'd brought that along."

"Which is my point. He might have seen this, not some brochure. I've left my purse around a lot."

"If so, I'm sure it's not a big deal."

"How can you say that?"

"We'll deal with whatever comes of it."

"I really like the boy, Fred."

"We both do."

"I'm getting nervous about this, really nervous. Even after we gave up trying, I always dreamed of seeing Debs again. But in my dream, it was either free and easy or a battle. Now we're in some middle territory, lost halfway between safety and danger."

Fred spreads his arms around.

"Kind of like this place?"

"Yeah, kind of like this place."

# 16

As the train emerges from South Australia's bleak yet beautiful nothingness and slowly creeps into civilization—perceivable only by the appearance of lights in these early morning hours—Deborah lets open the curtain. A sliver of sunrise snaps her out of tourist mode into the reality of who she is, where she is, and who she's with (and not with). Soon they'll be out of Port Augusta and then, a couple of hours or so later, Adelaide.

What is she going to face these next days, or even weeks? The indefiniteness is what's feeding her trepidation. The lack of control. Sure, she'll retain control of her actions, and those of her son, but the scope of that control has narrowed. That's what's scary. But a relief too in a way. Which is surprising. Never could she have imagined the suspension of her independence as anything but threatening. Yet it actually feels all right.

She shuts her eyes until a knock wakes her from a nap that went deeper than expected.

"Debs, we'll be arriving in an hour. Enough time for a quick breakfast if you want to join us."

"Hear that, Christopher?" she mumbles.

No answer and she realizes her son's not there. She opens the door to look down the passage to see Christopher, already dressed, walking with Fred towards the dining car. She turns on a light to see his suitcase open and filled with his clothes, packed neater than one could expect from a boy his age. Who is this kid?

A remark from an unfriendly taxi driver at the train station provokes a growl from Christopher that reminds Deborah her son is the still same kid. She doesn't catch what was said and the cabbie shrugs it off as he continues loading the Johnsons' more than ample luggage. No one bothers to enlighten Deborah about the exchange—perhaps figuring she saw and heard it—and she lets it drift from her thoughts as they drive into Adelaide.

It's her first time visiting this city and she can't recall Fred and Ruth ever expressing any affinity for it beyond as a potential base for a wine tasting trip. It's lovely in a subtle way, elegantly flat with green space aplenty, its symmetry charming, though to some it could seem sterile. Beyond the centre, a large patch of inviting parkland catches her eye.

However, the parkland remains in the distance as the taxi slows, turns, and twists through small downtown streets and comes to a stop in the semi-circular driveway of a high-rise condominium. It's a nice looking building, tall, modern, maybe five years old. But so not Ruth who's not only afraid of heights but has constantly bemoaned crowded streets and skyscrapers. Deborah's never known her sister to live in anything but a large house with a good-sized garden. Like the grand Victorian in Hobart she and Fred restored. Unlike many other couples, their fixer upper arguably saved their marriage. It also served as a haven for Deborah as a teen when she needed to evade an overbearing boyfriend or get away from her father. That house was cute, quirky, and historic. That house is a retirement house; this is the farthest thing from that.

"Here we are, home sweet home."

Ruth says it somewhat equivocally, as she and Fred get out, retrieve the bags, and pay the driver.

A glass-enclosed elevator with a superb view of that same parkland takes them to the sixth floor. Christopher finds it neat but Ruth seems uneasy at the swift ascent. They exit into a long corridor that feels hollow because the doors between the units are far apart. They go all the way to the end and enter a corner unit.

It's a spacious, ultramodern suite with elegant furniture that looks staged—lots of leather, chrome, sharply defined angles—and high-end appliances nicer even than hers at home. Seeing them reminds Deborah of Willie, makes her wonder how he is, but knowing now is not a good time to dwell on that.

"Ruth, really, this isn't like you."

"I know. Our old place became too impractical, requiring fixing all the time."

"Indeed," Fred says, "we've traded character for convenience. Sorry if it's not what you expected."

"Don't be sorry, I love it. If I could afford it, I'd live in a place like this. And what do I always say about character, Christopher?"

"If the people in a house have character, then the house has character."

"That's right."

"Mom, look, it's the same as ours."

He rushes to the table Deborah knows well and she finds it amusing how it's coming out of the wall almost exactly as hers does. Seeing it is disturbing and comforting at the same time, fortunately more the latter.

"It was made by a family friend," Ruth says. "But Christopher, did you know it was originally one table meant for us to share? Well, asking sisters born twelve years apart to share something: what could he have been thinking? We fought a long time over whose room it should go in, so long he ended up cutting it in half and refinishing both parts to make two individual pieces."

The story makes Christopher laugh. Deborah's glad Ruth omitted the proviso the tables ought to be considered sisters and never be apart for long. As well as the fact the gift was in honour of their mother who had recently died.

"Who made it?"

"Your mom never told you the story?"

"No."

Deborah becomes self-conscious but her son's concern about the table's history is diverted by a pair of framed school portraits, each of a young girl. One is white, the other Aboriginal. Deborah doesn't recognize them though the white girl is striking with shiny big blue eyes, a petite mouth, and long, thin blonde hair. Something familiar about her.

However, Christopher is more enamoured with the Aboriginal girl who's closer to his age. Her exotic face is attractive but tough, intense, due to her smouldering eyes. Maybe she resembles a classmate. Christopher picks that one up and his interest in this strange girl baffles Deborah. It reminds her of his unusual curiosity to the point of obsession about Uluru. Where did that come from?

"Who are they?" Christopher says.

"That's Wilma," Ruth says. " The younger is Carla."

"Yeah, but who are they?"

"Christopher, don't be rude."

"Sorry."

"That's all right," Fred says. "They're children of friends of ours with whom we've gotten close. We have no children ourselves, so they're the next best thing. Maybe we can add your picture too?"

"I don't have any school pictures."

Christopher says it matter-of-factly but Deborah can't help look away, doubting he's ever sat for one. She's never thought about it, isn't a fan of photos in general, and doesn't even own a camera. At a time like this, that can get awkward.

"Fred, how about you show them around?"

The rest of their home is as impressive as the kitchen and living room. Deborah admires how the hardwood floors are different in each room yet still complement each other. Of the two guest bedrooms, Christopher takes the larger one with the television, which is fine as Deborah's room has a balcony. Both rooms connect through a shared bathroom.

Fred and Ruth excuse themselves to unpack, check phone messages, take stock of groceries, and so on while she and Christopher settle in. Her son's notion of settling in is figuring out the TV channels; for Deborah, it's taking a much needed, non-moving shower.

When she's done, she checks on Christopher who's found cartoons to watch. She gets him to agree to take a shower when it ends, then joins Fred and Ruth in the living room. They greet her with a glass of Riesling. A pang of guilt for not having called Willie yet passes when she realizes it'd be too late in the evening there; she can call him tonight.

"We have news," Fred says.

"Good news," Ruth says. "About Daddy."

"Oh?"

Apparently, as they were crossing the Nullarbor Plain on the Indian-Pacific, her father's condition improved enough to allow his transport from the Melbourne hospital to Royal Hobart Hospital where he is more easily accessible to friends. Good news for him, no doubt, but Deborah can't escape the sense she's a victim of a bait and switch.

"So now I'll have to go to Tasmania if I'm to see him."
Fred shakes his head earnestly.

"We haven't told anyone you're here so if you decide not to go, we'll understand."

Yet they're looking at her, ready to say, "but to have come all this way," to any inclination of hers to call their bluff. The situation reminds her of the soft manipulations she used to endure from her older sister. How little has changed. It doesn't make her angry, just sad.

"I have to think about this."

Deborah says it knowing as well as they do that she'll give in. They drink their wine in silence until Christopher appears, all clean and changed.

"What's going on?" he says.

"What's going on, young man," Fred says, "is we need to stock up on food and I need a pair of strong arms to help. How about you come shopping with us? I'm sure we can find a treat."

This perks up Christopher. Just getting out ought to perk up Deborah too but the wine is sweet and her head starts hurting. She begs off but does go to her balcony to wave at them.

It's a magnificent day, not too hot, and the view towards the parkland is lovely. She could make some tea, sit out there to soak it in, maybe even slip into a nap. Only she's unable to ignore a troubling feeling that will only worsen if left unattended.

Deborah stares at the photos of the two girls a good minute before pulling the familiar looking one out of its frame. She turns it over. All it reveals is the girl's first name, Carla, and the year, 2010. She looks at the photo again, examining the girl's features. A soft rounded chin and such sparkling eyes above a small yet conspicuous nose. A milky complexion.

Oh God. She stares at the photo, puts a hand to her mouth, takes a deep breath.

Her head tells her to make that tea, get outside, and try not to think. She replaces the photo, her hands shaking a little, and heads to the kitchen. But instead of filling the kettle, she snoops, opening drawers and doors. Her efforts are fruitless except they do help stave off a full headache. She won't limit her search to the kitchen though she will draw the line at the master bedroom, at least for now.

Then, under the cutlery tray, she finds a red file folder. Inside is a legal document, a lease agreement. She's about to put the folder back when it hits her: lease? She assumed Fred and Ruth owned the unit. Fred, so mindful of maximizing every dollar, frowned on renting. More unusual is that the document reveals the lease is with Kiltepper Properties. Could be coincidental and none of her business. Though this possibility is shattered upon discovering the monthly rent for this deluxe three-bedroom unit in the heart of Adelaide, a unit that ought to fetch thousands a month, is costing the Johnsons a mere five hundred dollars. A year. That's it. And it's a five-year lease.

What is she to make of it? Does it have anything to do with why she's here? Are they tricking her?

The folder also contains a news article from the Launceston paper from last September. It's about the same bushfires Deborah read of in the Toronto paper. This article is about a particular one that ravaged a remote estate near Launceston. It lists her father as a survivor, but not the only one. The other survivor she recognizes by his picture. No wonder Fred and Ruth haven't been forthcoming about the details. Would have been nice to know this before making her decision to come to Australia. The fact Deborah never asked is no excuse. She lets a flash of anger pass through her, then shakes her head. Come on, Deborah, be honest with yourself: at the time you had no interest in anything that might have prevented you coming here. This realization, the full significance of which she's not ready to face yet and needs to let sink in slowly, oddly seems to have rid her completely of her headache.

As she reads on about the victims, including children and wives and others she once knew, it's difficult to understand how Fred and Ruth could have held this back from her. She knew these people at one time, cared about them. That remark to Fred and Ruth about a letter being sufficient haunts her now. Deborah can see why that reaction upset her sister, how it would have made Ruth hesitant about sharing news that deserved to be shared in person.

But she's frustrated too by a feeling of betrayal at seeing her own family still close to people who hurt her a great deal. Suddenly Deborah feels all alone, isolated, vulnerable. Not unlike that dark period in Canada after

Dwight's death and before Willie's arrival. She must do what she did then, focus on Christopher, rely on her love for her son, her need to do what's right for him.

This trip has been positive for Christopher and his behaviour is much better than she could have hoped for. He would never have gone, willingly and alone, with Fred and Ruth to a public space like a grocery store if he was still in Canada. She's never seen him enjoy himself as much as he has since they left. She can't forget he still he has an opportunity to know his grandfather and every boy ought to know his grandfather, regardless of any issues between the man and his own his mother. To take him back now, just so she can escape her fears would be cruel. Going to Tasmania is unavoidable, something she must do, if only for her son.

She puts everything back, pours a large portion of Riesling into her glass, and settles on the balcony where the afternoon sun gently soothes as the world walks, cycles, drives on by below her and the green of the distant parkland comforts her in her resolve to see this through. However, it doesn't address the fact her trust in others has been shaken.

# 17

Beep-beep-beep-beep.

"Nimrod," Willie says to himself as he struggles to unplug the refrigerator, finding the simple task not so simple and also profoundly depressing.

He felt like such a hero the previous Christmas when he surprised Deborah with the stainless steel, feature-laden appliances and got rid of the archaic almond decades-old scratched machines that came with the house. And then to follow that up moments later by guiding her into the living room to sag, not in the old cloth chesterfield with its dubious history, but in a welcoming leather sofa that looks stiff but is remarkably comfortable and forgiving. Oh, the look of delight on her face that all too brief instant before her scepticism took over, after which Willie had to convince her they were bought legitimately with his staff discount.

Beep-beep-beep-beep.

"What is that moron doing? Hasn't he driven a truck before?"

The plug finally cooperates and Willie slides the fridge clear and close to the hallway, careful to tuck away the cord and leave room to allow the old one back in. He'll never regret the deception, which he intends to maintain until they return. If they do.

Not that he'd blame Deborah if they don't. If anything, he'll blame himself for not stopping them. But he agreed with Fred this was an opportunity to work out his issues without scrutiny. With Deborah around, there would have been plenty of scrutiny. Though Fred never hinted as much, there may be a chance for Willie to benefit from Deborah reuniting with a family that is obviously wealthy. Wealthy, but not jerks. When Fred handed him cash to cover the next several months of rent and living expenses, he was respectful. He didn't come off looking down on Willie, and certainly not as if he was trying to cut Willie out of Deborah's life with a bribe. Fred wisely pointed out it would keep Deborah from inquiring too much if, when she calls from abroad, she senses he's in no difficulty.

Beep-beep-beep-clunk.

That's not a good sound. Willie looks outside. It's dark and takes a few seconds to spot Todd in his black pants and coat. Fortunately, the rest of the street is still quiet.

"What the hell are you doing with that truck?" Willie says.

"It's not yours, so don't worry about it."

"I want to make sure it'll drive off. Bad enough alerting the neighbours, most of whom are probably trying to sleep, because you can't back it up. Would have figured you'd know how to drive a truck?"

"I know how to drive a truck. Now let me inside so I can grab a beer."

Todd worms his way in, then scowls at the moved refrigerator.

"Why'd you unplug it already?"

"Relax, the beer's in the sink, with ice."

Todd helps himself. "At least you got my Coors Light."

He then looks around, impressed. He should be as the furniture and appliances are ready and staged to load. It took Willie a long time but the way Todd's gulping that beer you'd think he's done all the work. Todd finishes the can and motions Willie to follow.

Willie's hesitant to look inside the truck, but he has to. There they are, the ugly, old, barely reliable appliances and furniture that came with the house when they moved in. He'd have tossed them for junk except they belong to the landlord.

He and Todd work to get them inside and then load the truck with the good ones. They're working well together, as they once did, but never will again.

"You're sure no cops followed you?"

"Positive. I know what I'm doing."

"I followed you easy enough the other day."

Todd stops moving. "Listen, the Toronto police and the local police are too busy fighting over who's in charge of the investigation. Besides, neither has a clue about our enterprise. Not yet. I ought to know considering how much time I've spent with them."

His words contradict Willie's discussions with the police who seem quite cognizant of their scam. Willie decides to keep this to himself.

"They could be watching right now," Willie says.

"Right now, we're not doing anything illegal."

Todd's casualness grates on Willie. "That doesn't mean it won't lead to trouble."

"Listen, I'm doing you a favour. You've got no one to help you. So just shut up, get this done and if it turns out the spotlight were to shine on you, our old activities will no longer be evident."

"What's that supposed mean?"

"Nothing, nothing, just keep moving."

Willie wants to pursue it but the phone rings in the kitchen. He wends through the appliances and catches it on the fifth ring. It's Deborah.

He motions for Todd to keep quiet. Todd grabs another can, happy for a break, though he doesn't leave the room.

"Hey honey, where are you now?"

"Adelaide."

"Adelaide," Willie repeats, then glances at Todd who's not taking the hint. "So you got there safe."

"Everything okay?"

"You bet, just in the middle of . . . something."

To his relief, Deborah accepts this. If anything, she's the one who's troubled. She shares how she feels overwhelmed by all the changes since she left. How it's one thing to feel culture shock for a new country, another when it's one's native land. He's not sure what she's trying to say but it leads to her telling him an unplanned detour to Tasmania means the trip will take at least a week, maybe even a few weeks, longer. Willie's too distracted by Todd and what Todd might be thinking to catch it all until:

"I've half a mind to skip it and come home now."

"Oh."

A twitch from Todd indicates not only is he paying attention, he's also getting the gist.

"What do you think?"

"Of course, I miss you, would love to see you." He waves off Todd who's shaking his head. "What about Christopher? Does he feel the same?"

"Christopher's doing fine, actually. He's taking well to learning from Ruth."

Willie flinches, sensing what Deborah might: the fear this change in environment was all it took for her son, along with the corresponding fear his issues were their fault all along. It's tempting to persuade Deborah to come back immediately. One look at Todd, who appears ready to intervene and grab the phone, dissuades him.

"Probably best to let it play out and just keep an eye on Christopher. And yourself too. Maybe you need to get through some things."

More words along these lines fill the silences until Deborah relents. Willie hangs up, completely regretting everything he just said.

"She's not coming back yet, is she?"

"They're extending the trip to see her sick father. After that, who knows?"

"How will you explain this, if they come back?"

Willie has figured that out. He'll blame it on a claw back clause in his employee contract in case of employee termination. Todd tells him that's clever. A compliment on intelligence from Todd is about as valuable as a teetotal lesson from a barfly. Yet still comforting in its own way, and all he's got.

"Let's get back to work," Willie says.

"You miss them, don't you?"

"I don't want to talk about it."

"You want them back."

"Of course I do. But I'm glad they're not here to see this. Not even for an easy alibi."

"Easy alibi?"

"Christopher. I was with him the whole time after leaving the warehouse, except the ten minutes to get to his school, but that was hours before your father got killed. It's a relief to not have to put him through that."

They get back to work and now Todd's showing increased industry, though he drives off without offering to help Willie re-install the old appliances. Just as well, Willie thinks, as he opens a can of beer. It'll keep him occupied in this empty house, and keep him from worrying, for now.

# 18

Christopher helps himself to another potato and slice of beef and the last drops of the scrumptious gravy. They've been at Aunt Ruth and Uncle Fred's house a few days now and the only thing he misses about Canada is Willie. Before coming to Adelaide it was Willie and his cooking, as he quickly got tired of all the bought food while they were travelling. But in Aunt Ruth, Christopher has to admit he no longer misses Canadian food. Sorry, Willie. But he'll hold on to his wish of Willie joining them because it could only get better with three rather than two. Especially for his mom.

Everything was going great until they got to Adelaide and she started acting weird, her moods all over the place. Sometimes mad, sometimes sad. No, she was still all right when they got to Adelaide. It was that first day after they came back from the grocery store, which really wasn't all that interesting except you could buy wombat meat there and his discovery of Tim Tams. His mom seemed fine at first but slowly her mood darkened. Even now, after a few glasses of wine, which usually gets her chatty, she's keeping quiet. The tension at the table reminds him of that incident with those miners on the train. His aunt and uncle must sense it too because they're careful about what they say. They probably saw his mom like this when they were younger. Something's got to break. It didn't work last time she was upset but it's worth another shot.

"Mom, you never said if you've been to Uluru. Maybe we can go there while we're in Australia."

"I've been there." Her direct answer catches him off guard and he doesn't know what to say until she adds: "And we're not going."

"Why not?"

But his mom doesn't answer.

"It's very far, dear," Aunt Ruth says. "One has to plan for it long ahead. And it's most popular now, during the school holidays."

"Oh."

Christopher tries to sound disappointed but he doesn't really care about a lonely rock, just why that rock makes them all act strange. He's got to get Aunt Ruth to produce that picture. But how can he do that without giving himself away?

"Besides, we have other plans," Uncle Fred says.

"We're leaving here?" Christopher says.

"Wouldn't you like to see where I grew up?"

"Sure, Mom."

But Christopher doesn't mean it. Sure, he enjoys going to different places, seeing new things, but travelling will mean restaurant food again.

"Fred, Ruth, if it's okay with you, maybe we can go tomorrow?"

Aunt Ruth and Uncle Fred nod happily at his mom, as if they've been waiting some time for her to say this.

Early the next morning, just as daylight opens up the sky, they take their repacked bags down to the building's garage and put them in an old car that doesn't fit in among the other shinier and fancier vehicles. Like an overripe banana in a fresh bundle.

"You still drive this thing?" his mom says.

"We use a car rarely now, no need for a new one."

Makes sense to Christopher but his mom stares at it as if she doesn't believe them. Why would she care? It's still a nicer car than her Civic, which isn't much newer, and this one definitely looks more comfortable as it's bigger. He's pretty sure the air conditioning works too.

The streets are busy with traffic until they get to a highway that takes them into a stretch of farmland that's pretty but not nearly as interesting as the desert they crossed on the train. And the novelty of driving on the left side of the road doesn't last long. Uncle Fred's classical music station isn't horrible but, combined with the smoothness of the ride and the warm temperature, makes Christopher sleepy. He finds himself dozing off. Whenever he wakes, he tries to whip his eyes open, hoping to conjure up something new. There's rarely something new.

No one is talking either, except Uncle Fred who from time to time points out a "bucolic setting" or a "pastoral landscape" or a sign or building for which he describes some historical event, which they then talk about for no more than a minute, maybe two, and follow with a comment on the nice weather that ends the conversation and allows the dull music to take over again.

They stop for lunch and gas at a place called Mt. Gambier. The cheeseburger is okay but the fries are really good. Afterwards, it's much the same for another two hours until the water comes into view. Now this is spectacular.

"Is that the ocean?" Christopher says.

Uncle Fred shakes his head.

"No, That's the Great Australian Bight. Spelled B-I-G-H-T. Beyond it is the Southern Ocean and then Antarctica."

"Wait, there's no Southern Ocean. There's only," and Christopher counts them on his fingers, "Pacific, Atlantic, Arctic, Indian. That's it."

Uncle Fred explains this used to be part of the Indian Ocean but some organization decided to give it a different name. He doesn't give a good reason why that was important. There's not much more to say about it and the long drive continues with Christopher longing to be back on the train with Aunt Ruth teaching him things.

Another hour, maybe it's two depending how long he dozes, and they reach the Great Ocean Road, which excites Uncle Fred. Christopher wants to be excited too because it sounds neat, but he's so tired. The ocean's great whenever they get close enough to see the violent waves, but Christopher groans inside each time they get out to walk to another view over water. He stops counting at five.

Not even the Twelve Apostles can end the boredom Christopher feels and eventually he falls asleep for good, not waking until they stop at a motel in a place called Geelong. There they get two rooms beside each other. Uncle Fred goes out to get a pizza, which they eat in the Johnsons' room.

Christopher stays up long enough for a second slice before heading to bed via the connecting door. He gets into his pyjamas, lies down. His body's tired but his eyes seem to not want to stay shut. He comes back out.

"Where are we going tomorrow?"

"Tasmania," his mom says

Christopher knows this should mean something but his mind is too wound up to figure it out. Then Uncle Fred winks at him.

"But on the way, I'll have a surprise for you."

# 19

When working out the details of this odyssey, it seemed brilliant to Fred to visit the Melbourne Zoo as a way to fill the hours before boarding the ferry, which doesn't depart until dinner time. It's why he wanted to cover as much distance as possible the day before to allow more time at the zoo. He saw this detour as a way to bond with Christopher over their shared interest in animals, and one marsupial in particular. He doesn't feel so brilliant now, with everyone worn out from the overambitious drive. Fred grossly underestimated the time they needed to truly enjoy the Great Ocean Road.

A bigger mistake was in not fully grasping how much Christopher's underwhelming experience at the Toronto Zoo a few weeks back affected the boy. It's certainly contributed to making him despondent today. Not even the wonderful weather, ensuring an abundance of animals, is capable of invigorating his spirit. It's no surprise to Fred to find him with his mother and Ruth, the three of them yet again resting their legs at a bench.

It's nearing two o'clock and there's still one must see. Fred's passed up two sessions already, holding off until he sees some energy in the boy, but this is the last one for the day. With some encouragement from Ruth, who wants time alone with Deborah, Christopher agrees to follow Fred past the wombats to a pen where a Tasmanian devil is moving about.

"Well, there it is," Fred says.

Christopher gazes, unimpressed. "What is it?"

"A real Tasmanian devil."

"But he's so small. And not whirling. He's cute."

Christopher says it with disdain, which makes Fred laugh.

"He may look cute but he's a fierce creature all the same. Wait and see."

A dark-haired zookeeper in her early twenties, pretty in a tomboyish way, emerges from inside the pen. Despite her youth, she's mature and confident with an audience rapidly increasing in size. She introduces herself as Megan and the devil as Cyrus. She gives a brief talk about the creature's habits and history.

Christopher's transfixed.

Whether it's by the creature or a sudden infatuation with the young girl is hard to tell. Either way, Ruth would be ecstatic to have her nephew / student pay such rapt attention to her instruction. Fred makes a mental note for his wife to assemble a lesson about this. Maybe he'll do it himself.

The talk concludes with a discussion of Devil Facial Tumour Disease—DFTD—and its devastating impact on a large percentage of devils. Without a cure, devils will join a long list of extinct species of the island. Christopher's alertness intensifies at this; one can grasp the sadness of the animal's plight upon the boy's face. The crowd is sombre, politely so, but perks up when Megan attaches the carcass of a small animal to a long pole. The hungry devil—thankfully displaying no sign of DFTD—lets out a screech, opens its jaws, rips off a piece, and goes at it with ferocity.

"Wow," Christopher says. "That's some chewer."

The zookeeper smiles at Christopher.

"When he gets to the bone, if he's still hungry, he might eat that too."

"Uncle Fred, I want to see a real one."

"That is a real one."

"No, in Tasmania. A real one. Free. In the wild. You know. In the woods or wherever they live."

Christopher's more alert and responsive than he's been in a while, and Fred indulges in thinking himself brilliant again.

Ruth and Deborah approach and Christopher bolts to his mother to drag her to see the devil. By the time he gets her there, the zookeeper is gone and the crowd has dispersed. The devil, done his meal, has retired in a small den with only its snout visible.

It's a good time to leave the zoo and get to the ferry dock and check in early. Which is what's on the minds of Ruth and Deborah too.

They head to the exit but Christopher detours into the tent with the DFTD exhibit. They follow him in and find him checking out pictures of Tasmanian devils suffering the disease.

But then he becomes entranced by a poster of a creature that looks like a dog with stripes along its back. It's part of a smaller, linked display entitled, "Shared Fates?" A television screen shows a looping video Fred's often seen of the last Tasmanian tiger in captivity pacing impatiently in a cage.

"What's that?"

"That's a Tassie tiger, a Thylacine."

The voice behind them rhymes the last syllable with "sign", which is not the way Fred usually hears it pronounced.

"Tigers in Tasmania! Will we see any?"

"No, honey," Deborah says, "what they're saying here is, don't let devils go extinct like the tigers."

"Oh," Christopher says, his voice sad.

A cough from behind makes them turn around to see the man who just spoke shaking his head.

"Extinct? Don't be too sure. Maybe just hiding. People I know and trust say they've seen them."

The man's words indicate to Fred he's crazy, but his neat denim shirt bearing official looking badges indicates otherwise. Saying this to make the boy feel better is irresponsible, Fred thinks.

"Really, where?" Christopher says.

"People all over report sightings. Given the wildness of Tasmania, it's reasonable to think some are valid."

Fred wants to get the man to shut up yet not stifle Christopher's exuberance. It doesn't help that Ruth and Deborah appear interested too. The man leads Christopher to a map of Tasmania dotted with pins for reported sightings. He points to a spot just northeast of Launceston called Lilydale.

"Got a report of one around here the other day."

"Maybe I'll find one."

"Going to Tassie, are you? Good luck to you."

"Thanks, have you ever seen one?"

"No," the man says, then chuckles. "Not me. Not yet. Which is why I pronounce the last syllable to rhyme with fine. Get it?"

"Huh?"

Christopher looks at Fred who, though anxious to get clear of this fellow, can't resist a chuckle.

"I'll explain later, we have to get going."

Fred pulls Christopher away and the boy offers no resistance, intent on figuring out what it is his uncle will explain to him later. He alternates saying Thyla-seen and Thyla-sign over and over until he gets it, at which point he begins laughing. His mirth is contagious, bringing smiles to Ruth and Deborah as they chat away. What a relief to see everyone's spirit restored.

# 20

The unsmiling customs official hands the passport back to Willie.

"Enjoy your stay in England, Mr. Fitzmorris."

Willie takes his carry-on with all his remaining belongings through the baggage claim area. Another door, watched over by another customs officer, and he's made it.

A young mother and her son, who is maybe a year or two younger than Christopher, walk in front of Willie, slowly, holding hands. The boy is pulling a Looney Tunes backpack on wheels, a Maple Leaf sewn on its side. Willie unconsciously finds himself adapting to their pace.

"Where's Papa?" the boy says.

A man in his early thirties brushes past Willie to join the mother and son. The man grabs the boy who squeals with delight.

"Right here, son," the man says.

The father's sudden appearance disturbs Willie. He wants to get away from the young family yet can't take his attention off them. They pass through a sliding door and emerge into a concourse full of people waiting. No one is there to meet the young family, nor did they expect anyone, as they move off. Willie continues following them to a departures screen where the father stops to scan the lists. He taps the boy's shoulder and points up.

"That's our flight home," the father says. "It's on schedule."

"That's hours from now," the boy says.

"That's right," the father says, "enough time to catch the tube for a little sightseeing."

Now it's Willie's turn to read the board. Just below the Toronto flight the father pointed to is one to Sydney. Fascinating, the only two places on the list off limits to him, the only two places where he knows anyone, taking off minutes apart.

Going after them would undermine the freedom that cost him so much. Not just freedom from arrest but from having Deborah and her son experience firsthand the consequences of his actions. It's a big price he's paid to escape his unjust but inevitable fate in Ontario. Was it the right choice? Does it matter anymore?

By now the police will be all over the house, taking it apart and doing who knows what to not only his things, but also those of Deborah and Christopher. Their understanding is all he can wish for, based on the letter he sent along with some of their favourite items, including Deborah's special table, to the address in Adelaide. But it's doubtful he'll ever know what their reaction will be.

He inspects the fake passport, confirming again its expiration is in two weeks. He can still go where he wants for a limited time. If he were to take a risk, it'd have to be now. Only he's spent nearly all the cash he made selling the cars and what he got from Fred on that freedom. By the time he acquires more, legitimately, the passport will be useless.

Even if he could get the money, he couldn't go to Canada, or Australia, or anyplace anyone knows him as Willie Galloway. But at least he is free to make any other choice.

Willie strokes the beard he hasn't quite gotten used to but has to keep indefinitely, ready to face the fact Willie Galloway is no more as he goes forth in life as Patrick Fitzmorris.

# 21

The rising sun silhouettes the black mountains in a hauntingly beautiful and eerie pattern. She's never seen the island on which she was born and spent her childhood from this vantage.

The ominous dread the early convicts must have felt upon seeing a sight like this as their ships approached. Particularly those wronged by justice. The uncertainty of their future. Deborah can relate, in a way. Except her dread is of a different kind, tinged with paranoia instead of fear, informed by experience instead of reputation.

A more apt parallel is how her arrival and that of the convicts is in the hands of others. Of course, she has the option to free herself, though not without the guilt of disappointing the one she loves and cares for the most; that can be a stronger chain than any physical one.

It wasn't an easy decision to come here and it's likely more difficult decisions are to come. Fred and Ruth are holding back something. The article about the fire, the lease agreement, something's going on and she wants to figure it out on her own. Her mind since that discovery has been preoccupied in speculating about what lies ahead on this dark, mysterious island for her and Christopher.

More and more these thoughts lead to a possible outcome she would have thought unimaginable two or three weeks ago, let alone twelve years. But now, perhaps, those dozen years of separation have given her enough maturity to understand and utilize the power within her.

A large wave nearly knocks her off balance, but does knock out the seriousness of these thoughts, allows her to laugh away her mood and realize she's getting ahead of herself. No reason not to enter Tasmania as she entered Australia, as a tourist, and see what happens.

## 𝒦

Carla and Wilma look adorable in their hard hats, pink for Carla, of course, and deep blue for Wilma who would cringe if he called her adorable. Andy would have preferred both to wear the more visible bright yellow ones like his but he's learning to ease up about such things, adapting to rather than subduing Carla's girly nature and Wilma's intensity. Though now he wishes Wilma would have picked a brighter colour for aesthetic reasons. The shade of her hard hat combined with her dusky skin gives his niece a menacing countenance that undermines her affable disposition. For that matter, the pink one makes Carla paler than her mother ever was. They probably don't need them anyway; it is Sunday and the workers are gone for the weekend. Also, the chance of injury at this stage of construction is slim. But he'll err on the side of over-protectiveness as the girls are all he has left.

If not for the fire, all the work would have been done by now, but he is satisfied with the progress. The landscaping is nearly finished and all the steps and stairs are in place and stable. The rest is still on schedule to be ready by Christmas, though the guest cottage, only a foundation at the moment, will have to wait until after the school break. Any urgency for that project would be artificial; once it's done there won't be anyone to take advantage of it. The main house is sufficient now that the Kiltepper numbers are down to three. The practice of hosting business partners and clients at the estate has stopped and Andy has no intention of reinstating it, other than for special exceptions of a personal nature.

Indeed, if there's one positive outcome from the fire it's his resolve to work less and give more of his time and energy to the girls. A change no one, least of all him, could ever have imagined. Yet the loss of his family gave him no choice and once he accepted the need to sell off much of the Kiltepper empire, it opened up this opportunity to amend for the neglect he showed his family when prioritizing business, particularly in regards to Carla.

This refocus applies to himself as well and has allowed him to indulge in a deeply personal project: the Kiltepper museum. Planning, designing, and decorating an entire room dedicated to preserving family history has been therapeutic. As has digging up artefacts from the fire over many visits, which has aided his physical recovery. What a great idea of Crane's to fence off the site after the authorities cleared it as safe. Now each visit is optimistically archaeological rather than depressingly wallowing. Last week, he achieved the milestone of acquiring at least three showpiece items for each generation, all safely and securely stored in fireproof, waterproof containers awaiting the room's final touches for their unveiling to the world.

The journal of the first Andrew Kiltepper will be the centrepiece, along with other journals and maps, a few guns, an old side table his father made, a well preserved Tasmanian tiger fur, a helmet from each World War, a myriad of tools, toys, and a surprising amount of jewellery. Sadly, one piece continues to remain conspicuously absent. Andy still holds faint hope of finding the medallion.

Contrary to how some might view his museum venture, Andy sees it as beneficial, even essential, in achieving closure. By compartmentalizing the past, he can proceed with his other plans to pave the path for a new dynasty for his only blood relation, Carla, with the new estate as its grand symbol. The exterior is modelled after the original but with more resilient brick and siding instead of wood. The building will cover greater square footage due to larger rooms. The furnishings and interior elements will not be rustic and manly as before, but modern and inviting for women. Designed how Carla's mother, who for years harangued Andy to tear down the "old shack," might have designed it. It always infuriated Andy to hear that epithet, and Julia knew it, but at least she said it because she truly hated it, not as a foretelling of its destruction. There's no ghostly "I told you so" ringing in his ears. Though he will draw the line at installing a swimming pool; Carla can do that on her own when she's older.

Andy checks his watch and takes a seat on the front side of the veranda while the girls ascend the stairs to design their rooms for the umpteenth time, confident their father and uncle will fulfill whatever they come up with. It'll be worth it for the joy it gives them and the much needed calm these breaks give him in these moments. Lately, a rash of colds has been sapping his energy so the quiet before his guests arrive will serve him well.

A weathered white Holden Commodore rolls up the unpaved driveway, gingerly, as if the driver fears it will fall apart. He parks it aside Andy's SUV so that it's no longer visible, save for a line of white at the bottom. Good thing. The sedan is hideous and has got to be at least ten years old. Seeing it rankles Andy, an echo of an old wound. He has to be nice though. No doubt the long drive has worn them out and they're bound to be sensitive and seeing them sensitive will only compound his irritation at having to seek their help.

Fred Johnson emerges and waves tentatively, followed by his wife, Ruth, both smiling as if all is good and always has been good. Not quite, Andy thinks, but then chastises himself and takes a deep breath to try and cast off his displeasure at seeing this man's face again. He's never cared much for Fred, though he's not sure Fred is aware of that. Ruth, on the other hand, he's always admired. An angel whose pleasant demeanour made Fred's lesser traits tolerable at one time.

Until, of course, Ruth's father appointed Fred to succeed him nine years ago. Whether the grooming of his son-in-law was poorly handled or whether Fred was basically incompetent, it was a nepotistic failure. Any businessman worth one-tenth his salary would have known when he was in over his head. Johnson, though, partly because of the inexplicable regard both Walter and Andy's father held for him, was left to plod on, making mistake after mistake. Until Andy stepped in to compel his father to get Fred to accept a redundancy settlement, one far too generous in Andy's view, particularly regarding that condo in Adelaide, though not worth fighting his father over. And it did ensure Fred would be away from Tasmania.

The settlement would have helped assuage any guilt Andy might have felt for blackballing Fred among their Tasmanian business peers, if he had felt any. He never did because a recommendation from Andy could have tarnished the Kiltepper name. This justified what in reality was personally motivated. Only he doesn't have to admit it because he doubts Fred ever found out. Johnson had many options on the mainland—he was highly regarded by several suppliers and partners, several of which profited from his mistakes—so his decision to retire instead could not reflect on Andy.

Seeing the man now, feeling his own stomach knot up, it's evident the contempt won't go away. Knowing that, if not for Fred, Andy wouldn't be alive, only makes it worse. Andy rises to greet them but before he gets there, Carla and Wilma rush past him to hug Fred and Ruth.

"We haven't seen you for so long," Carla says.

"How are you girls?" Fred says.

"Fine," Wilma says. "Don't you love the new estate? Let me show you around—wait, do you have hard hats?"

Andy shakes Fred's hand and gives Ruth a hug. "Forget about the hard hats, it's safe inside."

"You can wear mine," Carla says.

Ruth tries it on, shakes her head. "Too small."

"Come on," Wilma says, "I'll take you for a tour."

Fred and Ruth follow the girls in while Andy brings up the rear. Only the walls are painted and the fireplace bricked and the lack of furniture makes the space look massive. The gourmet kitchen is fully operational, though, an exponential improvement on the simple but big wood stove that fed dozens at a time in the old estate. A massive window over a large double sink gives a picturesque vista of the rainforest beyond. Ruth lingers a bit too long for the girls who grab her to take her upstairs to see their rooms. Fred follows but Andy remains downstairs.

The way his girls are with Ruth and Fred reveals to Andy how alone he is in his contempt. Everyone likes Fred. His own father and grandfather thought the world of him for some reason. The girls adore him too. So why can't Andy let it go and join them?

Because they have never had to deal with Fred in business, have never seen firsthand what a fool he can be. A great organizer but no vision and an utter absence of the ruthless decisiveness the Kilteppers exercise as a matter of course. Andy can't count how many times he bailed out Fred on behalf of his misguided father who, rest his soul, should have been embarrassed for hiring him in the first place. At least he could have stopped inviting Fred to their gatherings at the estate.

But if Andy's father had done so, Andy might not be alive to indulge in this acrimony today. For Fred was a late show this time, arriving after the fire had done its worst. His quick action to get help is what saved Andy's and Walter's lives. The irony of this is almost as painful as the memory of the fire.

The visitors return without the girls. Andy leads them out the back where the lot really opens up. No sod has been installed yet but there is a massive patio off the living room already laid with stone. It has a magnificent barbie, fire pit, and patio set. Underneath the barbie is a fridge from which Andy grabs a couple of coldies of Little Creatures for the men and a Smirnoff Ice for Ruth. All three sit on the rattan sectional where it connects.

"Thanks for coming," Andy says, as he hands out the drinks. "Sorry Ruth, no clean glasses."

"I'm fine. This will be wonderful place when it's done. The girls love it. How are they coping?"

"They're coming around. Every day I'm thankful they had that school trip that week. Otherwise . . ."

Ruth nods and Andy finds himself at ease; it's always been effortless with her.

"And your father, how is he doing?"

Andy takes a swig of beer to cover the difficulty of asking. He still wonders, to the point of fixation at times, how an octogenarian could survive the fire, albeit in a coma, while all those in full health who could continue the Kiltepper line—two brothers and three nephews and, of course, Drew—had to perish. Not to mention his own father and the three wives.

"About the same," she says, "though I fear he may never speak again."

Andy takes another swig, this time to cover his dismay. One redeeming aspect of Walter's survival is that vague utterance. Andy's gone to the site of the fire numerous times, not only to search for items for his museum, but also in an effort to determine what Walter said. It was only about a week ago that he believes he figured it out.

"He will," Andy says, partly to convince himself, "because he spoke to me. During the rescue."

"Is that so?" Ruth says.

"I think it was about your sister."

"About Debs? I highly doubt that."

"He hasn't talked about her in years," Fred says. "At least not with us."

Their assured response annoys Andy in how easily it makes him doubt his recollection.

"He said your sister's—"

"Deborah's."

"Of course. He was in rough shape when he said Deborah's name. But he added, and it sounded lucid to me, 'Find them.'"

"Them?" Fred says.

In the silence that follows, the girls can be heard bounding about upstairs. Andy can see his guests' perplexity is genuine. He'd be able to tell with Ruth, a poor liar since they were kids.

A bang from the house is followed by a cry. Andy rushes inside to find Carla and Wilma playing cards on the floor of the empty dining room.

"Everything all right up here?"

"Yes," the girls say, in unison.

"What was that noise?"

They shrug, apparently having heard nothing. Andy goes upstairs. He unlocks the museum room, immediately blinded by the afternoon light shining through windows still to be tinted. The crates, which will remain locked until then, have accumulated a layer of dust. Beyond that, nothing seems amiss, the cause of the noise a mystery. Andy smiles: Spirits, all this will be for you too.

He returns to find Fred and Ruth in discussion. They don't notice him so he digs in for another two coldies, but puts one back upon seeing Fred has only half finished his.

"Sorry about that," he says, surprising them.

"Everything okay?" Ruth says.

"Yes, I think so. Now what do you think your father could have meant by 'them'?"

"Ruth and I were wondering too. Sure he wasn't talking about us?"

Andy drinks some beer to dilute his irritation.

"I'm sure he was together enough to know Ruth didn't need finding."

"What do you want us to tell you, Andy?" Ruth says. "No need to beat around the bush."

"All right, I'll tell you what I think. I think he was referring to Deborah and her child, the one she threatened to abort. It's possible she didn't follow through."

"This is why you wanted to see us?" Ruth says.

"Yes. I want you to tell me I'm right. I want you to say I have a son somewhere in the world."

As his plea comes out from his fire-weakened voice, Andy realizes how meek it makes him sound. How desperate. Any number of possibilities could explain Walter's words, including his not hearing them correctly. To their credit, the Johnsons aren't laughing or even showing a hint of condescension.

"You know something?" Andy says.

"No," Ruth says, "at least not anymore. I did for a while, until she left for Canada with someone. I haven't heard from her since."

"But did she have the abortion?"

"She told me she did."

"Do you have proof? Were you there?"

"Easy Andy. Deborah's leaving was convenient for you but it was awful for us. No point getting Ruth upset about something outside her control."

Andy sits back, drinks some more beer but it's not going down well. He feels another cold coming on.

"You're right. I'm sorry, Ruth, I didn't mean to push so hard."

Carla and Wilma come outside to join them and Andy could kiss them for their timing. The girls beckon Fred away to show him some animal tracks. He goes willingly. Ruth grabs Andy's hands and looks into his eyes.

"I think I understand what you're wishing for."

"I'd say it's rather obvious."

"I don't want to encourage something unlikely."

"But it is possible."

"I can't say it's impossible. I have no idea what she did nor where she is."

"Canada, you said."

"That was twelve years ago. Our mom was born there so Canada would be a logical destination. But knowing Debs, who we all know is never ruled by logic, she could be anywhere."

"I want you to find her. Start with Canada. I'll provide whatever's needed."

"And if we do find her?"

"Bring her back. Bring them back."

"I don't know if I'd be able to do that."

"Tell her your father asked to see her."

"That'd be a lie."

"Maybe not, maybe that was the gist of what he said. Listen, this could mean so much to me. It could mean so much to you, to Fred. I'm not just talking reunion. I'm talking fresh starts, you know?"

Ruth takes this in, keeping noncommittal, but Andy's confident he's getting through to her.

"You do know how bad Fred feels, still, about all that happened back then."

Andy pulls away his hands, sits back.

"These past months have been about learning to accept for me."

"Good."

"Then you'll go?"

"Of course. I can't tell you how often I've kicked myself for not doing so while we had the means."

"Wonderful. As I said, go in style, I'll cover it. If you succeed, I'll consider what happened with your husband water under the bridge."

Ruth's eyes turn cold. "Then we refuse."

"What?"

"This is not a junket, a bartering exercise."

"I didn't say it was."

"They're coming back."

Andy turns to see Fred and Wilma returning, but Carla isn't with them. He looks around, containing his panic, before realizing his daughter is sitting behind him, staring at him, and seems to have been there a while.

"Didn't want to go for a walk, honey?"

"Nah."

"Quite the outback guide," Fred says, bringing a proud smile to Wilma's face. "We spotted a wombat and an echidna."

"I just know where to look," Wilma says. "I can find them all."

"Even a Tassie tiger?" Fred says.

This draws a scowl from Wilma.

"You know they don't exist anymore. Tell him, Uncle Andy."

But Andy's watching Carla who's quiet, even for her, wondering what's on her mind. Then Ruth's hand comes into view to grab his daughter's hand.

"How about you girls show me where to wash up. It's warm out here."

Carla and Wilma each take a hand, pausing to check with Andy who realizes he'll be alone with Fred for the first time in years. If this is how it has to be then so be it, Andy thinks, suppressing his true feelings for a greater Kiltepper good.

"Yes, go, I need to talk to Fred about something."

"Oh?" Fred says. "What could that be?"

"A junket, I suppose you could say."

Andy sends a wink Ruth's way, and she sends one back.

"I don't understand," Fred says.

Andy gets two fresh bottles of beer, takes a breath, motions for Fred to sit down. An hour later, plus ten minutes to scramble to get school portraits of the girls, and another ten for goodbyes, and finally the Johnsons leave.

Alone again, he recalls the time Ruth introduced her new boyfriend. It was Christmas Eve and Fred Johnson made a good first impression that, sadly, didn't last. The idea of relying on Fred Johnson now for such an important endeavour is difficult, but he has little choice. Now he has to wait, to be patient, to be hopeful.

As hopeful as a young Deborah Pollard might have been in 1995. Andy was thirty-seven then, married to a childless Julia, and his sister-in-law had just given birth to Andy's nephew. There was a great celebration for the newest heir to which the Pollards were invited. The Kiltepper aversion to Hobart was as much a social prejudice as a business one so the two families only mixed occasionally. Andy hadn't seen Deborah since her mother's funeral when she was barely a teen. Now she was almost nineteen and stunning. Andy and Deborah danced frequently that night and he sensed her forming a crush he found charming, innocent, inconsequential.

Three years later, Deborah graduated university and began working in Launceston at Andy's office. His marriage to Julia had become strained, largely due to their lack of success in conceiving. He and Deborah began an affair only Fred and Ruth found out about when the four took a trip to Uluru, a place he always wanted to experience but one for which Julia had no interest.

Much as he cared about Deborah, maybe even loved her, divorce was out of the question. That was not tolerated within the family, one of many moral holdovers from the original Andrew Kiltepper. Unfortunately, the young girl had blinders on and his efforts to end it proved weak and ineffectual. When Julia got pregnant and an ultrasound showed a healthy boy, Andy had to terminate the affair once and for all. Deborah, who never took his devotion to his family line seriously, called his lineage reasoning a copout. She defiantly held on to the hope of a future between them, despite knowing he could never divorce Julia while she had the power to take his heir away.

Then Deborah became pregnant. She gave Andy an ultimatum and was so hysterical about it, he openly doubted her claim she was bearing his child. Oh that was an ugly period, only made worse when her father took the Kiltepper side. She cursed Andy, cursed her father, declared she would run off to have an abortion. Not even Ruth at her soothing best could have calmed her.

Andy couldn't hold himself back either—he's ashamed of how he acted now—and told her he wasn't interested in a little bastard. He gave her $25,000 to take care of the situation and do as she pleased. Go to Canada, he said, as she'd always talked about seeing where her mother came from. Travel the world. Just rid yourself of the idea of becoming a Kiltepper. These were the kinds of things his desperation to avoid Julia finding out made him say. The poor girl, devastated naturally, took the money and went who knows where.

Julia did find out about the affair years later while pregnant with Carla. It hurt his wife more because she had been fond of Deborah. She stayed with Andy after he caved in to her demands, which he did more to keep control of and access to his son and heir than out of love. It pains him now to look back at his behaviour, the steps he took to keep Drew, only for his son's life to end so tragically.

He never heard nor asked about Deborah after she left, or what she did with her pregnancy. Maybe she didn't go through with it, maybe she has a son. But if that's true, he also knows it will be a delicate matter confirming it, let alone harnessing such a revelation.

# 22

Not another long drive is Christopher's first thought after Uncle Fred directs his car through the streets of the ferry town into wide open countryside. Just like before he points at things, uses words like bucolic and pastoral. But, Christopher has to admit, this all looks and feels and even sounds different. Maybe his mom said something because Uncle Fred's put on a popular music station and the songs, most of which he likes though he's never heard them before, add a fun weirdness. So if it is to be a long drive, it could be an enjoyable one. And the longer they're out here where there are few people, the greater the chance to spot a Tasmanian tiger.

A real tiger too. Not those silly stuffed ones in the ferry gift shop. Or that cartoony one painted on the bus parked outside the terminal. It's funny there's so much about Tasmanian tigers here. Why would there be if there weren't real ones around? There wasn't a ton of panda stuff at the Toronto Zoo gift shop before the real ones came.

The pouch bulging out the back of the driver's seat reminds him of a marsupial. He slowly reaches in, imagining his fingers about to touch some gooey material, and feels about, keeping his eyes on the window. But his hands remain dry as he pulls out a map of Tasmania. Cool.

"Want me to show you where we're going?"

How did his mom notice? Ever since the ferry, she's been chattering with Aunt Ruth about things they did as kids, pointing out places they saw with the grandfather he's going to meet soon, and the grandmother who's no longer alive. Nothing is anything Christopher's ever heard about, all of it stuff that happened before he was born. You'd think not having seen each other for so many years they would talk about new stuff. Uncle Fred is mostly keeping quiet so he can concentrate on driving, except when he corrects a date or place or some detail. And of course his comments about the scenery. Christopher should have asked to sit up front.

"It's okay, Mom, I'll figure it out on my own."

She gives him a smile before resuming digging into her and Aunt Ruth's memories again, this time about some high school teacher they both had.

Christopher unfolds the map and the first thing he notices is the shape of Tasmania is like a chicken nugget. The second thing he notices is he has the darn thing upside down. He checks to make sure no one's looking before flipping the map right side up.

He knows they came in at the top . . . there it is, Devonport. But he can't remember if they went left or right. He looks out the window just in time to spot a sign for Launceston, which he locates in just a couple of seconds as there aren't many main roads. Cool. But wait! Just beyond Launceston is Lilydale. Isn't that the town the zoo guy mentioned, where people see Tasmanian tigers?

"Uncle Fred, are we going towards Launceston?"

"Hardly," his mom says, her voice cracking a bit.

"What's that, Deborah?" Uncle Fred says.

Christopher politely waits for his mom to respond to his uncle. When she doesn't, he leans into the front seat and repeats the question, which makes Uncle Fred and Aunt Ruth fidgety. What did he say?

"Why do you ask?" Uncle Fred says.

"Launceston is not far from Lilydale. The man at the zoo said there would be Tasmanian tigers there."

"That's not quite what he said," Uncle Fred says.

"Yes he did."

"No. He said people claim to have seen them."

"People don't claim to have seen them?"

"I'm sure the claims are real and even that the people who make them think they've seen one. But they're mistaken. There are no Thylacines anymore. Notice how I rhymed it with sign?"

"Yeah."

Christopher slumps back, not amused. This is the first time Uncle Fred's said anything to spoil his fun. Maybe it has something to do with his mom's odd reaction to his mentioning Launceston, maybe Uncle Fred's just saying that to make her feel better and not worry her son's going off chasing tigers.

"Besides, honey, we're heading the other way, to Hobart."

Just as Aunt Ruth says that, a sign appears with arrows pointing left for Launceston and right for Hobart. They go right, extinguishing Christopher's hope of finding tigers. For now.

They drive along flat farmland that continues into the far off hills. A few cars and trucks pass them and Uncle Fred gets by an occasional truck himself. No way a tiger's going close to a highway like this. What a drag. Now the drive is starting to be like the one to the Great Ocean Road the other day. Like then, Christopher's eyes start flickering.

"He's dozing."

"No wonder," Aunt Ruth says, "Getting up so early, I'm sure he's exhausted.

"We're all exhausted," Uncle Fred says. "At least we're on the last leg."

Christopher feels his mom tug the map away, which makes him try to resist and wake up, but his body doesn't obey. It wants to turn to his side and he can't stop it. Uncle Fred changes stations, turns the volume down, and he can't stop that either. Soon all he hears is the rumble of the car engine and the occasional voices of the adults.

How long he sleeps for he doesn't know, just that upon waking he finds the towns getting bigger and closer together. They reach a huge river, which they are about to cross, first over a strip of land called a causeway, according to Uncle Fred, and then a long bridge. On their left, the houses built into curvy hillsides make for a pleasant picture. Definitely not tiger territory but more interesting than what they were driving through before. He opens the map, figures this is Bridgewater, meaning they're getting closer to Hobart. He can't wait for the drive to end. It's almost lunchtime and he's getting hungry.

Unfortunately, the bridge is a lift bridge and it's rising in the air for a couple of barges to pass. Uncle Fred is frustrated and, for the first time Christopher thinks, curses. Finally, they cross and drive along the river into downtown Hobart. Uncle Fred slows down at a building where he pulls the car up a semi-circle driveway and stops. Could this be where his grandfather is? It doesn't look like a hospital. Too modern and no ambulances around.

When his mom told him her father was alive and living here and that they were going to make a visit, Christopher wasn't sure what that meant for him. He's had time to think about it and supposes it's kind of cool. Those kids bragging about all their Christmas presents usually get nice stuff from grandparents. Toys and things don't mean a whole lot to Christopher but the idea of getting gifts does sound neat. And according to Aunt Ruth, Grandpa Walter is nice. However, his mom seems nervous about seeing him again. It sounds like they had a big argument before Christopher was born. It must have been a big argument because she and Willie argue once in a while but she would never leave Willie for that long. Ah, she's missing Willie. That's probably why she's been acting strange.

Uncle Fred gets out of the car and looks back at them. "I'll check us in, you can wait here."

"You'll love this place, Debs," Aunt Ruth says, once Uncle Fred goes. "You too, Christopher."

It's a hotel, not a hospital, of course, and a fancy one. Christopher rolls down his window, leans back so he can look up at the vertical rows of glass. He spots a giant letter "K" in a soft neon green above the top floor. The same logo that was on the places they stayed in London, Dubai, Perth, but not Geelong.

"Aunt Ruth?"

"Yes, dear."

"When's our next class?"

She smiles at him then points at several children coming out of the hotel lobby in shorts and t-shirts. She explains the kids are on school holidays for a couple more weeks. Lots of time to find some tigers, Christopher thinks, though this time he keeps the thought to himself.

# 23

The tourist approach is working. Deborah can't recall the last time she was so pampered. It would have been in her youth when she was too restless or entitled. Now she's mature enough to appreciate such a fabulous hotel and its indoor swimming pool looking out over the busy harbour, with grand, dark, mysterious Mt. Wellington in the distance. Easily the best part. Although her belly, still sated by a superb lobster salad she had at lunch, makes a good case for the restaurant. Fred and Ruth are pulling out all the stops.

As clouds start to disrupt her view of Mt. Wellington, Deborah turns onto her stomach in the lounge chair. The lifeguard appears competent so Christopher, paddling and splashing contentedly on his own, ought to be fine. All she's missing is the feeling of the sun on her back. If they were at a beach, she could try to regain the tan of her youth.

However, a heat wave makes staying indoors wise. Perhaps it's just as well, as her skin might struggle to reacquaint itself with the sun down here.

Yesterday's journey, after a generally smooth but occasionally rough ferry crossing, and the long drive the previous day, took a lot out of all of them. She's glad Ruth agreed to put off seeing her father a couple of days. Turns out he has to undergo tests today anyway. Coincidence? White lie?

Regardless, it was the best decision. For now, relaxed like this, she's even looking forward to the visit, curious beyond words how her son will react to his grandfather. And vice versa.

So it would seem all her worldly stresses have been addressed. Except one: her inability to reach Willie. She's tried at least a dozen times at home, not just the landline but his cell phone, as well as hers, which she left behind. No word so far. She really has no one else to call to check in at the house. At least Christopher's been too busy to notice but he'll ask about Willie soon. It's worrying enough to make Deborah contemplate ways to get back to Canada on short notice, just in case.

The pool soon erupts in splashes and greetings as guests, choosing manmade comfort over natural heat as Deborah did, arrive. One of the newcomers takes a spot next to Deborah. It's Ruth, who's by herself. Deborah turns over.

"Where's Fred?"

"He's got business to take care of."

"What kind of retirement is that?"

For some reason, her joke strikes a wrong chord with Ruth. Maybe they had an argument. Deborah scans the pool. It's crowded now and it takes longer to spot the boy with dark skin wearing a black swimsuit with horizontal stripes. There he is. But that can't be him, can it? She looks closer. Sure enough, that's her son, talking to a couple of young girls as if they've known each other some time.

The larger of the two girls is dark, Aboriginal, and quite radiant with her wet black hair. She looks a bit older than Christopher. An excellent swimmer too, now racing to the other end of the pool, her yellow bikini moving like an eel. And here comes Christopher, not only chasing her but also keeping pace, almost matching the quality of the girl's strokes. Deborah knows her son is comfortable in water but she's never taken him for swimming lessons. Looks like he's a natural.

The other girl is at least a year younger than her son, maybe two. Her fair skin looks alabaster compared to Christopher's and almost albino next to that of the other girl. But she's a real beauty in a classic, wholesome Australian way, with a narrow face and lush blonde hair she hasn't gotten fully wet yet and probably won't. Kind of how Deborah remembers herself at that age. The girl's acting bored, as if she's above racing in a pool, but possibly masking her unhappiness at not being the centre of attention. Deborah can't help a smile, recalling her own princess phase that lasted longer than she'll ever admit.

"You're in a good mood," Ruth says.

Deborah points to the younger girl.

"Just look at that one, she reminds me of me."

"She does, doesn't she?" Ruth says, with a wry smile.

"I didn't mean to sound conceited."

Ruth laughs. "Didn't take it that way at all. You were a looker, still are. I used to be envious. Okay, I'm still envious, but too old to let it bother me."

"You still look terrific. But look at Christopher."

"Quite a swimmer, isn't he?"

"Yes, but that's not what I mean. He's actually playing with kids his own age. I can't recall him ever talking to kids he doesn't know. Not this quickly."

"No doubt he recognized them," says Ruth who then waves at the girls who wave back.

"From where?"

"You don't recognize them? You're usually so observant, Debs."

Deborah's suddenly hot inside. She has to take a deep breath before looking at her sister. Ruth, joking only moments ago, now looks solemn, her blue eyes betraying guilt and fear. Not unlike her expression when she announced to their father her intention to move out and live with Fred.

"What's going on, Ruthie?"

For an answer, her sister pulls out a pair of wallet-size photographs, duplicates of those on the table at their Adelaide condo. Carla and Wilma. Family friends. The familiarity she saw in Carla is more evident now, in fact impossible to miss. This can't be happening. They can't be doing this to me, not this way.

Deborah turns away from her sister only to see Fred, in business casual clothes, at the far end of the pool, talking to a burly but fit man in a patterned short-sleeved shirt and tie. A man with burn marks on his face and bare arms. Yet still handsome. The man is watching the kids, particularly Carla whose face, even with its dour expression, is blessed with a captivating blend of her attractive parents.

Coming here to Tasmania the possibility of such an encounter was always in Deborah's mind, a possibility she felt she was prepared for. Apparently not. Around Launceston, maybe, and only then if she couldn't avoid that place. But not Hobart. She can't stop staring at him, until his head turns in her direction, at which point she stands up, collects her towel.

"I refuse to be ambushed," Deborah says, and rushes off.

# 24

Christopher's flipping like a dolphin now. Carla is laughing and he knows she's laughing at him. He can put up with the bratty one who's as unimportant as all the school kids he's known because Wilma, the nice one, appreciates what he's doing. Maybe Carla's still upset at being surprised because, oh boy, did she ever jump when he walked up to them and said their names. Both jumped, actually. Wilma was ready to attack him to protect Carla and eyed him suspiciously until he could explain he recognized them from the photos in Adelaide. Even then, she was hesitant until he mentioned Aunt Ruth, which brought smiles to the girls. But when Wilma became nice to him, that didn't please Carla.

He takes another dive but, tired, comes up quicker, in time to see Carla whispering to Wilma and giggling. It pleases Christopher when Wilma shoves her cousin and tells her to stop acting like a baby. Carla only laughs.

"What other animals can you do?" Carla says, to Christopher, trying to mask her giggling and sound sincere, but clearly mocking.

Wilma tries to give Carla another shove but this time the smaller girl manages to duck away. It's sweet of Wilma to defend him but she's wrong if she thinks Carla's teasing embarrasses him. If anything, it's the opposite. Christopher climbs out of the pool and then gets down on all fours and struts around like a tiger. Carla's giggles turn to laughter, drawing plenty of attention.

"Can you do a roo?" Carla says.

Wilma shakes her head at Christopher but that only encourages Carla to stand and pump her arms up and down.

"Doaroo, doaroo, doaroo."

He begins hopping and Wilma looks away. Then he slips on the wet floor and falls into the pool. He's down there a few seconds before he leaps out, spouting water from his mouth.

"Gross, mate. Now do a Tassie devil."

Christopher climbs out again, smiling, happy, even though people are looking at him. He glances over and sees Aunt Ruth next to an empty lounge chair. Where did his mom go?

"Carla, that's enough."

The male voice is low yet has a command to it and, though directed at Carla, alarms Christopher. He turns to see a large man standing over them.

"But Daddy, he's funny. A funny bogan."

"Carla, go to your room and stay there the rest of the afternoon."

Christopher feels sorry for her as she sulks off, but not once she's gone, since that leaves him alone with Wilma. Well, not quite alone.

"Sorry about that, son. My daughter can be insensitive at times."

The man sounds nice but the way he talks bugs Christopher for some reason. Maybe it's because it's like how Carla talks, as if he's better than everyone. He's relieved to see Uncle Fred with Carla's father, though his uncle looks small next to him.

"Christopher, this is Mr. Kiltepper. He owns the hotel here."

So Carla wasn't lying after all, just bragging. The man puts out his hand. Christopher hesitates before shaking it.

"You can call me Andy."

"Sorry about splashing around so much."

"No worries, young man, just be careful, okay?"

Christopher nods, hoping they'll leave so he can continue swimming with Wilma who's quiet; maybe she wants that too.

Thankfully, the two men go around to the other side to join Aunt Ruth. Except Mr. Kiltepper, Andy, is only there a moment before he exits the pool area. Christopher's uncertain feeling about the man stays, which makes it awkward now with Wilma.

"So your dad really owns this place like Carla said."

"He's not my dad."

"He's not?" Christopher says, feeling guilty that this information pleases him.

Because now Wilma's sad. She wipes a tear and tells Christopher her father died in a really bad fire that killed a lot of people in her family, including Carla's mom. The word fire nags at him but he can't figure out why because now his guilt doubles for thinking what he was thinking of Carla.

"Uncle Andy is my father's brother, sort of."

"What do you mean, sort of."

"I was adopted."

"I don't like him," Christopher says, before he can stop himself, but this seems to stop her sadness.

"You will. Uncle Andy can be gruff but he's like the nicest, most generous man. The best man I've ever known, besides my own dad."

Christopher wants to believe it and for Wilma he'll try. Then, as if rewarding him, she flashes a big smile and swats his knee with the back of her hand.

"Hey, the three of us are going on a bushwalk in a couple of days. You and your mom should come along. You'll find out how cool he is then."

"Will we see animals?"

"Heaps. Nah, maybe a few."

"Wild animals?"

"We're not going to a zoo."

"Tasmanian tigers?"

Wilma laughs.

"We're not travelling back in time."

"Huh?"

"They're extinct."

"No, I don't believe that."

"Yes they are. The last one died at a zoo here in Hobart long ago. Ask your grandfather."

"You know my grandfather?"

"Gramps Pollard, you bet. We love him."

Apparently, Wilma's family and his mom's and Aunt Ruth's family have been close for a long time. So why has his mom never said a word about them?

Aunt Ruth comes by and, after getting wet from hugging Wilma, asks him to get ready as they're going out to eat. Sadly, when he asks Aunt Ruth if it's okay, Wilma says she can't join them.

"When we visit my grandfather at the hospital tomorrow, you can come, if you want."

"Maybe," Wilma says, and her sadness returns.

As he follows Aunt Ruth away, he figures out what he couldn't before, that Wilma's fire has to be the same one in the article in Aunt Ruth's purse.

# 25

Fred stands outside Deborah's suite, about to knock, when he hears his sister-in-law's voice. She sounds frantic but he can't make out what she's saying. He waits for several seconds of silence before knocking.

"Not interrupting anything, I hope," Fred says, as she opens the door and lets him in to a large suite with a view of Mt. Wellington that's impressive, even at this angle, and despite being obscured by a band of clouds unleashing dark showers on its peak. That gloom seems to seep into the suite, despite the rampant sunshine in the foreground.

"No."

"Just here to remind you of our reservation in twenty minutes."

"Right."

"Ruth's getting Christopher."

"Okay, good, I need to do a couple of things."

She goes to the bathroom and Fred walks around the suite. It's fancier than the basic room he and Ruth share, just as intended. A nice abstract of Russell Falls on the wall above the sofa dominates the room. Evidently Deborah sleeps here, given her suitcase is on it, open and half-filled. Several smaller scale impressionist renderings of various rainforests complement the larger picture while also sublimely matching the soft blue walls. And the suite even has a kitchenette.

Deborah appears again, wearing a half-hearted smile. Fred remains quiet. If he knows one thing about his sister-in-law it's that, whenever upset, she either can't hold back what's on her mind or can hold on forever. Pressing always ensures the latter, a shutdown. A full minute passes and, sure enough, she lets out a sigh and points to the phone.

"Just trying to get hold of Willie."

"Still no success?"

"I've left messages. Nothing. So unlike him. I'm afraid he's in trouble."

"With the police?"

"I'm sure he would have contacted me in some way if that was the case."

Fred, though sympathetic to her situation, can't help feeling frustrated at how Willie continues to be a complication. It's impossible to tell whether the man's unavailability will make things easier or more difficult for he and Ruth. Fred sits down next to the half-packed suitcase.

"You're not thinking of going back, are you?"

"Why shouldn't I, after the stunt you and my sister pulled?"

"You mean Andy?"

"Of course."

"I'm sorry about that. There is an explanation."

"Yeah, well, I'm not sure I'm up to hearing one."

"I understand."

The door opens and Christopher, with his wet trunks, rushes in, with Ruth behind him. The boy is on his way to the bedroom but stops suddenly.

"Mom, why's your suitcase out? We're not going anywhere, are we?"

Deborah ushers her son into the bedroom, closes the door.

"She's mad about Andy, isn't she?" Ruth says.

"Yes, but her main concern is Willie. Seems she can't reach him. She's contemplating going home."

"Fred, maybe we've taken this far enough. If she wants to do that, I'll support her."

"Honey," Fred says, grabbing his wife's hands, lowering his voice, "let's keep reminding ourselves, as we've done ever since accepting Andy's proposal, that what we're doing is best for everyone. We still believe that, right?"

The bedroom door opens and Fred detaches from Ruth's hands. Deborah emerges alone and tells them Christopher is changing for dinner. Ruth is about to say something but Fred gestures her to keep it to herself.

"You guys aren't off the hook. I'm not sure what I want to do. Maybe I'll know after I see Daddy."

Christopher comes out, dressed sharply in a blue button-down shirt and clean shorts. Fred can't guess what could have transpired in that talk, let alone what was decided, if anything. Neither seems upset, a good sign. Still, a trust has been broken—actually he and Ruth broke it months before and it was only discovered today by Deborah—and it may be irreparable.

The restaurant is only a few blocks away but the sun's rays—enhanced by humidity and unimpeded by the clouds that seem to be waging all out war on Mt. Wellington—demand an indolent pace along the waterfront. Colourful sailboats bob slightly in the gentle breeze, their masts chiming away as the wake of an earlier vessel laps against the docks. The easy stroll seems to act as an effective tension soother.

"Uncle Fred, is there a zoo here in Hobart?"

"There used to be."

"Did it have a Tasmanian tiger?"

Oh dear, more of this, Fred thinks, but manages a smile.

"Yes. In fact, it was the last zoo to have one, and it closed about a year after the poor creature died."

"Benjamin," Deborah says. "The tiger's name was Benjamin."

"No, I'm pretty sure the last one was a female."

"So now they're only in the wild?"

Fred shakes his head and shrugs, as if he has no answer, hoping to drop the matter. Fortunately, Ruth and Deborah oblige by looking away, leaving Christopher frustrated.

This passes by the time they get to the seafood restaurant. Housed in a restored heritage building, it's Fred's favourite in Tasmania, possibly Australia. Not only for its cuisine but also its ambience, which is haughty to some but just right for him. The string music, melancholic but lively, complements the city sounds perfectly as the final hours of the working day wind down. To take a boy like this to such a place, to observe his fine manners and admire his courage to try new dishes at the recommendations of adults, is a joy he never imagined upon meeting this nephew who is a unique blend of rawness and civility. Much as he adores Carla and Wilma, he'd never take them to such a place.

That said, Fred is perhaps more impressed with his sister-in-law, particularly at how, since coming to Australia, she's overcome or at least tolerated situations that previously would leave her in a sour mood for hours, if not days. He doesn't want to jinx it but Fred is getting a sense she's not too displeased at encountering Andy. And then, as if to confirm this, Deborah asks Christopher about his swim with the girls.

"I like Wilma."

"What about Carla?"

"She's okay, I guess, but she's grumpy."

"Well, she's sad."

"But Wilma lost both her mom and her dad, and she's fun. At least Carla still has a dad."

Deborah nods. "What did you think of him?"

"He's okay."

"Okay?"

"Actually, I don't like him. Wilma says he's nice and—oh, she's invited us on a hike on Wednesday. I'd like to go. Can we go?"

"You know," Deborah says, pausing to butter and swallow a piece of lobster, "that might be fun."

The surprise Fred feels at his sister-in-law's easy compliance is shared by a speechless and overjoyed Christopher. Deborah goes one further and suggests they skip dessert and shop for hiking boots while the stores are still open. For such a reversal, Fred has no problem foregoing his strawberry mousse.

The shopping goes quickly, as Deborah knows what she wants. On the walk back to the hotel, after a negotiation in which Christopher trades staying up late to take an evening swim for an ice cream, Fred is anxious to take Ruth aside. He offers to hold the shopping bags and signals Ruth to join him.

"What do you think, honey?" Fred says. "Think she'll stay?"

"Oh Fred, I think it's more than that."

"More. How so?"

"The way she was talking about Andy when you were helping Christopher try on his hiking shoes. I don't know that she ever got over him. It sounds crazy, after all that's happened, but Fred, how things are now after the fire has affected her in a way I can't describe."

"Try. I'm meeting Andy in a couple of hours. He'll want to know."

"Yes, of course, a status report."

"Now Ruth."

"Fine. I don't think she's angry with us. I think she suspects we're hoping to reignite what she and Andy had before."

"Matchmaking? Deborah? How on earth would that not make her angry?"

"I know, but considering her troubles with Willie . . ."

"Are you saying she'd entertain such a notion?"

"I am."

"Oh boy," Fred says, "I hadn't foreseen that."

"Unless that's what she wants us to think."

Fred nods. Two things would trigger a perverse mean streak within his sister-in-law: manipulation and betrayal, both of which he and his wife are guilty. It wouldn't take much to mask her anger until her vindication unleashed in an unpredictably but uniquely Deborah fashion. Which would be a shame considering how open and trusting of them she's been since coming to Australia. What they are doing is dangerous as it could turn a temporary rift into a permanent one. Then all their energy would only result in compounding Ruth's misery over the past twelve years. He must keep strong for both of them. It'll be hard as he's no longer as confident as he was when they were in Canada. The stakes are increasing for him too. Each day he spends with his nephew, he feels his attachment to the boy growing.

These troubling thoughts stay with Fred until he meets Andy at the hotel bar later, uncertain what to report. As it turns out, Andy is preoccupied with his own struggles with Carla who hasn't taken the arrival of the Canadians well. It's a fragile situation between father and daughter, always has been.

It was no secret that Andy doted on his son at the expense of his daughter. A natural, instinctual gravitation to the male side was aggravated by the caustic relationship with Carla's mother, Julia, not to mention the affair with Deborah. Of course, Carla's unaware of the history but it's likely she inherited the intuition her mother used to ferret out the affair and, from that intuition, senses a threat in the newcomers. It will be difficult for Andy to repair his relationship with his daughter. She's so unlike him, dainty like her mother, not tough like a Kiltepper, or even an adopted Kiltepper like Wilma.

Their meeting is brief, giving Fred a reprieve of sorts. When he gets back to the room, Ruth is still up, waiting to tell him Deborah insisted on going to see her father tomorrow without them. Fred shrugs at that, happy to get some free time.

"Not like anyone can control what Walter says anyway," Fred says.

"Funny thing is, Christopher is inviting Wilma."

"What's wrong with that?"

"Nothing. I'm telling you because I see this as an opening for us to let things develop on their own."

"Good point. Though I doubt that'll be easy."

"I know. There's something else. Our concierge sent an email. We received a package from Canada."

# 26

Deborah's concern about Willie, her anxiousness for any word from him, has made her as pathetic as a teenager, rendered her almost agoraphobic. Even straying walking distance from her hotel room is unsettling. At least the humidity has subsided, making for a pleasant stroll to the hospital. Even better, she's glad she's doing this; it no longer feels like an obligation.

It doesn't hurt being accompanied by three kids who seem happy to be with her. Bless her sister but it would have been oppressive with Ruth around. It was always Deborah's intention to see her father with just her son since they left Canada. But when Christopher asked to invite Wilma, Deborah was happy to say yes, as long as he did the inviting. She stayed in the lobby while her son took the elevator to the penthouse. A few minutes later he came out with Wilma. Then, to Deborah's delight, but perhaps Christopher's chagrin, Carla appeared in a delightful yellow polka-dot summer dress that complements the mauve one Deborah's wearing, and announced she was coming too.

Much has changed in the CBD since Deborah lived in Hobart; for one, the hospital appears less imposing. Seeing the police cars in front of the old police office makes Deborah think of Willie, and she has to suppress an urge to rush back to check for messages. Of course she can't abandon the kids and their presence provides some insurance against such impulses. Deborah drops a hand to straighten a pleat but Carla thinks it's for her, grabs it, and holds on all the way to the hospital.

They enter, get directions to her father's room, take an elevator, and stop at a waiting area. Deborah asks the kids to stay there while she goes in. If Ruth knew this was the plan, she would have insisted on coming along to babysit; what her sister doesn't know won't hurt her.

"You kids will be okay on your own?"

"Oh yes. Uncle Andy leaves us alone here all the time when we visit Gramps Pollard."

As if to support Wilma's claim, an orderly walks by, waves to the girls who wave back.

Comforting, Deborah thinks, but unsettling too. She feels envy, sadness, guilt because these children probably know her father better now than Deborah does. Or they adore him because they know him much less.

Stop, she tells herself. You've done a fine job keeping the negativity at bay, just another hour.

Deborah pushes open the door and her steps slow as she enters and sees him, older, weaker, but the same man nonetheless. He's partially bandaged with an IV attached, his head propped up on a soft pillow. He looks small in that mint green hospital gown, an indication of how well his tailored suits made up for his lack of stature. Her father, though not virile like Andy, carried a presence: intimidating to foes, comforting to friends. Ruth rarely saw the former but Deborah experienced both frequently. Which version would she see now?

"Ruthie?"

Deborah spots a pair of glasses on the table, hands them to her father.

"No, Dad, it's me."

He puts on the glasses. He doesn't smile yet his eyes show he's happy to see who it is.

"I don't believe it."

"Yep, it's me."

"You've come home."

Come home? What does that mean? Her father's vocabulary is compact but he's particular about the words he chooses and how he phrases them. She wishes she'd asked Ruth how he might view her return so she could interpret his meaning accurately. His smile seems a grin now, as if he's won the latest battle between them.

To this point, Deborah's resisted recalling their last exchange, tried to take a future look. But now it comes back, the day she came home and admitted to her affair with Andy, which he suspected. It was the pregnancy that shocked him. She hoped to get his support and shared her frustration at trying to get Andy to do right by her, opening up more than she ever had before. Only to have him spout the same bull Andy gave her about the Kiltepper lineage and the shame this could bring to such an illustrious family. Walter Pollard's loyalty was an asset to them but a liability to his own daughter. A betrayal from a man she ought to have trusted more than anyone in the world. Other than the deaths of her mother and Dwight, Deborah never experienced anything so devastating. It drove her decision to leave Tasmania and stay away even more than the coldness of Andy's efforts to pay her off to "fix" the little bastard he wanted nothing to do with.

"I'm glad you came to see me," her father says, more warmly, as if aware of what's on her mind and adapting himself.

"Are you really?"

"Forgive my initial reaction. I'm surprised and I only just woke up. It takes a while to get going."

"You need some time, something to drink? Eat?"

"No, no. Don't go, I'll be okay."

Then his manner changes, all traces of the old acrimony gone. His smile is sincere and he's not that good an actor to put it on, let alone sustain it. His eyes blink quickly.

"How are you, my dear? You know I've really missed you."

"Oh Dad," she says, unable to hold back, and gives him a hug.

"I understand I have a grandson."

"Yes, he's here. Christopher wants to meet you too."

"Well, bring this Christopher on in."

Whatever she wanted to say while alone with her father escapes her as she opts for the easy route. She finds Christopher and Wilma together, chatting, while Carla is on her own, colouring in a book. Normally, Deborah would expect Christopher to be the loner, not the pretty princess.

"Do you want to come in now?"

Her invite was for Christopher but the girls take it to include them and they bolt into the room before she can stop them. Christopher lags behind and seems trepid.

"Wilmsy, Carly," Deborah hears a moment later.

She gives Christopher a nudge. They enter in time to see the girls, one on each side of her father, giving him a peck on the cheek. Deborah doubts she ever did that. Her son's still by the door and has to be beckoned in.

"So you must be Christopher."

"Hello."

Her father looks him up and down and Deborah wonders what Ruth told him about Christopher, particularly whether they described his dark skin.

"You're a big boy, how old are you?"

"Ten?"

"Ten? Is that so. You look much bigger."

At this, Christopher shies away again, until his grandfather asks about his journey, what he's seen, and so forth. Watching her son talk about Australia erases any lingering reservations she may have had coming here. Deborah can't recall her father being so charming with children. Even Carla's spirits have lifted in his presence. It's rather bittersweet.

"Sounds like you've seen a lot, young man."

"Not everything."

"You can't possibly have seen everything."

"Gramps, he means he hasn't seen a Tasmanian tiger," Wilma says.

"Ooh, that's a toughie."

"Tell him about the one you saw."

"That's right. I saw the last one, a long time ago."

"Did you try to catch it?"

"No, my boy, this was at the zoo here in Hobart. I was only four."

"I already know about that one. Do you think there are any still in the wild?"

Her father looks around mysteriously, then beckons Christopher to lean over to whisper in his ear. It lasts a half-minute. Whatever he says seems to satisfy her son. Then her father asks the kids to give him some time with Deborah and they leave.

"So what does Andy think of your son?"

"Why would you ask that?"

"It's just a question."

"I didn't come to worry about that family."

"But Carla and Wilma are here?"

This stumps Deborah. She's not sure where her father's coming from, let alone where the crafty old man might be going, but knowing him as she does, it's bound to be somewhere she doesn't care to go herself. The good thing is she's not annoyed with him because she feels a measure of control she hasn't felt since before Fred and Ruth came to see her.

"Christopher invited them. They happen to be at the hotel, on vacation. He met them on his own."

Her father shakes his head, patronizingly.

"Honey, are you sure you didn't come all this way in the hope of reconciling what happened when you left?"

Deborah resents him for trying to put her on the defensive, but it doesn't work, she withstands it. If he were in better health she might go on the attack. Instead, she calmly shakes her head.

"I heard about the fire and came to see you. And to spend time with Fred and Ruth. To give my son a new experience. I'm achieving all those things."

Her words seem to touch him and he asks her to tell him more. He listens well and her confidence in what she's saying increases as she goes on. She tells him about her life in Ontario, including about Willie, though leaving out his issues with the police. She shares her wish that Ruth—she hasn't explicitly told her sister any of this yet because it's coming to her as she speaks—can help get her son back to school and that her ideal outcome would be to live in Adelaide, perhaps, and to have Willie join them at some point.

Her father's nod encourages her to go as far as to admit her pride is an obstacle but that she's ready to fight it and accept the financial support of her sister and brother-in-law until she's established. She concedes how idealistic it sounds, no doubt exactly like the immature, naive young woman that left so dramatically twelve years ago. Unlike then, though, her father shows no sign of bursting her bubble. Yet.

"That's why I'm here. I may not have known that setting out, but this has been a discovery for me."

Then it comes, as her father solemnly shakes his head. Though now he actually looks pained for her, which is worse than the patronization she's used to.

"Honey, it hurts me to have to be the one to tell you this, because it seems your sister couldn't."

"Tell me what?"

"Just remember it wasn't all Fred. He messed up but I didn't prepare him well. Too anxious to get on with my ventures. Ignored signs he wasn't ready. I suppose no one could have been prepared for the global financial crisis and I'd have made many of the same errors in his place. True, I would have known when and how to cut the losses, but poor Fred, well, in the end the Kilteppers lost millions just in Hobart. It's understandable how they reacted."

"What are you talking about, Dad?"

"We owe a lot to Andy, my girl, a lot. By we, I mean all the Pollards."

"Dad, stop it."

She shakes his shoulders. He peers up at her, his face and frame weaker even than when she came in.

"How could you say something like that to me, of all people?"

"I have to say it, because it's true."

"What does that mean, we owe Andy a lot?"

"It means the Johnsons are broke, and so am I."

The revelation knocks her back, an echo of the large wave on the ferry.

"Broke?"

"Honey, you've been gone a long time but surely you must recall how tight our families were. When personal and business matters mix together in such a way, everything gets complicated."

He's talking in circles now, she thinks, or it could be her head spinning in circles. Maybe it's best she drop it and mind her own business. Her father seems to grasp this and mercifully announces he's getting tired. He asks to have the kids come in again.

First he says goodbye to the girls, then he gets Christopher to promise to come see him again soon. Fortunately, they're too young to sense anything is amiss, though Deborah wonders how aware Carla and Wilma are of the situation.

At the hotel, she waits for them to change and then leaves them at the pool. She hastens to Fred and Ruth's door and knocks but gets no response. A visit to the front desk reveals the Johnsons are out for the afternoon. How convenient, Deborah thinks, and ponders what to do. She could hang out by the pool with the kids and wait, though there is another source for answers.

Deborah sucks in her breath as she enters the elevator and presses PH. The elevator whisks her up and directly into a foyer where she's greeted by a good looking Aboriginal man with a gracious smile.

"I'm sorry, I thought someone else . . ."

"Mrs. Palmer?" the man says.

"Yes."

"I'm afraid Mr. Kiltepper isn't here right now."

"Oh?"

The man introduces himself as Andy's assistant, Crane.

"Mr. Kiltepper is grateful to you for taking the girls to visit your father. They adore him. When they came up to put on their togs, they expressed how much they enjoyed it."

"Well, they were delightful."

"Good."

She returns to her room, somewhat troubled by the exchange with Crane. If her father and Fred did so much damage to the Kiltepper business, why are they so chummy with Andy now?

She tries calling Willie again. Though by now she's used to getting no response, each time it's no less infuriating. Nevertheless, she resolves to keep a vigil by the phone, a comforting, albeit continuously disappointing anchor.

It's not until evening, after Christopher's gone to sleep, that Fred and Ruth return. They may have stopped by the hospital to compare notes with her father because they seem prepared for Deborah's inquisition when she summons them to her room.

But as Fred relates the business setbacks and his personal failures, she sees what Andy's treatment of her family after all that has taken out of them. While Andy never ostracized the Pollards outright, he has never forgiven Fred and it's been awkward for years with the healing only starting after the fire. Deborah has no desire to add to their torment—nor hers for that matter—by probing for details. The truth about present circumstances is what matters most to her.

Things aren't as dire as her father implied. The Johnsons aren't broke. Both still have pensions. But their standard of living, aside from the condo in Adelaide, is a far cry from what they're accustomed to. Indeed, it's not much better than hers in Canada. As far as the condo goes, it's subsidized not by Andy but his father's estate and will remain theirs as long as they wish and continue to pay the token rent.

"I suppose this is what Dad meant when he said we owe Andy a lot."

"Not sure I would see it that way," Ruth says.

"I'm guessing Andy's responsible for me being here."

"That's true," Ruth says, "in a financial sense. He is paying for everything."

It's clear to Deborah how badly Ruth feels. She'll forgive her sister someday, though it's fine to let her squirm for the time being.

"It was his idea too," Fred says, but then checks himself.

"What Fred means is, it could only have been his idea. You have no idea how long I've wanted, we've wanted, to find you. We never had the means."

Deborah's wearying of this, exhausted by the emotionally draining mix of manipulation and good deed. Time to end this conversation. Fred and Ruth concur, then hand over a letter for her, addressed to their condo in Adelaide, which they had couriered here. She recognizes Willie's handwriting.

"It came with your table, which is at our condo."

Shaking a little, Deborah gently puts the letter and paper aside.

"So what was Andy's purpose in doing all this now?"

"Best you talk to him yourself," Ruth says. "You can tomorrow on the hike. Without us around."

"We're planning to skip that," Fred says.

"Oh no, you're not. I'm skipping it. I need time to evaluate things with no distractions. I want you to watch Christopher while I do so."

"But you will talk to Andy?"

"Let me figure that out."

They're probably unhappy about her vagueness or about having to do a hike, but leave without protest. Which is good as she'd rather not share the real reason she's staying back, which is to be there in case Willie calls.

It's quiet in her suite, save for the soft breathing of her son that accompanies a troubling, previously improbable realization that, in all of Tasmania, and even the world, the only adult she's not displeased with at the moment is Andy Kiltepper.

# 27

Oyster Bay, in concert with the silhouette of Maria Island blocking the distant Tasman Sea, appears to engulf the horizon, while in the foreground gently furled green carpets of grass act as a benign contrast. Scenes like this and others on the drive underscore Andy's visceral attachment to this island in a way his fellow passengers, sleepy prey to an early start and smooth roads, could never understand.

Except for Wilma.

She's been as alert as he has since their departure just after sunrise. The northeast carries significance for his niece who is convinced she descends from the Oyster Bay tribe that peopled this coastal area before the Europeans settled here. Sadly for her, she can only speculate on this. She's a pure orphan, with no known blood relatives, and no research has revealed otherwise to this point. She'll keep trying and Andy will support her quest, which has gained importance since the fire. And if anyone can appreciate that, it's Andy.

Carla, on the other hand, slumped in her seat and possibly in one of her moods, couldn't care less about family history. Or even the beautiful scenery that's passing her by. Which is frustrating for Andy as his daughter's been whinging for him to take her to Freycinet National Park for weeks. He's resisted to this point because he can never be sure she won't back out. The hike to Wineglass Bay was Julia and Carla's favourite and he would take them once a year to appease them. Then, during the first months after the fire, Carla showed no interest whatsoever. At Christmas, she suddenly began clamouring for them to go. Andy saw this as a good sign at the time but now, in her emotional state, he's not sure how she'll react. Had it been up to he and Wilma, they'd be halfway up the more challenging Mt. Wellington by now and no one would be sleeping.

Of course, no one is as alert as Crane, whose capable driving perhaps has made it too easy for the passengers to rest. Without the tight turns and steep hills of the inner roads they usually take it's a drive Andy could have managed. Would have managed, before the fire. He's become a cautious man, content to entrust such responsibilities to the long-serving family aide who's been with the Kilteppers since Andy's grandfather was alive. Crane's Aboriginal roots, unlike Wilma's, are not a mystery. He knows his parents and their parents come from the Oyster Bay tribe and can confirm it with records. As Wilma likes to point out, those records contain gaps in which she might fit. A slight resemblance between them—more noticeable in their manners and voices than their faces—is enough for Wilma to be certain they are cousins in some way. Crane is as fervent about his heritage but is sceptical about records. As he says, "You cannot be sure where you're truly from, only where others tell you you're from."

Andy isn't particularly keen that Fred and Ruth have come along. They're not in good shape so the hike will challenge them and inevitably they'll slow everyone down. However it is notable, encouraging even, that Deborah's allowed Christopher to come without her. From what Fred told him, and his own recollection of her controlling tendencies, Deborah's protective of her son. Her absence ought to provide greater freedom for Andy to find out more about this boy. To see what his makeup is, to see if his suspicions are correct. It helps that Wilma likes him and Carla's sibling-esque swings of indifference and hostility can be a positive indicator, albeit a poor reflection on his daughter. However, any scrutiny of Christopher will have to wait until the hike. When Andy took the front seat, he expected, hoped, the kids would share the middle seat, which would put Fred and Ruth in the back. Instead, it's Ruth in the middle with the girls while Christopher sits next to Fred in the back.

The road takes them inland for about twenty minutes before hugging the Oyster Bay coast. As they approach Swansea, Wilma gets animated, taps Carla until she wakes, and motions at a mileage sign for Campbell

Town. They usually stop there for ice creams when coming from the estate or Launceston. He's afraid Carla will badger him for a detour but instead, she asks:

"Dad, when are we going back to the estate?"

"Tomorrow, honey."

"Where are you going tomorrow?" Christopher says, directing his question to Wilma who nods.

"You have to come too. If there's anyplace you're going to see a Tasmanian tiger, it's there."

"There's no such thing as a Tasmanian tiger," Carla says, her intensity about this surprising Andy.

"You don't know that," Christopher says.

"Dad, tell him there are no—"

"Uncle Andy, is it okay if Christopher and his mom come visit us?"

"Fine by me, as long as his mom is okay with it."

"Great," Wilma says.

Andy directs a glance at Fred. "It depends on your plans, I suppose."

"We'll discuss it with Deborah," Fred says.

Discuss it with Deborah? What an odd response from Fred, as if he's making decisions. The Johnsons have done a marvellous job getting Deborah and her son here, but Fred shouldn't forget who's making it all happen, who's in charge.

"You guys should come too," Wilma says, to Ruth and Fred.

We'll see, Andy thinks, but just smiles.

"We'll see," Fred says, and Andy finds this echo of his own thought particularly grating.

Past Swansea, the road veers right, away from Campbell Town, towards Coles Bay where it turns right again straight into the park. Crane drops them off at the entrance, then drives away.

"He's coming back, right?" Christopher says.

"Of course," Andy says, "He's just going to visit a relative while we hike."

"Which one?" Wilma says.

Andy shrugs. Thankfully she doesn't pursue it.

As Andy suspected, the Johnsons struggle early on the uphill path. As does Carla, though for some purpose of her own; normally she has no trouble keeping up. Christopher's doing fine and, of course, so is Wilma. It doesn't take long before they split into two groups, and Andy forges ahead with the two older kids.

However, he finds himself needing a rest much earlier than usual. At least it's not as hot as it's been lately; otherwise that pesky recurring fever might kick up again. Luckily too, it happens at a natural stopping point, the lookout over Coles Bay.

He tells Wilma, who's eager to keep going, that he wants to give the stragglers a chance to catch up, not wanting to let on his conditioning isn't what it was. She's not happy about it but relents and plops herself down on a rock while Christopher walks to the lookout. Andy moves to stand next to him. He is unusually tall for a ten-year-old, just as Fred noted, but his skin is darker than Fred described.

"What do you think of this view?"

"It's nice."

"Just nice?"

Christopher shrugs. He seems restless. It appears to Andy he's more interested in scanning the expanse of brush fronting the azure bay than the bay itself, or even the loveliness of the coast and sea beyond.

"Stop looking at the ground."

It comes out more stern than Andy intends. In a softer voice, Andy asks what's on his mind.

"I wish Willie was here."

"Willie? Who's Willie?"

Christopher looks at Andy. Something seems to register in the boy's eyes. Andy tries to grasp what it is but can't before Christopher looks away.

"I mean, I was hoping we'd see some animals."

"Too many people around for animals."

"Oh."

Andy's trying to be nice, but the boy's apathy is exasperating. Now Wilma joins them to pester Andy to keep going. This day isn't turning out the way he had hoped at all.

"Go on, but wait at the top. Okay?"

"Come on, Christopher."

The pair are out of sight almost instantly. Andy waits a few minutes before spotting Fred and Ruth, which only piques his nerves further. But then he sees Carla with them, lively and engaged, and he starts to warm to the Johnsons' presence. They catch up, stop for some water, then continue. Andy adapts to their pace, a hit to his pride but a relief to his aching body. They reach the top and the four come together at the railing.

A layer of clouds rises above the rolling hills beyond. Their whiteness adds a fine texture to the pristine semi-circular beige beach below. From here, the glorious blues of the water seem still against the sand. It's an inspiring scene that lifts Andy's mood, a worthy reward for the effort to get there, one he appreciates more than he did on previous visits.

"Wow," Ruth says, then grabs Carla's hand, just as Julia would do. "Isn't this wonderful?"

But Carla's crying now. Not her normal tears of complaint but deeper sobs. No doubt she's recalling pleasant times with her mother. She'll never know how bad things got between her parents, let alone the part played by Ruth's sister. It's a tough situation for Andy who constantly feels like a bad guy around his daughter. He's not sure how to fix that. In the short term, he's grateful Ruth is here to console her.

Meanwhile, Wilma and Christopher are pacing back and forth among the rocks facing the view, clearly bored. Andy joins them, followed by Ruth and his daughter who's expression is alive again, though not in an attractive way.

"What's the matter, Christopher, not enough tigers here for you?"

"Shut up, Carla," Wilma says.

"Hey, hey," Andy says.

Carla jabs a finger towards Christopher.

"Idiot thinks he's going to find a Tassie tiger."

Christopher looks more startled than hurt by her mean tone and this seems to annoy Carla. She looks at her father, as if expecting him to join her mockery. Her face drops when he says nothing.

Then the strangest thing happens as Christopher gets down on all fours and starts moving about like an animal. Andy's mesmerized, too stunned to say anything. He can hear Carla's cackling but the boy doesn't stop. He's remarkably nimble, his agility fascinating to watch. Until the commotion of others behind him brings the realization how unbecoming this is for a Kiltepper. Andy lowers his head.

"Get up," he commands Christopher.

He has to repeat it a couple of times before the boy acknowledges him. Everyone but Carla is quiet, her laughter echoing as Andy moves to Christopher, his hands ready to lift the boy up, until another set of hands on his arms pulls him back.

"Andy, what on earth are you doing?"

The harsh insubordination in Fred's tone is what arrests Andy, not the hands from which he could easily break away. The tone is an evolution of Fred's earlier comment. Andy's too shaken—as well as too afraid of being recognized—to react as he normally would to such behaviour. He even allows Fred to guide him away.

"You want to alienate Deborah, after all we've done?"

The fact that Fred's right galls Andy but he has to concede.

"Sorry, I was caught off guard."

To this Fred says nothing. They rejoin the others to find the girls still at it while Christopher seems indifferent to the tension, oblivious even.

"Sook."

"Stop calling me that."

"Sook."

Her cousin keeps repeating it until it makes Carla cry and rush to Ruth who comforts her.

Wilma declares her intent to walk down to the beach with Christopher and go back to the parking lot the long way. Andy's of no mind to protest. Fred and Ruth wisely opt for the shorter route and return the way they came. He expects, even hopes, Carla goes with the Johnsons but she surprises him by wanting to do the round trip. It's more surprising because she never did so when they came here with Julia. It also means that, though his body would prefer to take the easier route, it's best he follow the children, if only to keep things in line.

He struggles to match their pace, even with the kids' slow progress from bounding about here and there searching for wildlife. Carla too joins the search until Andy reminds her about snakes and other critters. Then his daughter sticks to him, which is nice and lasts until they get back to the parking lot where they find Fred and Ruth waiting with Crane by the car.

A universally disappointing excursion, Andy has to admit. Fred and Ruth got unwanted exercise, Christopher saw no animals, Wilma was bored by the easy hike, his daughter got unnecessarily sad, and Andy lost a chance to test his theory. Worse, the boy's antics are unsettling. Andy's unsure what to make of it. Acting like an animal is so childish, not at all the way a Kiltepper ought to behave.

What's most vexing is how difficult he finds it to connect with the boy. It can't be an adult thing; Fred seems to have no problem. Nor for that matter does Ruth, and the boy seems to admire Crane, as most people do. Maybe it's Andy, maybe it's related to his difficulty with his daughter.

Poor Carla, who probably felt betrayed when he didn't join her mocking, especially considering his strong public views about supposed tiger sightings.

Of course, she can't know those views were ones he held before his experience at the fire, which to him still seems too real to discount.

# 28

A strange day, Fred thinks, as he and Ruth make their way down the hall to Deborah's suite. It was disconcerting to see Christopher revert to old habits on the hike but good to have Andy to see it firsthand and unprompted, unlike at the pool where it just looked like playing. Andy ought to be impressed by the boy's athleticism, not to mention his forbearance with Carla's taunting. But is that enough to get past being put off by Christopher's conduct?

"We're caught in the middle," Ruth says, echoing his own sentiments, "and we're getting squeezed more and more each day."

"How did your sister sound when you called?"

"Pretty chipper, actually, which doesn't help."

"You're right, Ruth, it is time."

Deborah lets them in and she is in a bright mood and glad to see them. Her suitcase, Fred notices, is put away out of sight. No clothes are lying around and the suite looks tidy; no indication its occupants are ready to move out. She says Christopher is at the pool with the girls.

"Did he tell you about the hike?"

"Only a bit, he was in a hurry. He did mention the invitation to the estate and made me promise to think about it. It's pretty clear to me how much he enjoyed himself."

Nothing in her manner shows Christopher said a word about the episode with Andy. Should he let it go or bring it up? A glance at Ruth indicates her thoughts are running along the same lines as his.

"The energy of those kids," he says.

"I appreciate you two going on that hike. I know it's not your thing so I feel guilty forcing it on you."

"It wasn't so bad," Ruth says, half-heartedly. Fred and Deborah chuckle. "But we did miss you."

"I needed the alone time to process everything."

"Glad to oblige," Fred says. "It appears you've at least restored your spirits."

"Yes, eventually. It was an up and down day."

She tells them she read Willie's letter, about which she shares little more than she's likely seen and heard the last of him. Thankfully, Ruth resists prying. Perhaps she's as perplexed as he is at her sister's calmness and lack of anger. Indeed, Deborah tells them she's coming around to being grateful to the Johnsons for getting her to come here, in spite of this news and their methods. Hearing this pleases Ruth until Deborah clarifies she's not fully there yet.

247

"However, the biggest puzzle for me was why Andy would go to all this effort."

"Was?" Fred says.

"We're not Andy's agents."

Fred's not sure what prompted his wife to utter that. The toll the past few weeks have taken on Ruth must be heavier than he thought. Things never go well when both sisters get defensive.

"I didn't mean it that way, Ruthie."

Deborah says it calmly, to Fred's relief, and now it appears his sister-in-law is as afraid of inflaming matters as the Johnsons are.

"At the risk of contradicting my dear wife, Ruth and I feel it's time for us to go back to Adelaide."

Deborah's stoniness returns and it's impossible to tell how she's taking this. He explains they intend to drive back in the morning, after a brief visit with Walter, and they'll make the flight arrangements and be ready for Deborah and Christopher if and when they want to join them. Ruth nods.

"We've been with you all this way. Maybe now is the time for you to sort things out with Daddy, with Andy, with Tasmania, with your life, on your own. Of course, it's up to you whether to do any of that and how to go about it. We believe it'll be easier to make those choices without us around. I know we've put you in a tough spot we take responsibility for that. Whatever you choose to do, we'll support and we'll be ready for you in Adelaide, as Fred says. We do hope you and Christopher end up with us when all is said and done."

His wife's lucid explanation impresses Fred who can only nod. Deborah maintains her stolidity a while longer before also nodding.

"I think you're right."

"Of course," Ruth adds, "you can come with us tomorrow if that's what you'd prefer to do."

"No, what you said about sorting things makes sense. It's best Christopher and I stay a bit longer."

"Are you going to talk to Andy?"

Deborah gives Ruth a mild don't-push-it look before smiling. "No better time than the present."

"If you don't mind, we'd like to say goodbye to Andy first."

"Certainly, Fred. After that, maybe you two can look after Christopher for a couple of hours?"

"You bet."

These past days, with Christopher spending so much time with the girls, Fred has felt neglected. It hits him that their leaving tomorrow could mean—depending on Deborah—tonight could be the last hours he spends with a boy for whom he's formed a special bond, the depth of which he hasn't grasped until this instant. That bond, combined with the joy he's had spending time in Hobart again, fills Fred with a profound sadness about their departure. It's tempting to change Ruth's mind to stay for it will be hard for her to leave her sister too. But if they don't allow things to run their own course, it could ruin everything.

Fred and Ruth hold hands on the elevator to the penthouse. Crane answers and escorts them into a good-sized room just off the foyer. It's a stuffy, old-fashioned study with bookshelves lining the walls and thick patterned carpets on the floor. There's a desk and several chairs. Except for one shelf filled with children's and family DVDs bearing colourful sleeves, the room could belong to an army officer from the early nineteenth century.

Andy enters and his greeting is not as warm as Deborah's was earlier. In fact, he's clearly annoyed.

"Who the hell is Willie?"

The one thing Fred and Ruth have argued about most since getting back to Australia was what to reveal to Andy about Deborah's personal life in Canada. Ruth, naturally looking out for her sister, preferred to reveal as little as possible; whereas Fred thought it best to be open about everything. Ruth eventually convinced Fred there was no point to mentioning Willie since they knew so little of what was going on. So now, just as he feels it's best to let Christopher mention the incident with Andy on the hike on his own, if he wishes, he also feels it's best for Deborah to be the one to tell Andy about Willie. The drawback, of course, is the awkward situation they find themselves in now.

"How did you hear about him?"

"Christopher mentioned a Willie as someone he misses. I didn't get the sense this Willie was a casual acquaintance, a pet, or a teddy bear."

Fred establishes it was his decision to withhold telling Andy about Willie before sharing the little they know, including the situation with the police and the murder. He's not sure whether to add what they learned since regarding the letter and table sent to Adelaide, but decides it's best to let it all out. No point returning home with anything but a clear conscience. Surprisingly, Andy listens gravely and does not pepper Fred with questions.

"You made a judgment call."

"Yes."

"Andy, you put us in a tough spot. It's going to take time to get over deceiving my sister. Which is why we're going back to Adelaide tomorrow."

"Really?"

"Yes. We'll see Walter early enough to give us time to catch the ferry back."

"Just the two of you?"

"We just told Deborah a few minutes ago. It's up to her to come along with us or not."

"What was her answer?"

"She'll tell us when she tells us," Ruth says, with some defiance that draws a rueful smile from Andy.

"I do see how difficult the situation must be for you two, how much I've asked. For what it's worth, I am grateful. Personally grateful."

"That helps," Ruth says. "We did this willingly and we are in turn grateful you made it possible."

This is something Fred didn't foresee when they left that estate meeting so many months ago. Yet it's minor compared to what comes next.

"There are some major changes in the works for Kiltepper, Fred, for which you'd be well suited. That is, if you'd be interested."

"Wow," is all Fred can say.

"We'll talk later, no need to commit now. I can't do much until Carla and Wilma are back in school."

Andy stands up and Fred and Ruth do the same. The two men shake hands before Andy guides them out the library into the foyer.

"About Christopher, do you know the truth?"

"No," Fred says. "We don't know."

"Would you tell me if you did?"

"I'd tell you if I knew. I'm not so sure I'd tell you what that truth was. That's best for Deborah to do, don't you think?"

This satisfies Andy who then sees them to the elevator.

Fred's pleased at how it went, particularly his response to the last question. Andy's theory—and even Ruth would admit her sister could sustain a lie of such magnitude—is something they want no part of exploring. To them, Christopher is their nephew, regardless of who might be his father.

"You do realize," Ruth says, once they're in the elevator, "we never addressed the gap between what they both think."

"I know. But like you said, we're in the middle, we're getting squeezed. That stops now. We have to step away and let them sort it out on their own."

"You're right, of course, but what if everything backfires?"

# 29

Deception has always been and will always be a part of the Pollards and Kilteppers. It's taken all thirty-five years of her life for Deborah to accept this as a given. And to do so without emotion or indignation. She now sees how much it was a factor in drawing her to Willie Galloway the moment they met. He was several years older, somewhat immature, not particularly attractive, certainly not wealthy; indeed the opposite of the type of man she probably would have ended up with, had she not gotten involved with Andy Kiltepper. But Willie was the opposite in one other way: he was not a deceiver. It wasn't in him. He was bad at lying, knew it, and rarely tried. This inability, so contrary to the surroundings she grew up in, was his appeal.

At least that was the situation, until she read the brief letter, which she opens up and reads again, this time aloud.

"Things are bad here. It might even make the news where you are. Trust me, only the minor parts are true. That said, I have to take steps to keep safe while making sure you and C aren't troubled. If you get this, then at least I salvaged your table and some other items I shipped to Adelaide. As for everything else, including the cars, I can't say the same. Sorry. I need all the cash I can get. I will always think of you and C. Tell him whatever you need to. Love, W."

Her response upon first reading was a good cry that dried quickly due to so many questions that drove her to the hotel's business centre to search for information online. She found plenty, most notably that her wonderful, adoring Willie was a fugitive from the law, wanted for murder and fraud. Fraud? Furthermore, her misgivings about the furniture and appliances, misgivings she only recently overcame, were well founded. A negligible factor relative to the entire mess but one that pains her more deeply than the absurd notion he could be a murderer. A second stream of tears lasted longer but, mercifully, ended before everyone returned from the hike.

Now, after her talk with Fred and Ruth, she can be clinical. Willie's a thief but she believes his claims about the murder. She see his actions, misguided as they are, as meant to help her and Christopher. The lack of details in the letter is a deception intended to protect them. She may forgive him for that, eventually, if she ever gets the chance.

That's doubtful.

Her desire to lament this loss is now offset by a need to figure out what to say to Christopher. Willie's fine being the villain but it's not likely Christopher will buy it; more likely her son will find a way to view his actions as heroic.

Willie's deceived her but she understands what drove that deceit. She's deceived her family but she knows what drove that. Deborah can make sense of what drove Ruth and Fred to seek her out. It's pretty clear given how happy they've been together to this point, and how quickly they set things right when their deceptions were exposed.

What remains a mystery is what drove Andy to it? Only now does the answer seem clear, though it's been discernible from the start. What's not clear is how she'll handle it. Given the news about Willie, it would be easy to give in and guarantee an easy life for Christopher. Andy's still an attractive man and his ego seems to have softened—in fact, he's a pretty nice guy now. It would be hard to not credit such an effort. And then there's lovely little Carla. How nice that would be.

But Deborah no longer is that spoiled kid. She's matured enough to recognize when something is too easy and, instead of falling for it, looking deeper for answers. When she does this, it's clear she can't go along with such a scheme. Best to be up front about it with Andy. Ruth is right too: she must do that on her own and soon. Andy may ask her not to be hasty in deciding anything, to give it time. But that would only lead him on, lead herself on, knowing all the while it can't and won't work. For even if Deborah could come around to accept such an arrangement, there's no way Christopher could get beyond seeing it as a betrayal of the closest and only father figure in his life.

Oh God, what will she say to her son? Maybe she needn't say anything yet. Considering Andy's ability to locate people, maybe there's a way to get him to help her find Willie. Should Andy mistakenly infer she's open to other developments if the search fails, what's the harm?

It could work. She keeps repeating that to herself as she applies a touch more makeup than usual, and takes the elevator up to Andy's suite.

Crane answers and confirms his boss is there. But instead of inviting her in, Crane asks her to wait in the foyer. It's less than a minute before Andy comes out, wearing casual slacks and a polo shirt. In her Harrod's skirt, she feels overdressed.

"How about we go for a walk?"

"Not tired from your hike this morning?"

"I had a good nap."

"I hope Christopher wasn't a burden?"

"Not at all. He and Wilma are peas in a pod and getting along famously."

His description of Christopher's reaction to the invitation to the estate matches the enthusiasm she saw in her son each of the five times he asked her to accept. She tells Andy what she told Christopher, that she'll think about it.

"That's terrific. Of course, if you have any questions, concerns, just ask."

"I will."

On the elevator down, the awkwardness is there but it's not as palpable as she expected. Once they exit the hotel, it lifts altogether, as if carried away by the pleasant breeze. Through Parliament Square, by Parliament House, towards the wharf on Castray Esplanade, she allows him to guide her around and show her landmarks she knows well from growing up in Hobart. But she was much younger then, not as appreciative of the import of certain monuments. He's a good guide, even if his recollection of the nearly identical strolls they used to take more than a dozen years before has lapsed.

"I never heard you speak this fondly of Hobart."

"It's a lovely city, I've never denied that."

"But it's no Launceston."

"Never."

"That sounds emphatic."

"Sorry, but Hobart is a sore point with me due to avoidable losses we suffered here several years ago. Trouble outside my control."

"Don't you think you're being hard on Fred."

"Ah, so you know some things."

"I've gathered a few facts. The rest I can derive from knowing you."

"Touché," Andy says, with a laugh. "Actually, I have stopped being hard on Fred, as you say. I'm making it right by him."

"That's hard to accept on your say so. No offence."

"None taken. Your image of me is outdated. So much has changed since . . ."

257

"Of course. And you know what? I haven't properly expressed my condolences . . ."

She suddenly feels shallow. Condolences. Sorry for your loss. Thoughts and Prayers. Just words. Combinations of consonants and vowels that can in no way express one's feelings without coming across as a palely empathetic indifference. Perhaps they make people feel better if you say them, but more likely they only make people feel bad if you don't. Yet what else can she offer? She wants to break down for him, to cry for those people she knew once but doesn't necessarily remember anymore.

"Thanks," he says, with a graceful finality, as if grasping her discomfort and letting her off the hook.

The toll the fire's taken on him is profound and how deep it goes would be impossible to imagine if she weren't witnessing it. He's obviously gutted, his vitality has diminished. But that has made him more pleasant, easier to be around. Which is probably why her own rage has remained dormant.

They reach Battery Point, once a landmark on their walks, from where they would take a detour to stop in at Fred and Ruth's house a few blocks away, enjoy a drink on their porch, whether the Johnsons were home or not. This time they head for Kelly Steps, which they take down to the dockyards and warehouses of Salamanca Place for the return to the hotel, the dark presence of Mt Wellington in view.

It's an easy walk but Andy seems tired. Then he begins coughing and turns away. He apologizes and tells her about how the pneumonia he contracted during the fire keeps returning.

"Should we get a taxi?" she says.

"I'll be fine. I want to show you one more thing."

"So how do you intend making it right by Fred?" she says, as they move on.

"I've got some work for which he's well suited."

"A reward for getting me down here?"

Andy laughs.

"I've missed that about you and I'm glad you haven't lost your sass. But I'm not hiding anything. Yes, I did make it possible for them to find you."

"You helped them? Or got them to help you?"

He stops, as if to interpret precisely what she's getting at, and then to construct a suitable response.

"Just tell me why," she says, beating him to it.

"Why do you think?" he says.

"I suspect you're looking for a new—"

They stare at each other. A spark of their old fire is there, but it's barely an ember and it's dying. He gives her a wan smile.

"A new wife? You?"

Andy slowly shakes his head. Kindly, sincerely, with no trace of malice. Yet his response hits her as hard as any rejection ever did, including his from twelve years ago. Which is stupid because she should be relieved; this is what she wants. Or is it? It was when she thought she knew what he wanted. Now it's not as clear. Somehow she manages a smile to cover the confusion and turmoil inside.

259

Then he laughs. Not a guffaw, not even close to the mocking way she knows firsthand he's capable of. It's a light-hearted laugh that demands a great effort on her part to suppress her own laugh, with partial success, resulting in what she suspects is an unbecoming grin. His expression, on the other hand, is one she's not seen on him before. Compassionate. Gentle. As if his life mission has transitioned from dominating people businesswise to accommodating them in personal ways.

"That wasn't my intent," he says, aptly easing the discomfiture. "Sorry if I led you to think that."

"I'm not disappointed, I'm relieved."

"Oh, I didn't mean to presume. Let me clarify."

He explains his goal is not to replace a wife and mother but to help reunite the Pollards, a family his actions and insensitivity helped tear apart. Helping them will heal himself or at least help. His sincerity is touching and Deborah appreciates his roundabout way of taking responsibility for what happened between them.

"I didn't share any of this with Ruth so you can blame me for any misunderstandings."

"You've changed a great deal, Andy."

"The fire's had a big impact."

He guides her into St. David's Park towards its ancient cemetery. It's as creepy a place as it was when she was younger and dates would try to coax her in, though she never fell for it. Andy slows his pace just as she wants to quicken it to pass through. He grabs her hand to make a turn

"Something I want to show you. It's not far."

"I don't much care for cemeteries."

"Relax, the graves are gone where we're going."

She follows Andy along a path amongst a series of headstone walls. He stops at one and points at the name: Morris Fitzpatrick who died in 1825.

"You remember my father and I researching the Kiltepper genealogy?"

She remembers him talking about it, at length at times, including how the subject bored her to tears. She hates computers and the idea of using them and spending all that time—and in some cases money—on that genealogy fad helped turn her off them. The desperation to find ancestors who ended up being criminals made little sense to her.

"Vaguely."

"Right, you weren't a fan. For what it's worth, our research paid off when we found this."

He points at the same headstone.

"Who is he?"

"My Kiltepper convict past."

So even the noble, honourable Kilteppers got drawn into this, she thinks, as Andy describes how this convict changed his name to Kiltepper to erase his shame, then launched a dynasty. A dynasty that will come to an end.

It's becoming clear the devastation of the fire for Andy goes beyond losing family members. It's about losing his essence, his illustrious family line. A knot forms in her stomach as she entertains a horrific thought: is he looking to her as a surrogate?

"You're still young, you can find someone else."

"A sports injury left me sterile. I have to accept the sun will set on the Kilteppers in my lifetime."

"You have Carla."

Now his face is showing some frustration.

"I'm referring to the male line. Never mind. I didn't bring you to this gloomy spot to mope about what's lost or what time has made unrecoverable."

Deborah doesn't ask why he did bring her here, though his demeanour indicates his earlier answer is incomplete; she's just anxious to exit this eerie park.

To her relief, he motions for them to do so. She starts off ahead, but then notices Andy lingering.

Doting on a family line this way, as if the people involved are mere parts of a valuable whole, seems absurd to her. But maybe that's just his way of seeing things, a way she shouldn't criticize just because she doesn't understand it.

"Carla reminds me of Julia."

Other than from an instinctual desire to change the subject, Deborah's unsure why she shared that aloud, but the remark doesn't seem to surprise him.

"Almost a replica, isn't she? Both good and bad. Which may be why I'm struggling with her."

"I think she's adorable."

This puts a smile on Andy's face. Good.

To end the evening on a positive note, Deborah tells him she'll accept the invitation to the estate. Of course, she always intended to accept, if only to arm herself with some good news to counter what she has to tell her son about Willie.

Christopher is still awake but fading when she retrieves him from Fred and Ruth's room. He stays groggy all the way down the hall and as she helps get him ready for bed. But he fully wakens when she tells him he'll have to get up early to pack his things. His delight at grasping why keeps her from saying anything about Willie, until he asks to call Canada right then and there.

"We have to let him know where we are, in case he decides to come."

"Honey, he won't be there. He's gone."

"You mean he's on his way here?"

Deborah shakes her head, scans her muddled mind for a way to explain that causes as little hurt as possible while being truthful. It's hard. She stumbles about her words, alludes to the investigation and the furniture, until eventually revealing Willie is in so much trouble he had to leave Canada and will never see them again.

Remarkably, none of it flusters her son whose indomitable faith impresses her when he says:

"Of course we'll see him again."

He sounds so convincing she almost believes it. This helps her decide to withhold showing the letter. But she won't go as far as indulging in her son's belief. Though she can understand and forgive most kinds of deception, she can never tolerate its root: self-deception.

# 30

Christopher's anxious to get going. It still bugs him they first had to have breakfast with Uncle Fred and Aunt Ruth to say goodbye, even though they'll see them after Wilma and Carla's school holidays are done. And now his mom's making him visit his grandfather again. Grandpa Walter's nice enough, and the idea of a grandfather is great, but those two are tense when together. At least their talk last night revealed what's probably really bothering her, even though she's wrong about Willie.

Just as he's wrong about the visit. Surprisingly, Grandpa Walter and his mom are happy to see each other. Truly happy, not fake happy like his mom can be with people. Christopher also likes how he and Grandpa Walter shake hands like men. Before he knows it, he's forgotten the estate, as he talks about the hike, about what he's seen so far and, of course:

"Tell me about the Tasmanian tiger you saw at the zoo."

"I'm afraid I don't recall much," Grandpa Walter says. "I was rather young."

"How big was it?"

Grandpa Walter puts two fingers to his lips.

"I do remember thinking it was a large dog at first, until I saw its stripes."

"How many stripes?"

"That I couldn't say—my don't you three paint a lovely little family picture."

Christopher frowns, glances over his shoulder to see Andy next to his mom. He repeats the question. But Grandpa Walter's grinning and distracted.

"Time we get going," his mom says.

"Yes, I am quite tired," Grandpa Walter says, before Christopher can protest. "I promise I'll have better tiger answers next time you visit. Okay?"

Christopher nods, but he's disappointed.

Until they get outside where the big SUV is waiting for them in front of the hospital. His earlier impatience to get going, to be with Wilma, returns.

Crane is driving, which is good, Christopher realizes, once Andy gets in the front passenger seat, as he didn't want his mom and Andy sitting next to each other in the front. However, the two cousins are sitting together and he would rather sit next to Wilma than his mom. How can he make that happen? Happily, he doesn't have to because his mom asks Carla to sit next to her. Carla looks to be grumpy again and shrugs. Which is when his mom takes charge and gently guides Wilma into the back row with Christopher. That was easy. Maybe too easy.

He doesn't want people to know how much he likes Wilma. What if they think that already? What if Wilma thinks that? He keeps snug to his window just as she keeps to hers. He enjoys the scenery for some time and it looks similar to what he saw on the drive from the ferry to Hobart. Sure enough, they cross a combination of lift bridge and causeway and he recognizes the highway. What was the name of this place again? Oh yeah, Bridgewater. This time the bridge is down and they cross quickly. He interrupts his mom who's chatting with a suddenly cheerful Carla to ask for a map. She then asks Andy who passes one down.

"Where is it we're going?"

He asks Wilma while he unfolds the map over his legs, dreading he'll do so upside down again. He doesn't and easily locates Bridgewater.

"We're going to the estate."

"No, I mean where on the map. What town?"

She leans over as far as her seatbelt will stretch. Her long and thick black hair brushes briefly against his shoulder and then on his neck. It sends a shiver that feels nice—if only she could unbuckle that seatbelt and get closer. She runs her index finger along the map. He can feel it on his thigh but can't look down, mesmerized by her pretty face that's focused on the map.

"There."

He manages to look down in time to where she's pointing before she catches him staring, he thinks.

But by then she's removed her finger. Now he's disoriented and it takes longer than it should to figure out where they were, where they are, and where they're going. It's embarrassing for someone as good with maps as he is. Wait, there it is. He now sees they are going in the direction of the Devonport ferry but only as far as where the road splits. This time they're going north towards Launceston, and a bit beyond. Then he sees that name again, Lilydale, the place the guy at the zoo mentioned. They're not going as far as that but pretty close. What a thrill. Only he's going to keep his thoughts to himself this time. No need to get Carla riled up. Or his mom.

He refolds the map and hands it up to her but she doesn't notice. Carla's sleeping head is on her shoulder while she's talking to Andy. It's hard to tell what they're saying but they're laughing in a way Christopher doesn't like. In a way that reminds him of Willie. He jabs her shoulder with the map.

"Hey."

"Sorry."

Christopher quickly looks out the window to pretend he was distracted by the scenery. She takes the map and resumes talking to Andy. But then, as more signs for Launceston appear, showing shorter and shorter distances, she gets quieter. They pass through the city and come out into a much prettier, forested area. Soon they turn off the highway onto rougher, smaller roads.

What a beautiful place. So green, so bushy, so wild, so remote. Perfect place for a tiger. The roads with their twists and turns and hills, you never know what you'll see at the crest. It's usually a narrow but unusual tree-filled view, but sometimes it's another vehicle that seems as if it's going to hit them. Unfortunately, it's virtually impossible to spot wildlife through the trees because the car's going too fast. Crane's a really good driver.

They lurch forward and swerve, startling everyone, before Crane scowls and slows. Behind them, a small animal feasts on road kill. It looks up at them.

"Sorry about that folks," Crane says.

"What was that?" Christopher says.

"That," Andy says, "was a Tassie devil."

"Wow."

"Disgusting," Carla says.

"It's neat," Christopher says.

"The boy thinks it's neat, Crane," Andy says.

Crane laughs, but in a nice way. "It's lucky I saw it. They so often turn into what they eat."

"Can we go back and take a picture?"

"I reckon we scared it off."

Christopher's fine with that. He's bound to see a bunch the next few days. This trip will be even better than Wilma promised.

"Aren't you glad you came?" she says.

Christopher chuckles to himself. He's getting used to her guessing his thoughts. He nods before resuming his scan for wildlife. The more remote they are, the greater the chance of seeing something. However, despite going slower on the dirt roads, it's not any easier due to their bopping around on the bumpy surface.

The dirt road eventually goes uphill to a narrow, smoothly paved driveway that looks out of place amid the wildness. Farther on, a car is parked in a shady spot under a tree. Who else could be here? Uncle Fred and Aunt Ruth? Maybe they changed their minds about going back to Adelaide. That would be nice. But no, he can tell this car, though somewhat muddied, is much sleeker, much newer than the Johnsons' car. It's also silver, not white.

The driveway opens up to a large flat gravel area in front of the largest house Christopher's ever seen in person. It's old-fashioned looking but the orangey brick and black roof shine like new. There's a big veranda that wraps around the house with freshly painted white railings. Then there's the front door. It's really old, beat up. Why Andy would have a door like that makes no sense. The wood it's made from reminds him of those special tables his mom and Aunt Ruth have.

They get out, approach the house. Christopher now thinks the door, the thickest he's even seen, as homely as it is, is fantastic. The old-fashioned style letter "K" on top is like the neon ones on the nicer hotels they stayed at, including the one in Hobart. Despite being refurbished, painted, and varnished, it only looks bad next to everything else because it's older and doesn't belong. The inside of the house, on the other hand, is all new, all shiny with appliances and furniture like those Uncle Fred and Aunt have in Adelaide, except bigger.

"Come on," Wilma says, grabbing at his shirt, "let me show you your room."

"Who else is here?"

"No one."

"Then who owns the other car?"

"Oh that. We always take two cars here. Crane has to do lots of errands that require the SUV and the car makes sure we're never stranded. It's too far for anyone to get out of here on their own without a vehicle. Except me, of course."

She leads him up a set of long, curving stairs to a hallway with many doors. Wilma points out the rooms: her uncle's, then hers, then Carla's, and then three or four guest rooms. One of these is closed and grim and reminds Christopher of a scary movie. All that's missing is a Keep Out sign.

"Pick any one you want," she says, then points to the closed room. "Except that one."

"It doesn't matter," Christopher says.

She leads him to a room at one end next to the closed one. It's bigger than his at home and looks out onto a rainforest about a hundred metres from the house. In between is a huge lawn, bordered by a wooden fence, that could fit at least ten houses like his in Canada. He can make out part of a large patio with a fire pit and a massive, shiny barbecue that's more like a kitchen. Directly below is the awning covering the veranda.

"Yeah, this room is great."

"Good, it's yours while you're here."

He tosses his bag on the bed and stares out the window. There's a movement at one corner near the fence. Christopher sighs with disappointment seeing it's just a sheep. Several of them, in fact, calmly grazing the massive lawn.

"Is this a farm?" Christopher says.

Wilma explains her uncle wanted a huge lawn but not the maintenance so he leases the land to a local farmer who uses it for overflow, whenever he has too many sheep and not enough land to feed them. Apparently, it's a Kiltepper tradition.

"Don't worry, they won't do you any harm."

"I'm not worried about me, I'm worried about those sheep."

"There's a fence that keeps them in."

"Some animals can jump fences."

Wilma gives him a look.

"You think a tiger no one's seen will threaten some sheep?"

He wants to argue, wants to point out what the man at the Melbourne Zoo said, but Wilma's tone is too close to Carla's. The last thing he wants is for Wilma to turn into Carla. He keeps quiet.

"Come see my room."

He follows her out. From the hallway, they can hear everyone in the kitchen, particularly his mom who is constantly complimenting the house. He's never heard her gush like that about material things before. He ignores it and follows Wilma.

Her room is bigger than his but the soft yellow paint makes it feel cosier. It has its own bathroom too. She's proud of the bed and tables and dressers she picked out on her own. They're nothing special to him. He's more interested in seeing the view. But it's the same as the one from his room, just closer to the sheep munching away. Not exactly the wildlife he was hoping for.

"Here, you want to see a Tasmanian Tiger?"

She pulls a newspaper from her bedside table and spreads it on the bed. He watches as she opens it to the sports page with a large picture of a team of cricket players at which she stabs a finger.

"There you go, Tasmanian Tigers."

She reaches under her bed for a green ball cap with a green and yellow logo of a tiger with a pair of red stripes matching the ones worn by the players.

"Very funny," he says, which makes her laugh.

"Keep it, I have another one."

"Thanks."

He puts it on, adjusts it, and decides that her joke is funny. He's about to chuckle when he sees a large framed picture of Uluru on the wall opposite the window. It's just like the picture Aunt Ruth has, but without people. So lonely yet so beautiful, it could be a painting painted a hundred years ago. But no, it is the exact same picture, taken at the same time. He can tell by the dog-shaped cloud.

"Where did you get that?"

"Don't you love it. Uluru is such a sacred place and so beautiful."

"But where did you get it?"

Wilma looks down, sighs. It's the first time Christopher has seen her like this since she told him about the fire at the hotel pool.

"It belonged to my father. It was his favourite because of that lone cloud, which reminded him of a puppy he had as a kid. Uncle Andy salvaged it from the fire. You can see burn marks on the back and one side but otherwise it's in great shape. Sometimes I imagine that lone cloud is me."

The fire. The picture and article in Aunt Ruth's purse. It's still a mystery to him but at least now he knows beyond a doubt they're all connected.

"When did your father take the photograph?"

"He didn't. He wasn't even there. Uncle Andy took it."

# 31

No matter how hot it gets at the estate, Andy sleeps with the air conditioning in his bedroom off. Three reasons. First: a tribute to previous generations who lived without such luxury on the old estate; second: to allow the sweet music of the morning birds to play undistorted by an artificial hum; third: to purify that special scent from the flora and fauna that wafts out with the mist from the rainforest. The clamminess, the dampness, the sweat, all acceptable trade-offs for such rewards. The scent is especially satisfying this morning with the estate no longer as sparse as it has been. Nothing approaching the consistently raucous density of before, of course, but a start.

Andy staves off his biological urges to indulge in the last aromatic breaths before the natural smells yield to manmade ones from the kitchen downstairs. Bacon, eggs, bread, pancakes, sausages, a myriad of aromas disperse and overwhelm the ephemeral ones from the rainforest. Just as the sun will clear the clouds of mist hovering over the estate. Meanwhile, the clattering of pans and utensils and the crackling of grease provides percussive accompaniment to the birdsong still in full swing.

No one other than Crane is up yet, Andy notes, upon descending the stairs. But then the door to the back from the kitchen opens.

"Oh, good morning, Christopher," Andy says.

"Hi."

"Been up long?"

"No, just looking around."

"The boy wanted to see if there were any critters about."

"Okay, good, so it's just us men."

Crane chuckles but Andy's remark has no effect on Christopher who takes the glass of orange juice offered by Crane and sits at the table.

Crane rings the dinner bell—salvaged from the fire—which startles Christopher. Moments later, the girls show up, with Deborah not far behind. Did she recognize the ring from her visits before? Deborah doesn't mention it and Andy refrains from pointing it out as everyone takes a seat at the dining table.

With Christopher sitting between his mother and Wilma, Andy notices the boy's skin is closer in tone to his niece than his mother, which is consistent with how Fred described the man Deborah says is the biological father. But also not a great deal darker than Andy's skin, which makes it consistent with the gradual darkening seen in Kiltepper males over recent generations.

"Uncle Andy, when are you going to show the museum to Christopher?"

"After breakfast."

"It's neat, you'll like it," Wilma says, in an aside to Christopher. "Especially one item in particular."

"Don't spoil it for him. Deborah, you're welcome to join us as well. You might find it interesting."

"A museum? How far away is it?"

"It's upstairs."

Her sceptical look is one Andy remembers well. Good, he thinks, hoping she'll decline. He'd prefer to take Christopher alone.

But she decides to come along and follows Andy up the stairs with Christopher trailing behind. The sound of Crane clearing the plates reminds Andy of instructions he needs to give his assistant before he leaves for his other duties.

"Mind waiting here? It'll only take a minute."

When Andy returns he sees them huddled, as if she's persuading a reluctant Christopher.

"Sorry about that, but welcome to the Kiltepper Museum."

Andy unlocks and with two hands pushes in the French doors. He beckons them into the room, now nearly filled with Kiltepper artefacts and treasures representing seven generations from the original to the present, each displayed museum-style on stands or encased in glass cabinets with identifying labels.

Pictures, books, candles, jewellery, army uniforms and a helmet from each world war, plenty of sports equipment and trophies, kitchen items, bric-a-brac, potpourri, knick knacks, and dozens of other objects he's sorted and arranged by himself. The majority, he explains, have been salvaged from the fire but a good number are from his house in Launceston as well as those of his siblings. The artwork that adorns the walls is mostly of Australian landmarks, lending context to the contents. Rather than guiding them to specific pieces in a set order, he lets them wander about in a desultory fashion.

What's frustrating about their muted reactions is they're not unique. Only Wilma, it seems, with only the barest connection to Kiltepper history, seems to appreciate what it means. Maybe he's delusional but he hoped for more from the boy.

He feels a coughing fit coming on and is about to liberate the visitors when Deborah is drawn to a ceramic bowl still in pristine condition.

"I gave that to your brother for his wedding. It survived?"

Andy smiles, his spirit restored.

"That's right, it used to hang in the kitchen in the old estate. It was one of the first items I salvaged."

"They never had children, did they?"

"They're the ones who adopted Wilma."

"Why is that wall empty?" Christopher says, as he points above the bowl.

"It's for a picture I let Wilma have. It belonged to her father and it's hanging in her room."

"I've seen it. Mom, you have to see it. It's of Uluru."

"Is it?"

The way Christopher says this to Deborah, as if baiting her, along with how she responds, as if wary of taking the bait, strikes Andy as peculiar. Has he missed something? Of course. He took that photo on the clandestine trip with the Johnsons and Deborah. Would she recognize the original?

Christopher moves to an empty glass case on a pedestal.

"Did somebody steal what was here?"

Andy laughs. "You could say that, in a way. This is reserved for a special item, a misplaced medallion. Deborah, you might recall the one commemorating the end of transporting convicts to Tasmania."

"Oh no, you lost that?"

"I hope to find it still."

Now that Christopher is showing more interest, it's time to reveal what for the boy will be the pièce de résistance. Sure enough, Christopher's face lights up with recognition.

"Is it real?"

"You bet. Want to touch it?"

Andy pulls out a key, unlocks the cabinet, and lifts the glass. It's unfortunate to have to keep the Thylacine fur protected this way for it looks much better without an artificial barrier. He encourages Christopher to pet it and smiles as the boy first rubs his hand along the back several times before using his thumb and middle finger to stroke the stripes.

"That's just how I did it when I was your age."

"How old is it?"

"Almost a hundred years. My great-grandfather used to hunt them. It took him years to realize they weren't the threat to sheep or humans others said they were. By then, of course, it was too late, but he did keep one as a pet. This one."

"What do you mean too late?" Christopher says, suddenly taking his hands away.

"I mean, before they became extinct."

"People have seen them. Not far from here too."

"Christopher, time you stop believing strangers' stories."

Christopher becomes sullen but his mom's not having it. It's not Andy's place to intervene but the boy's expression makes it impossible to hold back.

"What if it's my story? I hope you don't consider me a stranger."

"Excuse me?" Deborah says.

"I may have had an experience with one."

"Now I've heard everything. Andy Kiltepper, of all people?"

"Did you really?" Christopher says.

"I can't be sure. It happened while I was unable to move during the fire."

"Andy, let's not talk about that."

"Mom, I know about the fire. Wilma told me. Though she never said anything about a Tasmanian tiger."

"Wilma didn't say anything because this is the first time I've told anyone."

"Please, tell me more," Christopher says.

Andy revels in the boy's interest as he relates his recollection of the creature during his ordeal. When done, Deborah challenges Andy to reveal how he can know it was a Tasmanian tiger. He responds by returning to the empty case on the pedestal.

"I had the medallion around my neck for the party. Something snatched it from me, stole it while I couldn't move."

"And you think that something was this tiger?"

"I can't be sure, Deborah, but I'll reserve this spot until I find it. And when I do, then I'll know."

An awkward silence ensues during which Andy allows Deborah to study his face, read him. It seems she's cluing into something she keeps to herself. She ushers her son out of the room.

The door closing shuts out all the sounds of the house, leaving Andy by himself, feeling empty with an echo of the horror of the fire in his head.

Something has to give. This roundabout, passive approach—Ruth's approach—won't cut it. The Johnsons' help was essential as he would have been spurned in Canada. But he's yielded to Fred and Ruth too long, wilfully remaining ignorant that their objectives could run counter to his. No wonder Deborah was so off base about his intentions the other night. Waiting for her to understand him will take too long. Directness is needed, even if it results in her shutting him out.

Andy gets his keys to lock up the furs, but then Christopher comes back in, alone.

"Do you mind if I pet it again?"

"Not at all."

Andy steps aside to make room for Christopher.

"Can you remember what sound it made?"

In Christopher's still black eyes, Andy catches something that brings back the dark fear, the pain, and all his sense memory.

"If it made a sound, the roar of the fire drowned it out. But what I do recall is it smelled bad. So bad it delayed my unconsciousness, kept me awake for some time."

Christopher nods, entranced, inspiring Andy to rub his fingers across his throat and add:

"You know what? I'm pretty sure it drooled on my neck just before ripping off the medallion."

# 32

Coming here was always going to stir up difficult emotions, she knew that, though Deborah would have hoped those emotions would have, like the morning mist, given way to optimistic sunshine and a clearer, cheerier outlook. This eerie sensation, this haunting from the past that latched on to her the moment they arrived yesterday, just won't go away. Andy's museum / mausoleum actually exacerbates the feeling because the only elements still present, still alive, from that past are she and him. The estate is new and none of the children were born since the last time she was in Tasmania.

Her detachment is what now allows her to see with sharper clarity what she could never have seen had she never left. How Tasmania's remoteness, its wild isolation, absorbs the past, traps it, compresses and reshapes it. In a tranquil moment such as this, lounging on a sun-drenched patio, braiding a little girl's gold locks, this clarity reveals a ringing theme: like Andy, she is a part of this land, and this land is a part of her.

"You braid tighter than Mommy used to," Carla says, "and your hands are rougher. But I like the way you do it."

Deborah cringes, as she does at every broach of that subject, afraid the source of her unease could be Julia. This fondness for the daughter of a former rival, though completely natural and sincere, still feels like a betrayal, and that troubles her. Deborah barely knew Julia in those days but that didn't stop her despising Andy's wife when she ought to have been despising Andy. But she was too infatuated and, yes, too in love to ever consider that. How Julia who, truth be told, was always decent to her, would have hated Deborah had she found out. Deborah wonders now if she ever did, whether Carla knows anything. Considering the little girl's attachment to Julia and their rapidly growing bond, that's unlikely. Thank goodness.

At the far end of the property, near one of the gates leading to the rainforest, she sees Christopher with Wilma, paying close attention to his new friend as she points out various things on the ground and in the trees. His fondness for her is endearing and Wilma has a certain rough charm that might remind him of Willie. Is it a crush? Will he pine for her once they separate? However it plays out, this change in her son, which began with their arrival in Perth, is magical and has made everything worthwhile. The success of Ruth's teaching would have been enough. But to see him interacting with Wilma in such a—dare she say it?—normal way, she never could have hoped for that.

"What are they doing?" Deborah says.

"Wilma's just showing off what she knows."

Ah yes, the price for those two hitting it off is poor Carla being left out. But Deborah is happy to fill in as the young girl's pal until the girls go back to school and she and Christopher go back to Adelaide or Canada.

Funny that Canada has fallen, at best, to second choice when it was the only choice a few weeks ago. Now she only associates negatives with going back there: no job; no Willie; the residue of his troubles; Christopher's education; the long winter. Yet this is countered by a persistent sense, perhaps out of habit and fading with each day here, that Canada is still their home. Even though Adelaide is a more viable, balanced option, a city that gives her a good vibe. Their brief time there was comfortable, safe; one can be inconspicuous in Adelaide. Had she known that twelve years ago, she might have settled there and never gotten as far as Fremantle, let alone Canada.

She finishes the last braid and gets Carla to turn around. Deborah smiles proudly as Andy's daughter swings her head and flips the braids back and forth.

"Not bad, not bad, if I do say so myself."

"I have to see."

Carla skips away to the house to fetch a mirror.

It's not the guilt Deborah feels about Julia that's the real issue. It's the sense Adelaide is no more than an elusive dream she's unworthy of, one never to be fulfilled. The fear she and her son will get trapped in Canada or Tasmania. The latter outcome would be acceptable to him, probably preferable. So what's stopping her from considering it? Maybe Carla's mirror is a magical one that can reflect her own soul.

The window above her is mirror-like. Specially glazed to protect the museum contents from the sun and unpredictable temperatures. It bothers her not to be able to see in when anyone could be up there looking down on her. Indeed, it almost feels as if the entire history of a single family is doing precisely that. She looks away.

But that's it. How could she have missed it? She looks up at the window again, this time staring at it, as one would stare down a foe. The daylight blurrily and monochromatically reflects spreading branches at the tops of the eucalypts in the rainforest, their silhouettes distinguishable against a sky of several grey shades.

"I love it. Thank you, Auntie Debs."

Carla gives Deborah a hug she really needed.

"My pleasure."

"What's your pleasure?" Andy says, appearing behind Carla who turns and waves her hair around.

"Look, Daddy."

"Wonderful, honey. Now how about you join Wilma and Christopher to let us adults talk."

"I'd rather stay here."

Carla folds her arms until Deborah indicates she wants to talk with Andy as well. It's heartbreaking to disappoint Carla but Deborah has to harvest what's on her mind while it's fresh.

Once his daughter's out of earshot, Andy begins to speak as if there's something pressing on his mind. But Deborah's not listening. She's organizing her own thoughts. When she's ready, she stops him.

"I now realize, Andy, why you went through all this trouble to bring me here."

"But I already told you why."

"Yes, all that about repairing the bond between us and within my family sounds nice and sweet and I believe you are sincere. But it only explains why you brought me here, not Christopher. I'm sure that if I had no son, I wouldn't be here now."

Andy says nothing and looks straight at her, perhaps a little abashed, but certainly not hiding.

"I'm going to tell you a story," she says. "All I ask is for you to listen without interrupting."

"All right."

"This story is about a young woman, brought up in Hobart in an affluent family, fresh out of uni, who fell in love with an unattainable man and became pregnant with his child."

Andy sits back, says nothing. Deborah takes a deep breath.

"This woman, let's call her Debbie, spurned by the unattainable man, took the money he paid her to deal with the pregnancy and disappeared. She told no one where she went, not even her family with whom she was angry for not supporting her. That destination, which is only incidental to this story, was Fremantle, where a high school friend provided a haven from where Debbie could decide what to do. It wasn't an easy decision to keep the baby but once made there was no regret. I should mention this young woman was, if nothing else, determined.

"Jake Christopher Pollard was born February 29, 2000. With a baby boy but no work and a decent but finite amount of money, the single mother's future was stable though uncertain. She worked odd jobs, such as waitressing or cleaning houses. Roles for which she used to be the boss or client. But she kind of liked the reversal, it suited her in a strange way, a kind of personal victory.

"One night, serving a table of Canadian military men on leave, Debbie met Dwight, who was there with his best friend, Willie, who plays a part later in the story.

"She and Dwight hit it off instantly. Their shared alienation from their families—his drove him to join the army—made them feel like partners in crime. She did not mention her son until after accepting his invitation to Canada. Since her deceased mother came from Canada, this seemed a sensible choice. If things didn't work out with Dwight, she could find relatives as well as escape her family, including a sister who wouldn't stop pestering Debbie to return.

"The romance with Dwight proved more than a fling and developed into a full blown relationship in Ottawa. He restored in her the belief that not all men were—anyway, they married early in 2001 and soon after she became pregnant again.

"Then came the 9/11 terrorist attack on the Twin Towers, at the start of her third trimester. As part of

Canada's participation in the War on Terror, Dwight shipped off to Afghanistan. Their child was born while he was away. The boy was healthy at first but after a month succumbed to a fever and died. She was unable to contact Dwight before hearing he died on the mission.

"The two deaths, so close together, devastated Debbie for a long time and her depression impacted Jake's development. She was scared to let him out of her sight. It was easy to isolate herself and her son as she was okay financially due to the survivor benefit. Emotionally, though, she was bankrupt: this was the lowest point of her life. She resisted a strong pull to come back to Tasmania where her sister could help with her son; her pride vetoed that option.

"When Jake reached school age, Debbie didn't think he was ready to learn with kids his age and stressed over whether to send him to public school or hold him back. Private school was too costly.

"Around that time, Debbie received a visit from Dwight's friend, Willie, who came to Ottawa to pay his belated condolences. He brought a gift with him, a toddler's Toronto Blue Jays shirt with the initials CJP on the back. He was unaware of his friend's baby's death and assumed, because of his dark skin tone, that Jake was Christopher. She didn't have the heart to correct him. In Willie she saw a person who could be a friend, an ally she needed but couldn't know she needed until he was right in front of her. She moved to Willie's hometown, Oshawa, a place where she could nurture this friendship and no one could guess the truth.

"A remarkable bond developed between Willie and her withdrawn son who responded to this man in an easy, open way she hadn't thought possible. It enabled her friendship with Willie to transform into a romance they formalized by moving in together.

"A few years on, their untroubled, albeit modest, lives were disrupted by a surprise reunion with her sister coinciding with a few unusual difficulties that brought her home to face this unattainable man."

"Home?" Andy says.

She shrugs and looks Andy in the eyes, giving him time to absorb her words and read her face.

"Is it true?" he finally says.

"There is truth in it, as there is in all Tasmanian stories, right?"

"You know what I mean."

"You mean, have I been lying to my son all these years, holding him back? And Willie too?"

"Yes."

"Do you think I'm capable of that?"

"Yes."

"I suppose that's a compliment, in a way."

"You could take it that way, if it is true."

"That's right, if true. And if so, it would resolve the lack of an heir to keep your Kiltepper line going, wouldn't it? Which is what you're after, isn't it?"

"You've changed a lot, Deborah, you never used to be this bold. Brash, yes, but not so bold."

"You're not denying this is what you're after."

"I won't deny what I want is what you say."

"But I don't believe that's true at all."

She's been unable to precisely pin it down until this instant. She's been exploring the wrong causes, inferring the wrong effects, and relying too much on surface observations.

It's in Andy's face and she can hear it in his soft voice, the hollow words that accept her assertion but lack the passion or sincerity they deserve.

All about him is the sadness she sees traces of in his daughter. But for Andy it's not the sadness of a recent tragedy. He's not mourning the loss of a past as much as fearing a future of abject and inevitable loneliness.

# 33

"We should wait for Carla," Christopher says, adjusting the fit of the Tasmanian Tigers cap tight so it won't blow away or get brushed off by a low-hanging tree limb.

"She's not coming. Uncle Andy and your mom are talking so serious, she's probably found a spot to eavesdrop. Let's go on ahead."

"We won't get in trouble going alone?"

"We'll find out when we find out."

Wilma tugs at his shoulder to pull him along and shortly the world turns brown and deep green as they're surrounded by rainforest. It's creepy and exhilarating at the same time. Eucalyptus-filtered daylight comes through in bright strips, the only sign it's still early in the day. He ventures slowly at first to get used to the soft ground and watch out for snakes and spiders, as if he could spot them before they bit him. It's hot but he's glad he let Wilma talk him into putting on long pants.

With each step his world becomes quieter. The rustling of his feet on the vegetation sounds louder and the occasional sudden bird chirp startles him. He loses sight of Wilma who must be far ahead. He needs to hurry but can't help himself and stops. No sound. So peaceful. No people, just nature.

"Hey."

He jumps before turning to see Wilma behind him, standing there for who knows how long.

"How did you get behind me?"

She laughs. "That's my secret. If you can keep up the rest of the way, maybe I'll show you."

She's off again. Christopher's determined not to lose her this time. He copies her silent way of walking and is soon doing almost as well as she is. But when he looks up to the sky for just a moment, she's gone again. He spins a circle, no sign of her.

"Hey."

Some dirt lands on him. He spins again, this time looking up and down, but still sees nothing. He folds his arms and huffs, which is when she emerges from a patch of fronds, laughing, her beauty lighting up the surroundings.

"Sure you're up to finding a Tasmanian tiger? I could have easily pounced on you from there."

"Of course I am."

"Well, let's go find one and test you."

"Really?"

"Sure. Let's go."

"Let's go."

What began as a bushwalk is now a tiger hunt. Other than struggling to keep his cap secure, Christopher could not be happier. Not only is Wilma fun to be with, she believes they might find a Tasmanian tiger. Maybe she believed all along, he wonders, as she points out possible lairs and paw prints with seriousness. Not that he knows what tiger lairs or paw prints look like, of course, but he agrees with her all the ones they find are too small.

Though they find no tigers, they encounter other wildlife, including a wallaby with a tiny joey in her pouch. It's not frightened at their presence and lets them come up close. The thrill of this is nothing compared to the joy and surprise that comes when Wilma pulls him away as he's about to step in the path of an echidna. What a neat animal, a little ball of spiny fur shuffling roly-poly as it scavenges for food. Christopher's tempted to get on his knees and try to move in the same way but thinks better of it. However, they don't see wombats, which surprises Wilma as she always sees them. They also don't see her favourite, pademelons.

"What's a pademelon?"

She winks at him and says, "Tiger food."

He's enjoyed the bushwalk tremendously. The best parts occur when she compliments his ability to adapt so quickly. She's saying it to make him feel good like Aunt Ruth does. This is his world. It feels natural to him. He wants to explore and experience as much of it as he can, for as long as he can. In daylight. For now he realizes those strips of light aren't as bright anymore and that the rainforest is getting dimmer overall.

"We've been gone a long time."

"Not that long."

"Do you know where we are?"

"I know the woods as well as anyone. Been walking in them alone since I was six."

"But you haven't lived here that long."

"This is the same rainforest that backed on to the old estate."

"You mean we're close to where the fire was?"

"Yep. As the crow flies. Or the Wilma bushwalks."

"Take me there."

Wilma shakes her head, tells Christopher it's off limits, that her uncle lets her go wherever she wants, except there. Apparently it's dangerous and people are still investigating. It doesn't sound like she's any more convinced about that explanation than he is but she has no desire to disobey her uncle. Maybe she will when he tells her what Andy said to him about seeing a tiger during the fire.

"No way. He never said that."

"He did so."

"When?"

"This morning, in the museum room. He told me he saw a tiger when he was lying on the ground. He said it took some medallion about transportation."

As he talks, she shakes her head. He sees her doubts about the tiger never left. She was just playing along. He puts it out of his mind and suggests they search for the medallion and surprise her uncle. She thinks about it and he keeps smiling at her until she gives in.

"We can get close, but stay in the rainforest."

More sweaty bushwalking through denser bush and narrower tree passages brings them to a short path that leads to an opening. They must really be far from the estate now, he thinks, but is gladdened at seeing the sun still high in the sky. It is cloudy, which must be why it felt dimmer earlier.

They come upon a metal fence surrounding a flat, empty area. The sudden lack of trees makes it eerie. Inside the fence, pieces of the old estate are everywhere. It looks like a trash site. It's the first time Wilma's seen it, Christopher can tell, as she sighs heavily, though no tears come out. He wants to go over the fence but maybe this isn't a good time.

She shocks him by letting out a cry before hugging him and embracing him for a long time. He thinks he hears a few sobs but isn't sure. It feels nice and takes his mind off exploring. When she lets go, her face is tearless and strong Wilma is back. But only briefly, as if to prove she can take it, for then she breaks down again.

"What's wrong?" Christopher says.

He hopes for a short answer, so they can go explore, but it's not likely. He listens intently as she tells him how the only family she's known are the Kilteppers, how she was close to those who died and misses them. She stops abruptly. He suspects there's more she's not saying.

"Sorry for making you sad, for making you take me here," he says, now ashamed at his impatience.

"I still have Uncle Andy and even though we fight a lot, Carla is like a sister to me."

"Do you want to go back?" Christopher says.

"Not yet."

She stares at the decimation in front of them for a while and her eyes look distant, as if her spirit is about to leave. How it comes to him, he doesn't know, but when he asks what she knows about her actual roots, her smile says he asked the right thing.

Her Aboriginal pride is obvious as she shares the belief she is related to Crane who comes from the Oyster Bay tribe that inhabited the area where they went on the hike. She has no proof but bases her belief on dreams she has of destruction and burning homes by British settlers. What she's read and heard has influenced those dreams, she admits, but she's convinced the core is inherited from her ancestors. Her passion affects Christopher and he starts to feel the same sadness.

"What's hard for me is the Kilteppers are the type my ancestors hated, the type who killed them and everything in Tasmania, including your tiger."

"I don't understand."

"I'm not sure I do either or whether I ever will. All I know is it's sad for me to see this but there is a part that's not sad, a part that feels satisfaction."

Christopher takes a moment to digest this for it stirs something. "I kind of feel the same," he says.

"About what?"

"You know the picture in your room, of Uluru?"

"What about it?"

"Aunt Ruth has one, only hers has my mom and Uncle Fred and her in it."

"So? Many people take that same picture."

"No, you don't get it. It's the exact same picture with the exact same cloud formation behind them. It had to be taken by the same person. You said your uncle took the one in your room so that means he took the picture Aunt Ruth has. It seems weird, the four of them together on a trip. Maybe it wouldn't be if Aunt Ruth wasn't so afraid to show the picture to anyone."

"How would you know that?"

"Trust me, I've given her plenty of chances to do so but she never does."

Wilma takes a while to think about this, during which the sun seems to be rapidly descending. He's tempted to point it out but she's caught up piecing a puzzle together in her head. Her expression changes constantly until finally her mouth opens wide.

"Oh my God, could it be?"

"What?"

"How old are you, Christopher?"

"You already know I'm ten."

"Ten? You're only ten? Really?"

"Yes, why is everyone surprised by that?"

"Who else is surprised by that?"

"Well, Uncle Fred. Andy. Grandpa Walter."

Wilma nods as if another key piece falls in place. For her maybe. The longer she keeps working at it, the more ignorant he feels. She grabs his arm, puts it against hers.

"It makes sense. It could be."

Wilma's excitement is contagious, until she explains. He wants to tell her she's crazy, that it's impossible, but

297

gets this strange fear doing so might convince her more. So he says nothing other than to say he wants to go back.

She leads him through the trees into a much darker rainforest. And creepier. Yet more beautiful too. What a relief to be back in the woods again, and to recognize parts from before. They manage a quick pace as his mind rattles with Wilma's crazy notion that Andy is his father, that they are cousins, that Carla is his half-sister. All based on a photograph and the possibility there's Aboriginal blood in the Kiltepper family. The more it stays in his mind, however, the more it seems harder to disprove. Except the part where, if it is true, he has to be older than what he's been told he is. That couldn't be. His mom would never do something like that.

These distractions cause him to stumble several times. At one stumble, with Wilma up ahead, his hat falls off once again. As he picks it up, he spots an indentation in the ground. A paw print. How did they not see it before? Unless it's fresh. He's about to call out to Wilma but decides to inspect it himself. The shape isn't like any of the others they spotted so far. He hastily arranges a few fronds in a diamond pattern, holds them down with a stone. He rushes to catch up, managing to do so without her noticing, At least she doesn't show any sign she's noticed.

Though it's dark in the murky rainforest, Wilma manages to guide them back to where they started while there's still daylight. They find Andy and his mom talking closely, drinking white wine, while Carla is sprawled out in a lawn chair next to them. With her sunglasses on, it's impossible to tell if she's sleeping. Smoke comes from the barbie, the smell of hot dogs making Christopher aware he's starving.

Andy greets them with a smile but then takes Wilma aside. It's hard to hear but it sounds like he's scolding her. Carla wakes with a smug grin on her face. When Wilma comes back, she's unhappy as she apologizes to Carla for going on ahead without her. Andy seems satisfied with this.

"You two must be hungry, after all that."

The barbie is filled with hot dogs and burgers. Christopher fills a plate with two of each but Wilma is content with a single hot dog, though she loads it with mustard, ketchup and relish. She beckons for Christopher to eat with her, away from the others.

"Holy dooley, can you eat any faster," she says, laughing and pointing at his food.

He looks at his nearly finished plate, then at her half finished hot dog, then at her. It's good to see a smile on that face again but he can't smile back because his mouth is stuffed. And he's still starving. He goes for two more two hot dogs. When he comes back, Wilma's frowning. Not at him but at Carla who's on his tail.

"Go away, brat."

"Don't you want to know what I found out?"

"What did you find out?"

Wilma's mocking lack of interest sounds phony. Christopher wonders if she sent Carla back to spy. He's certain of it when what Carla reveals confirms some of Wilma's theory.

"Isn't that cool?" Wilma says, though it doesn't sound cool to Christopher.

"What does it mean?"

Carla asks several times but Wilma ignores her. He struggles to finish the last hot dog and doing so makes him feel sick. It could be the hot dog, or the feeling something's not right.

"What does it mean?"

Wilma torments her cousin by giving out half-truths that only increase Christopher's confusion and make his head spin. He feels woozy and slumps over. He barely hears Wilma calling his mom who comes over, takes him away, and helps to first vomit and then get to bed. He's still nauseous but manages enough of a smile to have her leave him alone.

When she's gone, he tries to sleep but he's too agitated. The only thing that calms him is closing his eyes and imagining that paw print.

# 34

Deborah takes her breakfast tray outside, settles in at the picnic table. The smell of the dew blends agreeably with the fresh coffee and toast; the colours seeping through the rainforest highlighted by the rising sun mix well with the yellow of the eggs and the orange of the juice. So quiet now. Even the sheep are sleeping off yesterday's grazing.

As she adjusts her sitting position, her foot kicks at an object beneath the table. She reaches down and pulls up the green ball cap Wilma gave Christopher. Fascinating girl, that Wilma, fiercely proud of her Aboriginal heritage yet cultivated like a Kiltepper. Does she grasp the beauty of the contrast, the power it can give her? She seems mature enough. And how sweet to give her son this cap. Deborah shakes off the collected water; he ought to know better than to leave it outside. She hangs it off the table to dry.

Poor kid, so sick last night. Too sick for her to attempt another talk about Willie, let alone show the letter. It might be best to wait. But until when? Until they're in Adelaide? She still has to address when that will happen. The longer they're here, the harder it'll be to prise her son away from Tasmania and his friend before she goes back to her school. He may even ask to attend that school.

That option is worth examining. Contrary to her vows twelve years ago, a future in Tasmania is not out of the question, if it's what's best for her son. Her recent talks with Andy have softened her bitterness, if not eradicated it altogether. He's more sensitive to the needs of others and she's more accepting of his ways. They've struck a fine balance in agreeing to leave things be. The Andy Kiltepper she once knew, upon hearing her story, would have demanded a DNA test to prove or disprove it once and for all.

It's great they're on the same page on a number of matters. For one, it's clear to both there will be no romantic ending. This by itself allows them to talk about the past, even reminisce, and the future as easily and casually as they did when she was in school and fell for this stately handsome man who was no match for her charms.

The sun is a quarter of the way above the trees now and she has to turn sideways to avoid its glare. The avian concert is in intermission and it seems too quiet. Normally her son would be up by now. True, he was sick, but he went to bed early, and should be feeling better. Or at least hungry. Deborah takes the last bite of toast and last sip of orange juice. The coffee, still half full, has cooled off.

Oh that sun. She reaches for the damp cap, puts it on, and only then realizes it shouldn't be here. She distinctly remembers Christopher playing with it as they were talking last night, then gently tossing it to the end of his bed when she kissed him good night. How did it get here? Did he open his window and toss it out? She's directly underneath his room right now so that's possible. But if he had thrown it down, it either would have gotten caught on the awning or flown past the table. Not under it. Possibly a critter moved it, but that doesn't explain why he would toss it outside in the first place.

Panic.

Deborah jumps away from the table, spilling the cold coffee and scraping her thigh on the wooden edge, before rushing into the house and running up the stairs. She's making noise but doesn't care. She runs into Christopher's room. Empty. She checks all the rooms on the main floor, which takes a while. By the time she's back upstairs, the others are up. She pushes them aside as needed to inspect their rooms. All empty. Only at Wilma's does she stop, frozen by the Uluru photo.

"What's wrong?" Andy says, his voice snapping her out of it.

"Christopher's gone."

"Probably out for a stroll like yesterday."

Deborah lets out a deep sigh.

She tells Andy he's wrong. It takes all her patience to suffer the inane questions—other than Carla asking if there's a note; a quick search reveals there's not—and pointless but reasonable suggestions of where he might be on the grounds. To each, Deborah has to explain her son would never have left the cap behind if he were only going a short distance. He would, on the other hand, leave it behind if he were to go where he'd be afraid of losing it.

Or if someone had taken him.

"Impossible," Andy says. "We're too remote and the security systems would have alerted me to any unusual movement."

"Then where could he have gone?"

"Bet he went to find a Tassie tiger," Carla says.

"At night?"

Deborah then realizes of course he would have gone at night when such animals would be about.

"But he'll get lost. He'll get hungry."

"He'll be all right. He's pretty clever out there. His only difficulty will be mozzies but I told him how to deal with them. We'll find him before he gets in trouble. I have an idea where he's gone."

Wilma's assurances calm Deborah who feels she can trust this Aboriginal girl. And before she knows it, Deborah finds herself agreeing to the sensible plan of waiting until the sun is higher. It helps to see Wilma getting herself dressed and putting together a kit and efficiently making breakfast for her and her uncle in preparation of a search party.

A half hour passes before the sun has risen high enough to begin the search. Andy and Wilma will go while Deborah stays back with Carla in case her son returns another way. Wilma has a wild look about her, a mix of concern about her friend as well as excitement at an adventure. Her face has no makeup but to Deborah it seems adorned with war paint, and she finds that comforting.

But once they're out of sight, Deborah sits at the picnic table fidgeting, staring off, panning and tilting her head between the rainforest and the sky in which grey clouds are forming. She's seen clouds like that before. They look benign at first but quickly darken. Carla sits next to her and snuggles up.

"Are you worried?" Carla says.

"Of course. Look at those clouds."

"I'm not worried."

"You're not?"

"Nah, Wilma knows what to do in the woods. She could be a bushie. And Christopher's really just an animal, isn't he? Belongs in the wild."

"You don't like my son, do you? Why is that?"

"He's weird. And . . . I don't want him to be my brother."

"What?"

"I heard you and Dad talking yesterday. I didn't know what it meant until Wilma explained it to me."

Deborah and Andy talked a lot the day before, not noticing Carla hadn't gone with the other kids for hours. She recalls what they talked about but can only speculate how it might have been interpreted by such a sensitive eight-year-old girl.

"And from all that you concluded Christopher is your brother?"

"Yeah, but I'd be okay with it if it means you'd become my mommy."

Deborah looks at Carla, briefly relishing such a possibility, before accepting the choice she's made. She shakes her head slowly as she strokes the young girl's cheeks.

"The trouble with eavesdropping is it's easy for people to misunderstand what they've heard."

A wet drop, a little girl's tear, not rain, falls on her thumb. She gently wipes it away. Deborah sighs before smiling at Carla, with whom she shares the common tragedy of losing a mother while still a child. This connection helps fortify the decision she's about to make.

"But honey, I'll always be nearby as a friend."

Deborah emphasizes her declaration by staring into Carla's eyes, committing herself to a promise that now seems inevitable.

This makes her wonder about the mindset that drove her to leave twelve years ago. All she recalls  is the anger, the emotion, the pain in a logical sense. All that remains in her heart is a feeling that's stayed with her since, that she was an exile, a refugee guilty of a crime. Everything else is an emotional snapshot that can be described but never again experienced.

It's funny how people tend to view the past, and how they hold on to emotional memories of people and places as still photographs, ignoring the fact that the past moves with the present, that memories shift and demand new angles for new circumstances while those original emotions evaporate.

She's as guilty of this as anyone, given her fixed stand on so many things coming back here. She now realizes her issue with Tasmania is relevant only in a context that's a dozen years old. Now, in this time, those events require no apology, demand no shame. She is where she has to be, as is her son; no need to cloud that truth with obsolete emotions artificially kept alive by what, pride?

Deborah chuckles, drawing a glance from Carla, but she doesn't explain it. She only answers with a smile, a confident smile knowing she doesn't have to worry about Christopher because he will return to her. This is where he belongs. Where they belong.

# 35

After two hours searching and shouting, Andy has to take a break. They've found no footprints or other sign of Christopher and he's winded. His exhaustion is aggravated by an onset of another fever and his confidence in his ability to keep up with his agile niece is waning. But he's a Kiltepper, he can't quit. Though it's tempting to take his niece's hints to let her continue on her own.

Fortunately, Wilma is amenable to stopping and these restful minutes help restore his energy. They share a granola bar, drink some water, and together observe the darkening sky.

"What do you think?" he says.

"Worst case, we've got an hour. There's enough wind so if we're lucky, the clouds might pass us by."

"Another hour? How far did you two—no, don't tell me we're going where I think we're going?"

"I'm sorry, Uncle Andy. He was so persistent. I swear we never went inside the fence."

It's pointless to berate her; he can deal with that later. Perhaps he's better off letting this issue go altogether.

"How did it make you feel?"

"Awful," is all she says.

Awful. That's the main reason he's kept the girls away from the fire site. How else could she feel? Now he second-guesses indulging his archaeological interests. He could have razed the property, planted new trees or just let nature re-cover the land with rainforest and take it back, while he redirected all his attention to the future.

"Christopher!" Wilma calls out.

Andy detects anger in her voice, though it seems targeted at him, not Christopher. She readies herself to take up the search again and though he could use a few extra minutes, he does the same.

It's strange they haven't even found a footprint, as if the boy has turned into Tarzan, bounding about the trees vine to vine. Then again, they can't even be sure they're going the right way. It makes sense he'd retrace the path the kids took yesterday, but it's not a given. Unfortunately, they have little else to go on.

They approach the destroyed estate at a point where the fence is at an elevation above them. Andy barely recognizes it from this angle. He always takes the SUV along the dirt road, never ventures beyond the fencing. As they close in, he sees Wilma slowing, as if spooked.

"Uncle Andy," she says, making him stop. "Why did you tell him you saw a Tasmanian tiger?"

Ah, his sharing the Thylacine experience must be what inspired Christopher to persuade his niece to disobey. Given the curiosity that must have been in her, she couldn't have resisted long.

"He told you that?"

"So you did tell him. Why?"

"I don't know."

"Then you didn't really see one, did you?"

"I wasn't making up the experience, if that's what you mean. Whether what I saw or sensed was truly a tiger, I can't say."

Wilma's staring at him, no doubt shocked he would admit even that much, considering how he's mocked others for intimating less. Perhaps she's angry too because she could be attributing that story to Christopher's running off, as Carla implied.

"You had to know you were leading him on."

"Trust me, if I had known this would happen, I never would have said a thing."

"I wish you'd have told me about that," she says, with less harshness.

"I never intended to tell anyone."

"Then why tell him, of all people?"

"I wanted to establish a connection with him."

Wilma smiles, as if she's caught him in a trap.

"Exactly."

"What do you mean by that?"

She shares her theory, which apparently started developing in her mind at Wineglass Bay, that Christopher is Andy's son. She adds how her theory is supported by several factors, including the Uluru picture in her room and his conversation the day before with Deborah, as related to her by Carla. That Wilma would give credence to Carla's interpretation of an adult conversation is unlike her.

Through it all he listens, slowly shaking his head, awaiting the chance to straighten her out once she asks a direct question. It doesn't come and she seems content to have gotten it out.

A mutual glance at the sky brings them back to their priority for which these other matters can wait. They agree to split up. Wilma consents to searching the perimeter of the property, promising to keep outside the fence, while he goes inside.

It's been weeks since his last search for objects here and the site looks undisturbed. No sign of Christopher or anyone or anything having been through it recently. It also looks picked clean. Maybe it's time to clear it and let it return to nature. The thought of doing so gives him a pleasant mild rush amid the frustration of the search.

He returns to find Wilma waiting, equally upset at their lack of success. It's approaching lunchtime and they're out of ideas. They decide to return to the house from where he can call Crane to organize search parties to attack the rainforest from multiple points.

A downpour begins as they set off and doesn't let up before an unexpectedly calm Deborah and an anxious Carla rush out to greet them.

"We're not giving up," Andy says. "Just coming back to arrange reinforcements."

"He'll be okay, I just feel it," Wilma says.

"I believe you," Deborah says.

He goes inside to dry off, get some medicine, and change clothes before going into town. His head starts feeling woozy as the search has taken more out of him than he thought. He needs rest but can't afford to give in to his body's wish to collapse on his bed. But he does move slower, more deliberately, and this helps.

When he comes out again, Deborah and the girls are gone. It's still pouring. He looks around until he notices a commotion in the familiar forms of his girls racing to the rainforest with Deborah not far behind. Andy struggles to catch up but slows upon seeing the object of their quest.

It's hard to recognize Christopher at first, what with his dark face striped and patched with dirt, his hair a wild mess as he slowly, somewhat gracefully, comes to meet the women. Carla is the first to reach the boy and gives him a hug.

"You stink."

Carla says it loud enough for Andy to hear and then gives way to Deborah who holds her son long enough for Andy to join them alongside Wilma who's standing back. No one is minding the rain.

"Honey, we were worried sick," Deborah says.

Christopher nods to show empathy for his mother and what he's put her through, while also standing his ground unapologetically.

"So did you find it?" Carla says.

"Find what?"

"Your tiger?"

Christopher's amused by her question, which sounds sweet, absent of her usual taunt. Instead of responding to her, Christopher walks past the females to stand before Andy. Their eyes lock a moment before the boy opens his palm to reveal an object covered in dirt.

"This belongs to you?" Christopher says, a crack in his voice.

Andy accepts it, thumbs away the dirt with the help of the rain to get to the white metal, to reveal the shapes of an emu and kangaroo. Further rubbing causes Andy to feel faint as he sees the words "TASMANIA FOUNDED 1803" on the bottom, and then, in a semi-circle in the upper half, above the animals: "CESSATION OF TRANSPORTATION".

"Where did you—how did you—?"

"A tiger let me have it but only once I promised we'd leave her alone."

"Wow."

Carla's jaws remain wide open after she utters this. Her face expresses a wonder Andy hasn't seen in his daughter since she was a baby.

# 36

The bell tings and echoes in Christopher's ears. It's the final week of this school term. He's seated at the front, watching his classmates scurry in, waving hi to some. English is his toughest class, the only one he struggles with, so he's glad he was early enough to grab a prime desk.

It would have been neat if he could have gotten Aunt Ruth, now that she and Uncle Fred have moved to Hobart, to teach here. But by the time the Johnsons arranged their move from Adelaide, the new school term was underway. He struggled at first with how things were done in the schools here, but figured it out on his own. And Mr. Eccles is a good teacher, in fact they're all pretty good, so he no longer needs Aunt Ruth's help.

He did need it to convince his mom to let him take that test from which they jumped him to the same grade as Wilma. Now he doesn't feel so big and awkward. He's even made friends, though none quite as special as his cousin. Too bad she's not in the same school, or even the same city. In fact, now he only sees Wilma on visits to the estate and it's been a while since the last one. The Kilteppers rarely go to Hobart and aren't likely to now that Uncle Fred is running things for Andy here. The job his mom took to help Uncle Fred has kept them both busy, which means that while he can't wait for the school break, it's doubtful they'll go to the estate. And since most of his friends are going to Fiji, or New Zealand, or elsewhere, he might get lonely.

Mr. Eccles enters the classroom and doesn't have to say a word before everyone shuts up. The kids are much more polite here. Or more scared. The teacher's face looks serious as he glances about the room and then approaches Christopher. Probably to nag, as he's done every day this week, about the topic of the story he has to write about Tasmania on his two-week break. It seems unfair to ask students to do work on their break, but the other kids have submitted their topics and none have complained, as far as Christopher knows.

"I need you to go to the Principal's office."

Christopher shudders, his heart beats faster, as those terrible old feelings about school echo inside him. Though he can't imagine what he could have done. He leaves the class, taking his books when the teacher suggests he does, and makes his way down the empty hallway, alone.

In the Principal's office, he finds his aunt seated across from the Principal, not smiling. The Principal gets up to leave them alone. Aunt Ruth dabs a tissue at her eyes when she tells him Andy's sickness has gotten so bad he won't survive much longer. She's come to take him directly to the estate to be with the Kilteppers at the end.

When his mom explained what was going on with Andy's pneumonia and how he was constantly getting the flu the past few months, Christopher never imagined anything like this could happen. Not to a robust, healthy-looking man like Andy. But once he knew, he could tell it was getting worse by how much sadder her and Aunt Ruth's faces became each time Andy's name came up.

"Where's Mom?" he says.

"She and your uncle are already on their way."

It's a long drive and it takes a while before Aunt Ruth gives into his request to listen to Triple J. Only she keeps interrupting the music to talk about cheerful things such as the AFL playoffs—he's still not sure why she and Uncle Fred are Sydney Swans fans—and what he'll do during his school holidays. Her efforts do help pass the time but do nothing to stop the gloomy sadness growing in him for Carla and Wilma the closer they get. It only continues increasing at the estate, despite the clear skies and a pleasant spring breeze, and the same old calm sheep grazing away as if time stood still.

The rainforest is a shiny, inviting green, though a bushwalk would be far from Wilma's mind. This girl, usually so calm and cool, is moping around as badly as Carla who at least has his mom to comfort her whenever she needs it, and she needs it a lot. Carla's been nicer to him since that day he found the medallion, but she's still a spoiled brat.

Even Crane looks old, weary—though still hearty—escorting Christopher to Andy's room, crammed with adults. His mom looks stern, as does Uncle Fred. But they don't look as bad as Grandpa Walter who was released from the hospital two weeks ago and has been staying at the estate. He looks guilty, as if he should be the one in the bed, not Andy who, despite his thin face and body, is in better spirits than the people around him. It looks like they're having a heavy discussion with Uncle Fred talking and Andy listening closely.

"To sum up, progress is at about seventy-two percent for Hobart, and between twenty-five and thirty-five percent elsewhere. We'll get to ninety and seventy percent respectively by the end of summer."

"Good, Fred, good. Keep it going."

"Count on me," Uncle Fred says.

"Come in, Christopher."

Andy smiles as he beckons Christopher to him. They shake hands. Christopher's surprised by how weak the man's grip is. He takes the chair his mom pulls out for him, unsure what's about to happen, if he's supposed to say something. Then Andy looks at his mom who rests a hand on his shoulder.

"Honey, we're discussing a number of changes, some of which will affect you."

He listens intently as his mom, with the help of Uncle Fred, tells him what those changes are, most of which don't affect him. He manages to contain his glee when she informs him Wilma and Carla are moving to Hobart to stay with them for the next school term. It's what his mother says next that stirs him.

"I'm going to Canada next week and want you to come along."

"Willie?" Christopher says.

His mom nods. She tells him the police came to the hotel while they were at the estate that time, on behalf of Toronto police, for any information to help them find Willie. Of course, she didn't know where he was but showed them the letter Christopher only found out about a few months ago. It was enough to convince them she was telling the truth.

"Do you know where he is now?"

"No honey, no one knows where he is. Though there are indications he might be in the UK."

"Then why not go there instead of Canada?"

She explains they can help Willie by having Christopher come to sign a paper swearing he was with Willie at the zoo that day. That way, if Willie returns, he won't be in as much trouble.

"But I could have done that back then. Are you saying if we didn't come here, Willie might still be there and be all right?"

His mom looks hurt by his question and unsure how to answer it. Aunt Ruth looks guilty too. He didn't mean to make them feel bad, it just came out.

"The important thing is we can fix it now."

"Yes, mom, let's go, let's fix it."

She's clearly happy with his response. They all are. He smiles and it takes several silent seconds to realize they don't need him anymore. He's glad to leave, eager to find Wilma who he finds sitting outside by herself, whittling a piece of wood into something he is unable to identify. She barely acknowledges him.

"So you're coming to Hobart?"

"That's what they tell me."

She says it as if he did something wrong.

"Aren't you glad?"

"Glad my uncle is about to die, glad to discover he's been selling Kiltepper companies for months, not giving me a chance to continue . . ."

"You know I didn't mean that. But do you really want to run businesses?"

She shakes her head. "You don't understand a thing."

"Try me."

"I'll give you a hint. Black Line. Look it up."

She rushes off. Christopher wants to tell her he doesn't have to look it up, that his class just studied the Black Line and he gets what she means. That she feels she's being corralled to eastern Tasmania like the Aborigines back then.

He's hurt by her anger towards him and figures it's better to let her be. There'll be time to fix it. She'll come around. Unless, maybe she wants him to follow her.

He starts to go but Carla intercepts him.

"Don't worry about her. She's just mad because she's got a boyfriend here. She'll get over it. I'm glad we're going to Hobart."

Boyfriend? Such a possibility never occurred to Christopher. Could be Carla's lying. Still, it bothers him. Why does it bother him? Because he thinks it's supposed to bother him and it's supposed to bother him because he wants to be her boyfriend? No, he doesn't. Maybe back then, when he first knew her, but not now. The idea of Wilma showing another boy tricks she showed him is what's disturbing. Especially if that boy is some athletic footy-obsessed meathead who fakes interest in nature.

"What's his name?" Christopher says.

Carla smiles in her usual snarky way, then stares, as if waiting for him to get upset. He matches her gaze and, in doing so, realizes that, though she's a very pretty girl, she's kind of ugly when she's like this. And his lack of reaction has a bad effect on her and further detracts from her natural attractiveness.

Her unpleasant smile transforms into a look of terror. As if she hasn't fully grasped what's about to happen to her father until this moment. Christopher wants to say something soothing, if only to prevent her from bursting into tears. But what can he say? His mom would know. Then Carla shocks him by jumping at him, giving him a warm, long hug, before rushing off into the house.

His attempts the rest of the day and the next to make up with Wilma come to nothing. Her moods only worsen as Andy's condition worsens, as if she's trying to absorb every pain her uncle is feeling. She spends a lot of time with him, even more than his own daughter, and is virtually unapproachable.

Andy dies the next morning.

Late in the day, after the many visitors, business partners, and other strangers are gone, while Crane prepares a meal for them all, Christopher finds an opportunity to get away to the rainforest, away from the sadness and crying. It's not that their tears and moans bother him but that he can't contribute his own. This makes him self-conscious about looking as if he doesn't care. Which isn't true, he does care. He will miss Andy, a man he grew to like as Wilma predicted. However, to be honest, a man who is still a stranger to Christopher.

No one else can be seen or heard but he suspects Wilma's behind him. If so, it's a sign things will be all right between them. It may be rough for a while but they'll get through it. The best thing to do is act like he thinks he's alone. Not hard in this place.

Christopher enters and quickly finds it useless to try and keep his suit from getting wet and dirty. The damp odour is nostalgic and reminds him of his search for the tiger on a night that no longer seems real. Entering the woods so confused and emerging with the medallion, as well as a deep understanding of many things, including himself.

It did take his mom some explaining to fill gaps, clarify what was true, what wasn't true, what others believed was true, and even what others suspected might be true. She revealed things not even Aunt Ruth and Uncle Fred will ever know. Only she and Christopher know everything. He'll protect the truth the same way this rainforest harbours its secrets and those of its inhabitants.

He steps further in to touch the bark of a dying eucalypt covered with wet moss. It feels fragile and some of it crumbles in his hands. It's surrounded by brown and green fronds just as tender. These look dry but he can sense the moisture trapped within. He crouches down to rub his hands on the ground, which is hard and durable. He shuts his eyes to let the woods envelop him. In doing so, he discovers the rainforest, for all its mystery and enigma, offers inspiration in the form of that elusive story idea for Mr. Eccles' class. He has no pen or paper so he has to repeat the words in his head: *The impossible creature sniffs for food amid the char, embers, ash, and decay* . . .

A rustle from behind, followed by clumsy steps making no effort at concealment. Then a voice that's uncharacteristically vulnerable.

"Did you see one that day? Did you really see a . . .?"

Her voice trails off.

It's the first time anyone's asked since Carla the moment he got back. Perhaps everyone chose their own answer, one that matches how they want to see things, for that is what people do. Except Wilma. She doesn't want to hide behind made up things, for her truth is sacred. To her, his response will mean a great deal. And so he must compose it with honesty, if not necessarily truth.

Yet he can't hold back a wry grin at something Uncle Fred might appreciate: in his story for school he won't have to pronounce Thylacine, though here it's another matter.

He waits for the grin to subside before he rises, stands tall, and turns to face a grieving girl whose rugged natural beauty matches the setting perfectly, magically. He wants to go to her, hug her, but can't. He's too mesmerized by her deep, dark, hollow eyes. Through them he perceives an even purer truth that spindles the past, present, and future as he gives his answer.

# *About the Author*

Peter Hassebroek published his first novel, *Upbound*, in 2008. In 2010 he published, *Melange and Other I. T. Stories*, a collection inspired by his past career, which was followed by a second novel, *The Dancer's Spell*, a year later.

A creative diversion into screenwriting and video art resulted in a number of visual productions and a screenplay collection published in 2016: *Greenplays, 3 Scripts by Peter Hassebroek*.

*Thylacine*, Peter's fifth book and third novel, began as a screenplay and fittingly marks a return to fiction.

Peter lives in Whitby, Ontario, Canada with his wife, Yolande, to whom he's grateful for her unwavering support and encouragement.

To contact Peter, or to find out more about Peter and his books, please visit the website:

www.peterhassebroek.com.